To Marye Anne,
My newest aunt.
Welcome to my
family. Love,
　　　Karen

AFTER MOSES

A novel by Karen Mockler

Karen Mockler

MacAdam/Cage
155 Sansome Street, Suite 550
San Francisco, CA 94104
www.macadamcage.com
Copyright © 2003 by Karen Mockler
ALL RIGHTS RESERVED.

Library of Congress Cataloging-in-Publication Data

Mockler, Karen, 1965—
   After Moses / by Karen Mockler.
      p. cm.
   ISBN 1-931561-37-0 (Hardcover : alk. paper)
   1. Eccentrics and eccentricities—Fiction.
2. Inheritance and succession—Fiction 3. Brothers and
sisters—Fiction 4. Ohio—Fiction I. Title.

PS3613.O28A68 2003
813'.6—dc21

                              2002156265
Manufactured in the United States of America.
10 9 8 7 6 5 4 3 2 1

Book and jacket design by Dorothy Carico Smith

AFTER MOSES

A novel by Karen Mockler

MacAdam/Cage

For Rick, Tom, Tish, and Jim, my own siblings, who taught me a thing or two about a thing or two.

CHAPTER ONE

She told him he didn't need to walk her home.

"I'm not," he said.

They left the rental car and meandered together down the shoulder of the highway, not back into town, but farther out into darkness. They weren't looking at each other, but he could not have seen her anyway. She was wearing a black dress, black pearls, with a black scarf tied around the straw hat she carried in her hand, and there were no lights on that stretch of road, besides. Several times they wandered out toward the center line, until a set of headlights approached from behind or ahead and they sensed, more than saw, their error.

Once she stopped at a large rectangular sign just off the shoulder, wrapped her hands around one of the posts, and, for a long time, leaned her forehead against the metal.

"Are you all right?" he asked her. "Are you sick?"

"Johnny," she said, "I'm not like that."

So he waited silently beside her. The night air was muggy but no longer hot, and he watched a satellite glide across the sky. When a semi passed and its headlights fell upon the sign, he realized that they had crossed into Indiana. He peered up the road to her motel lit in pink and yellow. He took her by the elbow and they set out once more.

When they reached the motel, she unlocked the door of her room, then went to get some ice. Johnny turned on the TV, switched on the air-conditioning, and posted himself by the open door. He planned to make his exit as soon as she returned, but he had always had trouble parting with Emily. It didn't seem right, somehow.

She returned carrying a plastic bucket full of square ice cubes with hollowed-out centers. She glanced at the air conditioner, seemed to hesitate, then shut the motel room door. After she set the bucket down on top of the TV she kicked off her shoes, reached in the bucket, and popped an ice cube in her mouth.

"Have some," she said, talking around it. "They're the good kind."

When he didn't respond, Emily lifted the ice bucket off the television and padded toward him on her bare feet. Johnny fingered the doorknob and she stopped. He felt her watching him, but when he put his hand back in his pocket and looked up, she was looking somewhere else.

"You all right?" he asked.

She was considering the motel carpet with lowered lids. "I'm all right," she said, nodding slowly.

He looked at her toenails. "Why black?"

Emily looked too. "In the beginning it was purely aesthetic," she explained. "I liked the way they looked all bruised, like I'd mashed them under a garage door."

Johnny nodded.

"Later on, it became more of a ritual."

"Shoe too," he said.

"I know," said Emily. "She had her own reasons."

Shoe was Johnny's big sister. For the last six years, Emily had been her best friend. Johnny had been scared to call Emily with the bad news, but there was no one else to call her, so he had done it. He had tried calling other friends of Shoe's as well, but some had been impossible to track down. Others said they'd fly out for the funeral and hadn't. He hadn't really thought the others would. Only Emily.

Now she extended the ice bucket toward him, but did not come any closer.

"I hope we can keep in touch," he said.

Emily cracked one of her crooked smiles. "We're sobering up." She picked daintily through the ice cubes. "At least use the toilet before you go. I'll let you break the seal."

Johnny did not break the seal, but slipped it from the toilet seat while Emily looked on. When he handed it to her, she draped the sanitation label across her chest like a banner, then marched from the room like a proud contestant in a beauty pageant.

Now he was alone. When he had gone about his business, he put down the toilet lid and sat. Time to leave, he thought. Johnny stared at the shower stall and didn't move a muscle. When Emily knocked on the door, he rose and slowly opened it.

"You tired?" she asked. The toilet banner had disappeared. So had the funeral attire. She had changed into her nightgown and was sucking on another piece of ice. "Because if you are, maybe you should stay."

Johnny nodded.

She offered him her toothbrush. Johnny did not refuse. She stepped onto the toilet lid, turned and seated herself on the toilet tank, elbows on her knees, knees pressed together, face in the palms of her hands.

"I'll ask for an eight o'clock wake-up call," she said. "If we leave here by eight-thirty, we can get the car and still be at your house in time for the will."

Johnny lowered his head and spat into the sink. He thought about it while he rinsed his mouth, then straightened and nodded his head.

Emily turned out the overhead light in the main room. Johnny turned off the television. They turned down the bed and crept inside it, settling at a distance from each other. Except for the humming of the air conditioner under the front window, there was silence.

For a long time, neither of them moved and nothing happened. Johnny lay with his hands behind his head and paid close attention as, one by one, his fingers all grew numb. Under the sheets, Emily shifted. Her foot nudged his in the dark and disappeared.

"Sorry," she said.

"Oh, I don't mind."

The air conditioner rattled suddenly, violently, and he swallowed under the cover of its noise. "Do you want to talk about this?" he asked her.

Emily laughed. "I always did."

And because the world was a hostile place without Shoe in it, as they talked they crept toward one another in the dark, until she lay inside his arms, where she remained until long after sunrise, when the motel phone rang to wake them.

The rest of the family was gathered in the living room when they arrived, silently awaiting their lawyer. The two entered and took seats side by side on the piano bench. Emily still carried her straw hat, but instead of putting it on she turned it around and around until it finally settled on her knees. Johnny still wore his suit. He hadn't showered in days, and his dirty blond hair fell away from his forehead in a rakish way it never did when it was clean.

His father frowned across the room at him, and Johnny decided he must look pretty bad. But when his sister Ida stole a look, her eyes ranging slyly from him to Emily and away, he wondered if his father had something else in mind. Irritated, he got to his feet and paced the house from back to front, but the house irritated him further.

It was one of those big houses built to look old, but without success. There were approximations of a parquet floor, half-hearted banisters, and bedroom windows criss-crossed by flat strips of metal to make the glass look paned from the outside, though that did not make it paned; from the inside, anyone could tell the glass was just one big sheet. There was nothing genuine or stately about the house and the kids all figured this out. It was something that crept into their sensibility before they could prevent it, making them into vigilant anti-snobs and complicating almost all their social interactions.

Because there aren't enough noble old houses to go around, Johnny thought. Sometimes in life you had to hold out for the real thing—Johnny understood that too—but he and his sisters had found other real things to hold out for. They hadn't fought their battles on the material plane. And he had felt okay about those battles, and his place in them, until their fiercest warrior had gone and lost hers.

After the funeral, several people had expressed to Johnny their surprise that someone as impetuous as Shoe would have made legal arrangements, at so young an age. But Johnny knew she was not impetuous. She was deliberate. That was what troubled him.

He stopped pacing and leaned against the front door until the knock came. Johnny showed the lawyer in and stood by while the man offered condolences to Johnny's parents. Frank Hurley been their lawyer for years and apparently Shoe's as well, an old friend of the family, with wrinkled cheeks and a wandering eye. Johnny stared at his kind, worn face for comfort.

Frank told them the will was brief, and it was. Shoe's life insurance policy left $85,000 to Moses, her five-year-old son. Most of the paintings Ida had given her through the years would go to him as well, save three in particular that Shoe had stipulated would go to Emily. Johnny got all her ski equipment, camping and climbing gear, and topo maps. The care of Moses would fall to Ida. There was no mention of the father.

At the end came a curious specification, or request,

that in the event Emily was still unmarried at the time of Shoe's death, Johnny marry her himself. To that, no one reacted much at all, save Emily, who laughed aloud.

Johnny was less amused. He'd known for years that if anything ever happened to Shoe, she wanted Ida to raise her son. Shoe had told him so late one night, a bottle of Johnnie Walker between them on her kitchen table, the stove lamp the only light burning in the house. She'd told him how it would be, how Moses would learn the virtues of their small Ohio town: the quiet pleasures of walks down by the river, the twisting, shady country roads, the bird sanctuary with that brilliant indigo bunting, how to feed the horses down the hill, which cemetery was haunted, how to take the tracks to dodge the law or cross the river or hear the wild kittens mewing among the rocks after dark. He'd learn all the things they'd learned as kids. Ida would show him everything, Shoe had said, as only Ida could. Ida should have been the mom.

But Shoe had been a great mom. She had adored her son. Sitting in her kitchen at midnight, Johnny had thought it was just the whiskey talking.

"It'll do Ida a world of good." In the near-dark, Shoe had taken a drink from the bottle, then wiped her mouth with the back of her hand. "And, you know, I'll be dead. So she won't have any choice."

Now Johnny wondered if this request to marry her best friend was supposed to do him a world of good as well. Maybe he was supposed to think he had no choice either, because Shoe had gone to an early grave. But he believed an early grave was what his sister wanted, and he believed he knew her reasons. To hand over the maternal reins was just the start. The main thing was that at thirty-four, the world she'd courted so violently for so long had worn her out. Maybe dying was the only way she could return home and still save face. She seized that opportunity as she had seized them all her life.

As a result, he predicted the demise of the family. It would start with his mother, since Shoe was her safeguard against disappointment. Without his wife, Johnny's father would grow silent and ever more remote. In effect, he'd disappear, and Ida couldn't make it on her own. Though they had lived their lives as opposites, Johnny knew that at core his sisters were more alike than different, and Shoe had really been no more of a survivor than Ida. No one in the family was much of a survivor, Johnny thought, except him, and that was largely accidental. He had never made up his mind to die as Shoe had, but then again, he'd never made up his mind to live.

After the will was read, Frank Hurley lingered briefly to talk with Professor Tumarkin. Mrs. Tumarkin sat on the couch beside her husband and stared at her hands. She wore a tailored navy skirt and jacket despite the heat. Her nut brown hair was neatly clipped across the nape of her neck, her lipstick still in place. But now she also wore the vacant look she had worn ever since the sheriff's phone call came from Boulder County.

Her firstborn had been found off a rough mountain road west of Nederland, Colorado, dead from a gunshot wound to the back of the head. It had taken more than a week to find Shoe's body, although another body was found less than a mile away on the same day she went missing, killed, like her, with a small-caliber bullet. The victim was a local drug dealer, found farther up the same dirt road, shot through his windshield and slumped behind his wheel. Her truck surfaced before she did, thirty miles south of Nederland on a side street in Idaho Springs. Fingerprints lifted from her truck matched fingerprints from the dead man's truck. These were the only connections between the dealer and Shoe, as far as anyone could tell. Police were looking for the man those fingerprints belonged to and for Shoe's gun, which was missing.

That was all they'd told the family, but Johnny had his own ideas about his sister's murder. He had pictures in his mind. Not of the killer, but it was not the killer that mattered to him anyway. As far as Johnny was concerned, his sister had killed herself.

Not that her death was drug-related. He doubted it, in fact. Maybe the killer had wanted her truck and nothing more. But Johnny held against his sister whatever brought the two of them together in the first place— whatever things she may or may not have done to place her in that wrong place at that wrong time. And whether she'd lost her life with intention or quite the opposite, Moses would never see his mother again.

Emily and Johnny rose slowly to their feet and went to stand in front of Mrs. Tumarkin, whose skin was somehow gray.

"You look like you need to lie down, Mom," Johnny said. "Why don't you?"

His mother gazed past him through the long windows onto the overgrown lawn. All week there had been thundershowers. It had never dried out enough to cut, although Johnny had promised he would do that much before he left.

"I've been lying down all my life," she said, rising, and disappeared upstairs.

Johnny sunk his hands into his pockets and spread the tips of his shoes.

"Well," said Emily. "I have a plane to catch."

Johnny would not look at her. "I'll walk you to your car," he said.

They moved outside together, although no longer side by side. Emily closed the front door behind them and trailed him along the front walk. When they reached the curb, she fiddled with her key, but the car was already unlocked. She climbed in, shut the door and rolled down the window. Johnny was standing in the middle of the street, looking west.

"This is it," he said.

"I guess you're not going to marry me," she said, and smiled.

Johnny smiled too, a toothless smile directed at the concrete. "We wouldn't want everyone to think we were just doing it for her sake."

Emily sat back in the driver's seat. She draped her wrists over the steering wheel. "I don't suppose we could just issue a disclaimer with the wedding invitations."

Johnny forced a laugh and sidled closer to the open window. This is really it, he thought, distraught and yet determined. They would not meet again. The feeling he had always had for her would remain an unnamed mystery. He'd never settle it now. And when she found what she was looking for—because he knew she hadn't yet—he wouldn't hear about it, and he wouldn't know what it was. He sidled away again, across and down the quiet street. When he reached the neighbor's mailbox, he stooped over and peered inside.

"I hope you don't think I put her up to this," he called.

"God, no," said Emily. "Please."

"She wrote that will with every intention to die, and then she just makes a big joke of it at the end—and you laughed!"

"No," she said. "I never laugh at jokes."

"What?" He started back toward her, his dirty hair flapping with each step. "That's true. Why is that?" Before she could answer, he thrust out a hand to stop her. "Don't tell me," he said. "What for? She's ruined everything. Now we'll never know what would have happened. She's altered the course of history, for all we know."

Emily had been watching him in her car's side mirror. She shifted her eyes back to the open window. Beyond it, Johnny was pacing in the gutter. "Are you referring to the murder, or the will?" she asked.

Johnny shrugged, shifting his weight from one wing tip to the other. He had left his jacket in the house and rolled up the sleeves of his white shirt, but his tie was still tightly knotted. "Everything. What difference does it make? They're one and the same. That fucking provision—"

"What's the big deal?" said Emily. "Since it is, as you

said, a joke."

"It's not a joke." Johnny stole another look at her, then scowled and looked away.

Emily sighed. She lifted one hand from the steering wheel and held it out the window toward him, but when he realized what she was asking, he thrust both his hands deep in the pockets of his pants. She sighed again. "We'll talk about it later," she said.

"No, we won't." There was no way to talk any of this over with Emily. She had been Shoe's best friend. She would always take Shoe's side. "I can't even look at you now," he said.

"I noticed that. But you seem to be suggesting—" Emily swallowed, "that if she hadn't mentioned us like that in the will, you might have had something to do with me."

He was silent.

"And now you won't."

"How can I?" he shouted. "I will not endorse her death!"

They both turned and glanced up at the house to see if anyone was watching. But there was no audience. The windows of the white house were closed and empty.

"But you aren't being honest now," Emily said quietly, firmly. "This isn't about her at all. Just tell the truth."

"I am telling the truth!"

"In that case," she said, "you're cutting me off just to spite her. And that seems rather willful."

"That's right," Johnny said. He feasted his eyes on her face for the last time, before he lost that face to life forever, as he had lost his sister's to death. "Now that

Shoe's gone, there's a lot more will to go around."

Emily lifted her wrists from the wheel and was about to turn the key in the ignition when she stopped.

Since she was fifteen or sixteen, Emily had seen into other people's lives. Her field of view was nothing like that of a psychic, neither eerie nor of any practical use. She couldn't see what was, what had been, or even what might be. She only saw what should have been.

These visions usually involved strangers, though she had imagined better lives for people she knew in passing: teachers, a grocery clerks, a doctor. The satisfying futures that played out for her were not, she understood, intended for the light of day. They weren't likely to ever take place. But she'd always thought what she saw with Johnny was something different—not a vision, but a daydream. Never mind that the daydream's details were fixed and a bit peculiar, like a short, haunting clip from a film without dialogue. Never mind that all of her visions were. She had thought the scene from her life was different because it wasn't relegated to something that should have been; because it still might be.

Johnny had set her straight about that today.

Because of what she saw, Emily knew that some of the world's best stories would never come to pass. While all of the raw materials existed—the right people, places, the requisite longing—they would seldom come together in the necessary way, because a story's rightness did not make it, in turn, inevitable. The two qualities were unrelated, and would remain forever strangers to one another, like two aging lovers she had once seen on the bus—lovers because in her mind she had seen them, winding their way up a steep, narrow street at dusk, arm in arm, on the first trip either one had ever made to Paris—a man and woman who got off at different stops without ever noticing each other. The fact that these visions weren't imminent was endlessly sad, but so inescapable that Emily had never fought it. And she didn't fight it now.

It is a tragedy when lovers are torn apart. But where lies the tragedy in a love affair that never comes to pass?

The tragedy, Emily reflected, was hers alone, just as the vision had been. And yet the picture she saw in her mind of a single rainy afternoon, the same slow-moving Saturday that she had seen for years, was not improbable. It not only should have been, but could have. Until today.

"I saw us," she said suddenly. "The two of us together."

When she stole a look at Johnny's beautiful face, it had gone still. He stood just out of reach with his eyes downcast, willing her, perhaps, to stop.

"I don't mean to upset you," she said. "It's only that I saw it all so clearly and I never have before, not in my own life. I have to tell you what I saw."

Johnny nodded carefully, as if he were balancing something on his head, or as if he were afraid his head might crack apart.

"It's a Saturday," she said, then switched to past tense, so as not to alarm him. For her, the rainy Saturday was still to come, but that would have to change. She'd recast the future as a memory, and then let it fade. "The rain came in the night, just before dawn. At first there was thunder and lightning, but by daybreak the noise and spectacle had stopped and it was only falling softly. It fell all morning, and into the afternoon. And we didn't want to get out of bed. We just stayed in bed."

"Sounds depressing," Johnny said.

"It wasn't, though. We had a big four-poster bed against one wall. That bed was our kingdom. It was late summer. All the fruits were coming ripe on the trees outside. We could smell them through the open window."

"I thought it was raining."

"It was. The window was stuck. It was one of those windows like they have in school, the long rectangular kind that hinges at the top and swings out at the bottom, but without the mottled glass. The rain slapped the glass, coming down, but none of it fell inside the room. And we didn't care anyway."

"Because of the smell?"

"That was part of it," said Emily. "We also liked the noise." She smiled suddenly. "We had a pear in bed with us."

"Red?"

"Yellow. It gave off this scent, like from the fruit trees, but because it was so close and dry, also very warm. We thought it might still be alive. We'd been smelling it for hours, but we were waiting—"

She broke off when she saw him squirm. Gently, she raised a hand and pressed the palm against her own head. This somehow seemed to help.

"Go on," Johnny said.

Emily shook her head. She was thinking that she talked all wrong, that she secretly despised the way she talked and had for years. She sounded stuffy. Serious. Like no fun at all. It was no wonder he didn't want her. If she were him, she wouldn't want her either. "I have a plane to catch," she said.

Another careful nod from Johnny.

But it is very bitter, she thought, just the same. Because she could only tell him what she'd seen, and it was this translation, this poor execution, that was objectionable. The vision behind her eyes was lovely and without fault.

She looked at him once more, because his face was very dear to her.

"That's all," she said. "Now I'll be off."

When this met with no objection, she was.

As she drove along the old bricks of Main Street, past the water tower and out onto the highway that would take her once more past last night's bar and their motel room, she reminded herself that of course, the same held true for almost everyone. People are heartbroken the world over, she told herself. And I've broken one or two of those hearts. I've disappointed men by rejecting them as he rejects me now. That's probably why my visions always embrace lonely people, not happy ones. Because there are so many.

Not that her visions helped them. She understood that. They only helped Emily, and only for a few minutes, while she basked in the glow of what might have been. When it came to other people's lives she would keep on dreaming; from now on she'd be more disciplined about her own.

Emily didn't know if other men would follow him. Surely she couldn't love them, but she made herself no promises. She would take them as they came and perhaps settle for someone less than he, someone more like herself. Whatever happened, she'd seek no sympathy for her situation. There was no use. People would tell her there was nothing to mourn, and that was what she mourned, as much as anything.

But it was in the produce aisle at the grocery store that real despair seized her. After that day in August, Emily stopped eating pears, for she had already known the perfect one, that rainy afternoon in their bed. She recalled the tender tautness of its skin, how far their teeth pressed into the warmly speckled surface before it broke, that first run of juice. There was no use in buying other pears. She knew full well they never would suffice.

CHAPTER TWO

From mid-August until the killing frost, they loaded the red wagon with whatever flowers they could glean from the family gardens. This they pulled behind them, along the shady half-mile stretch of sidewalk past the university, down the long hill that reasserts itself as a highway upon leaving town, and in to the entrance of the cemetery where his mother, her sister, was buried.

This was a ritual they both enjoyed. She taught him some things about flowers—not to pull the plant up from the root, for instance, and which blooms kept best, once they were separated from their source—and the boy learned quickly. By October, he proposed they stop killing flowers for his mother and give her living ones instead. His aunt agreed. They made an excursion to the local nursery just as the mums were entering their last-of-the-season sale. She stood back and watched her nephew bend over blooms of unusual hue—not the standard yellows and pinks, but the rusts and brilliant scarlets. This satisfied her deeply.

They were always on excursions, those two. Was there anywhere they didn't go? You were sure to see them out somewhere, consuming experience, and if you saw the one, you saw the other. They were a pair, though rarely hand in hand.

They especially liked to sit out under the water tower in the town square, one of Aunt Ida's curious contradictions, for she was morbidly shy and yet she loved the town. She loved watching its people. She enjoyed all sorts of bustle, mercantilism, enjoyed fights and machinations and intrigues, from a distance.

So they were peculiar. When they ventured to the center of the town—and they ventured there on days they didn't venture into the country—she wore her Salvation Army wig, or an old chiffon scarf gently knotted beneath her chin, or even the straw hat that Emily had left behind after the funeral. She dressed in all sorts of get-ups, not to draw attention to herself but rather to draw it away. When the leaves began to turn, she donned one of her autumn coats, the purple velveteen or the furry fake leopard that Moses loved to pet. In disguise, Ida did not mind people looking at her because it felt as if they were seeing someone else. She even liked to flirt, when the opportunity arose, but it was all a fanciful experiment. Her real life sprung from her imagination, like a strange and peerless flower fed on nothing more than rarefied air.

Anyone who bothered speculating thought that now, with Moses come to live with the Tumarkins, Ida would change. By this they meant that with her newfound responsiblity she would mature, and in so doing, become more like other people. Either this or vice versa. The order didn't matter; the outcome would be the same.

Instead, she seemed to become more of what she was before. Without being bad himself, Moses was a bad influence on his aunt, because he allowed her to indulge in everything that inspired her. She could not be bothered with the world's opinion when she was with Moses. He made her laugh as if she were in love.

For Moses, life with his mother had always been an adventure, and it remained so with his aunt. These new adventures bore a different sort of stamp from the old ones, but they were no more predictable and of equal delight. Sometimes they walked together to the library, sat down at the table with the short chairs, turned on the ancient phonograph, plugged in their headphones, and listened for hours on end to scratched records telling fairy tales. Sometimes at home they shut themselves in the basement and painted together, she at her easel, he at his. They wore matching paint smocks, which Ida sewed from old curtains, telling Moses there was a costume for every occasion.

Ida taught him to cook. "Now, when you go to first grade next week," she said one day, standing beside him at the stove while he stirred a bubbling pot of chocolate, "you may not like it very much, but when you come home, I'll be here, and we can make ourselves a treat..."

Moses never asked her about his new school. He sensed that he'd survive it, as she said she had, and he knew that if she said she'd be there when he returned, then she would.

It was true she seldom touched him. She seldom held him and she never kissed him at all, but sometimes she rested a hand on his unruly hair or, if she was excited, grabbed him by the arm. Best of all was when she read him books. Then Moses would climb into her lap and they would stay like that for hours on end.

The only time when Aunt Ida wasn't available to him was when she shut herself in the basement and locked the door. She rarely did this while he was home, especially once he'd started school, but sometimes after they'd eaten their afternoon snack she would return downstairs. Then Moses knew that she was painting a different sort of painting from what they did together.

He'd go upstairs to see his grandmother, who was not quite well. Sometimes she didn't eat with them, and Aunt Ida brought food to her on a tray. Ida said his grandmother was sick with sadness, but never said what she was sad about. Moses decided it must be his mom. He made a point of visiting his grandmother often, to try and cheer her up. Usually he found her in the master bedroom, where he climbed into the armchair beside the bed and she propped herself up on thick pillows and they talked.

Afterwards he climbed trees out back until he spied his grandfather walking home from work across the college playing field, just beyond their backyard. Moses would run out to be the first to greet him. If the field was empty they'd kick a soccer ball back and forth, or Moses would bring gloves and a softball and they'd play catch. His grandfather said this practice would develop his hand-eye coordination skills, but Moses didn't care about that and he didn't think his grandfather really did either.

In the beginning, Moses tried to trick himself into thinking his aunt was his mom. This took some concentration, since their voices were different. He was most successful at the playground, when Aunt Ida sat on a bench at the proper distance and read a book. He could watch her from the corner of his eye with her long, dark hair, and start to believe she was her sister. But even this illusion was hard to hold on to for very long, and it made his head ache.

After his birthday that September, he gave up trying. His grandparents gave him a bike. Uncle Johnny got him a fishing pole. Aunt Ida wove Moses a basket. She told him he could put it on his bike and pedal home with all the fish he'd catch out at the lake. When Moses blew out his six candles, he wouldn't tell them what he'd wished for, but he did say he'd know soon whether or not the wish had come true. He wished, of course, for his mom to come back to life. She didn't, though.

Aunt Ida had a friend they'd sometimes go to visit, a small man with a mustache. Sometimes the man would stroll along the brick streets of downtown with the two of them, tossing his spent cigarettes onto the sidewalks or into the gutter. Aunt Ida would always reproach him for this, but although they disagreed, they never fought, and though at first Moses found Henry hard to understand because of his funny accent, he soon got used to it and memorized the arguments on both sides.

Henry would take them bowling and on some

Sundays to mass at the Catholic church, then afterwards drive them deep into the country until they arrived in another town, it didn't matter which, where they would drink coffee, Henry would smoke his cigarettes, and Moses and Aunt Ida would eat big pieces of pie. He ate cream pie, she ate fruit, always the dark kinds— boysenberry, blueberry, blackberry. Once, when the diner was out of dark fruit pies, Aunt Ida sighed and ate nothing. It was then she told them about the huckleberry.

Out West, she said, somewhere in the Rockies, grew the finest berry of them all. It was little known outside its region. In gourmet magazines, when berry season rolled around, it didn't even garner mention. And since it was a strictly Western wonder, she shouldn't know the first thing about it, she explained, living two thousand miles away, but Moses' mother had once smuggled home two pints on an airplane and Ida had baked up a pie for her, right there in Ohio!

His aunt tried to describe the huckleberry to them, starting with its rich violet color and a tartness that only ran skin-deep. Underneath, she said, was a flavor so fierce that even a modest bite—if you could show such restraint—would explode in your mouth, lingering for minutes on end.

While she described this huckleberry in hushed tones, Henry forgot his cigarette and the smoke swirled up from the ashtray through the late morning light from a nearby window that looked out on the town's main thoroughfare.

"Incomparable," Ida concluded.

"Impossible," said Henry.

"Practically," she said.

They were silent for a time, then Ida announced her intention to one day go and harvest the berry herself. She reminded Moses that of the three of them, he alone had lived in the land of the huckleberry. There, she said, they must've eaten huckleberry pancakes every morning. You are the only one of us who knows those mountains firsthand, she told him. You are our resident expert. You have come to tell us all. But try as he might, Moses could not reach that far back into his magical past.

As for Henry, Moses came to like him a lot. The afternoon they painted themselves up like Indians and chased each other, whooping, through the woods—the only time Moses had to run full strength to keep up with his aunt—had been Henry's idea. He and Ida were not really grown-ups, but when Moses' aunt was forced to talk with other people she would sometimes pretend to be one for stretches of time, discussing subjects Moses didn't understand and didn't care about. He and his aunt were always relieved to get away.

Henry lived just beyond the long hill that carried people out of town. He lived, in fact, off the same street as Moses and his family, but while their house sat just north of campus, where the street grew quiet, Henry lived to the south, just past the cemetery. There, the road strained to become a highway and begin its journey down through farmland and other towns toward the great Cincinnati, a city his aunt promised to take him to one day, though cities scared her.

Henry lived alone on the top floor of a peculiar old farmhouse with sloping floors, and the walls of his house were hung with paintings, all by Henry himself. While Aunt Ida painted dreams, it seemed to Moses that Henry painted nightmares. Even the pink pig looked gloomy, and one painting frightened him so much he had to close his eyes just to walk underneath it.

This painting hung in the shadows of the middle room. The room itself had a lonely window that captured a narrow column of sunlight each day. The painting, of a man with a howling hole where his mouth should be, was too far from the window to get any light at all. One day, trying to get past it, Moses bumped into a chair. When he opened his eyes, his aunt was standing in the doorway to the room beyond, her back to the light, watching him. Later, she told Moses that she didn't like that painting either. "Poor Henry," she said, and sighed.

In the kitchen, though, there were no paintings, and sometimes Henry cooked them food from his native Texas: fudge, beer beans, or barbecued ribs. Henry said these things were all he ever ate, but Moses didn't believe him—there were spaghetti noodles stuck to the kitchen ceiling, and besides, Moses knew he lied about other things. For instance, they had heard Henry tell his landlord there weren't any mice, even though Moses had seen one with his bare eyes, skittering across the tiles of the kitchen floor.

Aunt Ida seemed to think this lie was marvelously funny, although she never lied herself. When the landlord dropped off some back-breaking traps anyway, Henry was so upset that Ida had to box them up, tape the box tight, and set it on a high shelf, out of view. Afterwards, she persuaded Henry to buy a set of humane traps. They drove with him to the hardware store and as soon as they returned, Ida set the traps with different kinds of bait—cheese, oats, peanut butter. These traps were ineffective, it turned out, but they all enjoyed checking the small gray boxes, lifting each one and shaking it gently from side to side, hoping for a thump.

One afternoon, Moses did find a mouse in Henry's toilet, still alive, its tiny claws scrabbling against the tank. He grabbed a colander from under the kitchen sink, scooped out the sodden mouse and quickly tipped it into the empty bathtub, then watched with great pleasure as the mouse shook out its gray fur. Moses went to the refrigerator and brought it back a square of longhorn cheddar.

Moses felt he should keep the mouse, once he had saved its life. Henry thought he should let it go.

"Not in the house," said Ida.

"Why not?" Henry said. "This is its home."

"What about the traps?" she said. "I thought the whole reason you bought the live traps was so you could move the mice out of here if you ever caught them."

"I never said that," Henry said.

"Well, that's no good," Ida said. "There's no sense of progress if you just let them go. You might catch the same one over and over and not know it."

"I'd know it," Henry said.

"Me too," said Moses.

"I just look them in the eye."

"But you may not always live here," Ida said. "And when you leave, the next tenant may not be so kindly disposed toward mice. So we have to move them if we want to save them. Otherwise it's just a game at their expense."

"I don't want to disorient them," Henry said.

"But they'll do all right," she said. "Mice have good instincts, you know. Much better than ours."

Henry eyed her suggestively. It was a long time before he spoke. "My instincts are magnificent," he said.

She blushed and looked the other way. "A field," she said.

They put the mouse into an empty potato chip canister. Then Moses and his aunt took the secret path through Henry's backyard down to the cemetery. They released the mouse on his mother's grave, to keep her company. Some night Moses hoped to sneak out and visit them both. He'd go in his pajamas so if anybody asked what he was doing, he could tell them he was sleepwalking. This kind of lie, he sensed, was neither the kind his aunt would laugh at, nor would mind.

One night after dinner, Aunt Ida and Moses settled onto their front porch to wait for Henry. It was not much of a porch, not for a big white house that wanted to look older than it was, just a concrete platform with five feet of railing. There was hardly enough room on it to unfold a chair. Ida said it was more of a stoop, like they had in big cities back East, where all the buildings were pushed together.

Moses had never been back East, and although his aunt hadn't either, she had read lots of novels set in those cities and seen movies too. She told him that if theirs was a real stoop, there would be three little girls down on the sidewalk in front of them, skipping rope. Moses pictured three girls from his first grade class, and waved.

It was not altogether dark when they sat down to wait, but the dark was on its way. Daylight savings time was ending soon, and after that it would be Halloween. He and Ida had driven out into the country the day before and carried back pumpkins from a huge patch. These sat behind them on the porch.

Many leaves had already fallen from the trees; some were bigger than the span of his two hands put together. These were sycamore leaves, his aunt told him. Moses said he'd never seen such leaves before. You didn't in the West, she said, because there wasn't enough water.

"There was a lot of water," Moses said. "There were streams everywhere."

That summer, in fact, before his mother died, he had been learning how to fish. And he remembered lakes where they had camped with Emily and Uncle Johnny. Sometimes Moses had slept out under the stars.

"How come you never camped with us, Aunt Ida?" he asked her. "You like nature. You like lakes. How come you never came to visit?"

"Because you always came to visit me," she said.

"Was the first time when you made the huckleberry pie?"

"That was the first time. You weren't born yet, but we

gave you a piece anyway."

"I remember," Moses said.

They were still laughing at that when a car turned into their cul-de-sac and parked across the street. It wasn't Henry's car. Moses had never seen it before. A man got out and started away down the sidewalk. The man was very tall.

In her lap, Aunt Ida held a plastic bag, filled with maybe a dozen apples. When the man had moved out of earshot, she pointed to the bag. "These are called Delicious apples," she told him. "Do you know why?"

"Because they're delicious," Moses said, patting the bag.

"They should be," Ida said. "But it's a trick."

They eyed one another knowingly in the gloaming.

"They're pretty enough," she said. "They sell them to the people in supermarkets who don't know any better. Always remember, Moses, that beauty doesn't equal delight."

"Then why did you buy them?"

"These aren't for me."

"Who are they for? Henry?"

"Not him either."

Moses sighed and set his chin into his hands.

"I know some good stories about apples," his aunt said. "It is the world's most literary fruit."

"What about the huckleberry?"

She turned and smiled at him broadly. "It's the world's best-kept secret."

The air cooled around them and held the smell of dying leaves. Moses put his hands inside his pockets to keep them warm, and watched the tall man on the opposite sidewalk hit the half circle of the cul-de-sac. Now, if he kept going, the sidewalk would lead him right past them.

"Who is that?" Moses asked.

"I don't know," Ida said. "I think he's lost."

"He's tall."

"He is."

"He's the tallest person I've ever seen."

The man turned up the driveway of a house two doors down. The porch light wasn't on, and when the man knocked on the front door, nobody came. He knocked again, then started back toward the street on his long legs. As he approached, the sky lost the last of its color and their voices dropped to a whisper, then stopped. It seemed to Moses that the man was looking at them through the dark air, turning his head from side to side like a slow-moving sprinkler but then staring hard each time his gaze came their way.

"Hello," called Moses, when the man had reached the bottom of their drive.

"Hello!" returned the man. He had a deep, booming voice, but friendly too, laughter-ready.

"Nice night," continued Moses. It was the thing his mother always used to say after dark, to strangers on the street.

The man stopped. He passed a slow hand down his face. "That it is," he said. "You seem to be enjoying it, you and your sister."

"This is my aunt," said Moses. He thought a moment.

"I don't have a sister."

"Well, that can always change," said the man.

Moses did not see how, but having never thought of it before, he opted to wait before deciding the matter for certain. The man might know something Moses didn't.

Before Moses had a chance to ask him, though, the man raised a hand in farewell. "Have a good one," he called.

He turned and ambled slowly back across the street. He didn't look their way again, but they looked his, Moses with his light brown eyes, chin in his palms, Ida from the corners of her dark ones. The tall man fit himself back inside his short car and turned the key in the ignition. Just as the headlights came on, Henry arrived.

Ida lifted the sack of apples and made her way down to Henry's car. The tall man was still across the street, engine running, but Ida put her back to him and stayed that way until Henry got out. Then the three of them slipped around the side of the house, through the backyard and beyond, onto the university playing field.

Maybe the tall man will follow us, Moses thought. He glanced over his shoulder a couple times, but it was an old moon overhead and he couldn't see anybody. From the playing field, it was a straight shot down the hill to the stables. Past the stables was the barbed-wire fence. By the time they reached it, Moses had forgotten all about the friendly stranger.

He watched as Aunt Ida gathered her long skirt in one hand, the apples in the other, and slipped through. A few steps into the field, she broke open the plastic bag.

Lifting the first apple, she moved away across the pasture. Moses saw the shadowy band start toward her, taking on animal shapes as they approached. Soon she was swept into their midst and Moses lost sight of her.

"They're huge," Henry said. "They'll crush her."

Moses glimpsed her again, one arm upraised, the first gift received. She dipped back into the sack.

"No, they won't." He set his hands between the sharp spurs on the fence and pulled down, the way his mom had once taught him, hunting mushrooms in the forest. When he had stepped through and planted his sneakers on the far side, Henry followed. From this side, the horses seemed much larger. They whirled around his aunt, but she fed out her prizes slowly. Suddenly the band of horses shifted toward him, then he saw why. Ida was stepping carefully back to the fence where he and Henry watched, as the horses rustled around her.

"She's a magician," Henry said.

Moses knew his aunt was no such thing. She didn't hypnotize the horses or enchant them; she just liked them. When the horses came forward and surrounded him, too, his aunt handed him the last apple and pointed. "That one there—he didn't get one." It was a horse the color of sand with a black mane and tail, a little smaller than the rest.

She took Moses' free hand, and while the horses spun above him, swiping for a bite, she parted the fluid shapes until they reached his horse. Moses lifted the apple. He and the sandy horse beheld one another. Then, with one sweep of his head, the horse took up the apple and disappeared.

With nothing left to give, Moses felt a pinch of fear between his shoulders, but it was only physical, nothing like the fear he felt in Henry's middle room. His aunt still had his hand, and when she pulled down a wire on the fence, he stepped through. Soon they were safe again.

Yet Moses felt different than he had before they walked into the field. For one thing, he hadn't understood before how safe they were. And he hadn't known that safety could feel exhilarating.

CHAPTER THREE

For his mother, safety had never been any such thing. To combat the shackles of safety, she confronted fear. This felt like a ritual on occasion, but was often just a habit. Sometimes it was a habit she could reason with; sometimes it kicked in like a reflex and she could not. If she thought some situation held possible humiliation, she sought it out to prove she wasn't afraid of humiliation, just like she wasn't afraid of pride, loneliness, danger, pleasure, pain. It didn't matter if the situation itself held no possible reward for her: The reward was in the doing. Conquering her fears felt less like recklessness than good housekeeping, as if she were keeping her affairs in order, or in the event of an accident, her underwear clean. Shoe tried to stay on top of her fears, and then one day ran out of them.

She contemplated suicide. But though twenty-seven seemed old at the time, she felt she owed her body something for all she'd put it through, and it said: Let me live.

"Fine," Shoe said. "I'll find another way out of this pit I've dug us into."

She was tending bar in Ketchum, Idaho, when she did. It was a quiet Tuesday night in November, and nineteen degrees outside. When Max came in, she was playing checkers with one of the regulars at the far end of the bar.

He was wearing a jean jacket, no hat, and his hands were bare. He stopped just inside the door and straightened out the length of him, took a survey of the room and let the room take one of him. Then he made his way over to one of the empty bar stools and Josh, the other bartender, took his order.

Max was rangy, sly. He wore a thick gold chain around his neck and even in the bar's dim light, Shoe could see that his tan wasn't natural. He didn't belong there, but he struck up a conversation with a couple of the locals and before long they were buying his drinks. Women watched him from booths and corners.

The next night it was the same. He was gregarious or something along those lines, and it was this social facility that first alerted Shoe to trouble, because she distrusted such people. She couldn't understand their motives, and motives meant more to her than acts. Only motives, she contended, got to the heart of the matter. When she caught him looking her way, she realized what she felt was more than distrust. She felt fear. So the third night, she got his beer and brought it over.

"Nice night," she said, setting it down.

Max laughed loudly. It was colder than the two before

and still he hadn't gotten himself any winter clothes.

"Give me Orlando any day," he said.

"Seems like I read the average household in Orlando makes thirteen car trips a day."

"So?"

"So it sounds like hell on earth." Shoe gave his glass a gentle tap. "This one's on me," she announced.

Max lowered the palm of one long hand onto the countertop, scarce inches from hers. The motion was so slow, so deliberate, she saw each finger flatten against the old wood in its turn. Then he raised his pale brown gaze to her. This, too, took long enough to be laughable, but she didn't laugh.

"You look great tonight," he said, and smiled the sterling smile he smiled for everyone.

"Hey, thanks," Shoe said. "It's called makeup."

He narrowed his eyes at her. "What's your real name?"

Shoe didn't want to tell him her real name. She didn't care for it.

"What's yours?" she asked.

"Helmut."

Shoe eyed him. "No shit?"

"No shit."

"So why do you go by Max?"

"Who says I do?"

"Everybody."

Max laughed, delighted. "I go by Max because my name is Helmut."

"But Helmut is cool."

"Max is cool."

"Not as cool as Helmut! Helmut is like Yul Brynner and a junkyard dog rolled into one. Helmut is tough."

"Nobody's tough enough to live down that name."

Shoe shrugged.

"And why do you go by Shoe?"

"Because my name is Susan."

Max turned on his stool and surveyed the room, addressing her over his shoulder. "I want to kiss you, Susan. But not until you're ready."

"Your wife won't mind?"

Max spun himself back around. He looked amazed, but the amazement only hovered over his features, much like his tan. Shoe knew she hadn't genuinely amazed him. Not yet.

"I'm not married," he said.

Shoe didn't think he was. But she would've laid odds he was cheating on somebody, or about to.

"And now I know why," he added.

She laughed. So did he. Then they stared at each other until somebody across the room shouted for her. She walked off, and didn't see him leave.

The following night was Friday, and the bar was packed. Shoe hardly thought about Max until he walked through the door, straight up to her at the counter, and slapped down a plastic bag of puffy orange candies. She took a step back in surprise.

Josh, popping bottle tops next to her, shook his head. "I'm disappointed, Max. Thought you were a man of taste. A man of distinction."

Max smiled his cunning smile.

"That's trash candy, man." Josh set the beers onto a tray and carried them off.

Max tore into the plastic and held the bag out to her. Shoe selected a circus peanut, took it gently between thumb and forefinger, and held it up to the bar's weak light.

"What you're holding there is the fruit of civilization," Max said. "A culmination."

She nodded as that sweet, strange, cloying smell wended its way inside her. "Yes," she said. "And yet a thing unfettered by convention. Stark-raving inspiration."

Their eyes locked. Then Shoe popped the candy in her mouth and moved away down the bar, where the mayor had just materialized.

Shoe thought she understood her life well enough. Her body had thrived on the existence she'd chosen; her heart had gone stiff and stale from lack of exercise. She made up a Bloody Mary for the mayor and thought, Well. Maybe I'll fall in love. It was a thing she'd never gotten around to doing, not in earnest. She couldn't think of any better solution to spring her from her malaise.

When Max had finished off his beer, she wandered back to remove his empty glass. "Care for another?" she asked.

"Thank you," said Max. "But I'm beat."

She glanced up at the clock over the bar. Barely eleven. He had stayed till near closing the previous nights.

"I guess you're leaving our fair town soon," she said. "In search of greener pastures."

"Is this your town?" asked Max.

"Nope," she said. "I guess you're leaving this fair town soon. You've got bigger fish to fry."

"What makes you think I'm leaving at all?"

"Aren't you? It's not like you live here, Helmut."

"I am living here, at present. I'm alive, Susan, and I am here. I can assure you I'm not living anywhere else."

"Not tonight," she said.

"No," said Max.

"Let me get you another," she said.

Max shook his head. He pushed the remaining circus peanuts toward her, tossed a five-dollar bill onto the bar and walked out.

Shoe paced for the rest of the night. She scarcely spoke to anyone, just popped circus peanuts in slow succession, stood before the plate-glass window and gazed out into the dark.

She had lived in ski towns since leaving Ohio, which ensured she could ski any old time and, more important, be close to the mountains underneath that snow. But it also ensured a culture particular to ski towns, an easygoing, nonjudgmental culture that, bit by bit, drove her mad.

People were friendly and fun-loving, but fun in a ski town was designed for the body, and conversation was largely limited to the body's sphere, what it could do and had done and hoped to do next week. It wasn't enough to trek into the backcountry for a weekend of skiing. You had to talk about the thing before you did it, while you were doing it, and all over again once you were done. You had to discuss the logistics, and Shoe never gave a rat's ass about the logistics. That wasn't where the adventure lurked.

For nearly ten years, she had drifted from one ski town to the next in search of something new, but it was always more of the same. Sex offered little relief, since sooner or later the guys always wanted to talk, and whatever they said bored her to such tears that she finally felt forced to give up sex.

She did not really think there was another option out there for her. She needed the mountains. She could not be out of them for any length of time. But she was lonely.

That night, after the bar finally closed and everyone made their way somewhere else, she stepped out onto the sidewalk, tipped back her head, and studied the sky. No snow, no clouds, no moon. The air was so cold it hurt to breathe. The stars seemed sadly far away. Then she heard a noise, dropped her head and saw him, loitering across the street. The shop window behind him, still done up for Halloween, framed Max in little orange lights.

Shoe crossed the street and climbed up on a pile of snow the plows had left behind. Even from this vantage point he seemed tall.

"There isn't anywhere to go this time of night except the 7-Eleven," she said.

"Let's go," he said.

Five minutes later they were there. What bliss, she thought, standing with him in 7-Eleven's candy aisle as it closed in on two a.m.

"I'm thinking about picking up some Twizzlers," she said. "Any thoughts on that?"

"I know why you do what you do," Max said.

Shoe wondered if, finally, someone might.

She bought a pack of red rope licorice and they munched up several strands on the walk back to the room she rented over the garage of a house. The licorice ropes were long enough that they could place opposing ends of the same strand in their respective mouths and, for a good stretch, chew on them freely as they marched through the cold. Each time their faces came within a few inches of each other, he bit off his end and she was left with the remainder flapping against her chin. At the time it reminded her of the game of chicken, and she seemed to win each time, but later on she decided she was wrong, that it had been nothing more than foreplay and that if anybody had won, he had.

Once they reached the chilly room and dug under her covers he said, again, that he knew her. Although he was by no means the first suitor to make that audacious claim, he was the first one she believed.

And so they became two. In the evenings, Max came around before closing, downed a beer, and told her bits and pieces about his life: A working-class childhood in Buffalo, New York, college on a basketball scholarship, and, of late, the sweet taste of success.

Max was an art dealer and a consultant. That was what brought him to Ketchum. He did a lot of work with galleries, and there were new ones booming in all the resort towns out West, where wealthy tourists and very part-time residents shopped for local landscapes to hang on their walls. He wasn't much for landscapes himself, but he didn't have to like the paintings to recognize what other people liked.

After closing they walked home through the dark, still streets. In the mornings they went their separate ways. Yet it was her days, even more than her nights, that were transformed by him, because she'd always felt loneliest during the day. He wasn't with her in those hours, but she held the expectation of him, and the recollection. She replayed his words and gestures in her mind. She felt the tidal pull of one emotion, and then another. Until Max, she had often entertained herself by savaging the people she found around her in the privacy of her own brain. With Max, there was no room left for that.

They started sex during her period and they did not use condoms and then her period slid by and Max told Shoe he'd never liked to use them, that he was too big and they made his penis hurt and she said ah, and birth control wasn't discussed again. He rolled her legs up around her head, propped her up on pillows, anything he liked. She wasn't in it for the sex; she just wanted to be with him as many hours as she could because she wasn't bored when she was with him. She liked to watch him do things, anything at all. He wore a deeper look of mischief than anyone she'd ever known. Deeper, she suspected, than her own.

She took Max to be deliverance. And why not? Suddenly she was afraid all the time: Fear was built inextricably into the equation. She feared Max because she loved him and loved him because she feared him. She didn't know him, of course, and didn't know herself, not quite, because she didn't know that it was God who brings deliverance, that it was God, really, she'd wanted all along.

CHAPTER FOUR

Moses started first grade that fall, but it was his grandmother who taught him to read, how to add and subtract. When he was older, she said, she would help him with his Latin, though it was Spanish his mom had been teaching him in the months before she died. Sometimes he showed his grandmother his latest painting, or the feathers of birds that he and his aunt had found down by the river or out in the woods. His grandmother was always cordial. She gave each of his creations and discoveries fair consideration. Better than all of this, though, she liked to speak of other places.

"Bring me the atlas," she would say, and Moses would go to the lowest shelf of the great bookcase across his grandparents' bedroom, where the heavy book was kept.

Looking at the atlas seemed to be her keenest pleasure, but she was secretive about it. Once, when Professor Tumarkin had arrived home unexpectedly early, Moses had seen her slip the large book underneath the comforter, and she never had it out when Ida was around.

It was an old book, and the binding, already reinforced with duct tape, had begun to sag. Some of the countries in the book had vanished, his grandmother told him, since the book was made. "The world is always changing," she explained. "There are countries here I'll never visit now."

"Did the people drown?" Moses asked.

His grandmother looked alarmed. "What people?"

So Moses explained how he had once heard his mom and Uncle Johnny discussing the ocean, how it was rising and covering islands where people lived.

"Oh, heavens!" cried his grandmother. "That's global warming. I'm speaking of politics."

Then, for the first time Moses could remember, his grandmother laughed. She laughed until tears squeezed out of her eyes.

"I shouldn't," she apologized, covering one of Moses' hands with one of hers and squeezing it. "It's terrible, really. The world is in such a state."

But for all that, her mood seemed improved. She sat up straighter, then actually climbed out of bed and crossed to the dresser mirror to apply some lipstick. It looked strange with her hair, which was strange already. Most of it was the same brown as his mother's, but the inch of hair closest to her head was pale gray. She returned to the bed, picked up the atlas, licked her index finger and began his first geography lesson.

They started large, with the seven continents, and Moses soon mastered those. Yet there were some things that didn't make entire sense, and these things made it harder to remember. Why, for instance, was Australia a continent when Greenland was not? His grandmother told him Greenland was too cold, so people couldn't live on it. Moses wanted to know, then, why Antarctica, so white on the map, got to be a continent. And why was Asia a separate continent from Europe when it was obviously one piece of land? Who had decided that, and who had decided where the dividing line would be? How, before the astronauts had flown so far above the earth, did anybody know the shapes of anything? Moses was certain that without a sidewalk laid out before him, he couldn't walk a single mile in a straight line, let alone chart the Mississippi or the way the Gulf of Mexico scooped out the land.

He had many questions, but he usually referred these to Ida in the end, because his grandmother didn't like these sorts of questions. She treated them as distractions, not sources for speculation, and grew impatient. His aunt could speculate endlessly, but his grandmother seemed to regard that kind of thought as a waste of time. It was the places she liked to talk about—the land, the climate, what the people ate and why. She had done a lot of reading about the world, and she wanted to do more. Moses became her information runner.

"Bring me a book on Bulgaria," she would say, and hand him a slip of paper with the word written in her small, cramped hand. He couldn't read a word like that yet, but the librarians could, if he forgot the country.

"Any book?" asked Moses.

"A book with pictures," his grandmother said. "With

color photographs, if you can find one."

Sometimes his grandmother followed him down-stairs. She dusted or ironed and didn't retreat until Aunt Ida showed up. She started to join them for dinner, too, at the big oak table in the dining room, a table that always made meals seem like a fancy affair to Moses, since he and his mom had usually eaten on the couch.

When Moses' grandfather took a plane from Cincinnati out to California for his job, Ida decided this would be an opportunity for the two of them to dine out with Henry. Just before they left the house, she brought dinner to his grandmother. Moses carried her water, stuffed with the ice cubes he'd personally selected.

His grandmother was sitting up in the bed, examining the evening paper. When they entered, she put down the newspaper but didn't smile. She never seemed to smile around his aunt.

"We're going to Henry's for dinner, Mom," Ida said brightly, as she laid out the tray on her parents' bedside table. "Moses is going to learn about real Texas hospitality tonight."

"If you really want to teach him about Texas, take him there."

Ida turned and smiled at Moses. "Being with Henry is like being there."

"He's a person. Not a place. To know the world, one must travel."

Delivered to Ida, this motto sounded like a scolding, but his aunt seemed to take no notice. They left the tray, and then the house. Out on the playing field, Ida ran circles around him in the grass, then flung herself onto a shallow pile of leaves. When a student passed them, heading home from class, Ida picked herself up from the pile, turned her back, and brushed the earth's debris from her hair and jacket. Then they marched past campus, briskly, holding their breath until the sun went down and the dark had truly come to free them, which it did about the time they reached the cemetery.

"We'll cover the mums," she said on reaching his mother's grave. "There's supposed to be a frost tonight."

He helped her drape the flowers with towels they'd brought from the kitchen.

"They won't die tonight," she said. "But even when they do, they'll come back in the spring. Okay?"

Moses nodded, and they headed up the old brick path that led them to Henry's farmhouse.

That night the moon was nearly full. After dinner they walked back out into the cold and down to the railroad tracks. As the three headed south they studied the moon, still climbing the sky, long spindly clouds drifting slowly across its face.

"Luna," Moses whispered. "Luna linda."

They could see the rails stretch away before them, see the two straight lines somehow converging in the distance. Though Moses watched that point of convergence closely, he noticed they never got any closer to it. Finally, he mentioned this and Aunt Ida said they would never reach that place because it didn't actually exist. She said it was an illusion, like shimmering puddles on the highway in summer that look like oil slicks, but aren't anything at all.

Henry said this was a bare-faced lie, but Ida wasn't feeling argumentative. She shrugged and raised her face back to the moon.

"I've been there," Henry said. "To the place the rails meet. But I wouldn't recommend it, to you or anybody."

"Why not?" Moses asked.

"I was in an altered state. You know what acid is?"

"I think so."

"It's a dangerous drug. It does things to your brain. How do you know what it is? You shouldn't."

Moses couldn't remember, exactly, how he knew. "Little pieces of paper." He thought of Henry's church. "People eat it like communion."

Henry shook his head. "It ain't right," he said.

They followed the track until they were deep out in the country. The last clouds cleared away as they walked, until the moon shone down so brightly they could see the black, crisp shadow of every tree in every field they passed. The moon even stretched their own shadows long and lean behind them, when they turned to look. Once the track began to curve off to the right, Ida stepped off to the left and down. Moses and Henry followed her, and the three set out across some farmer's fields.

They never met the farmer, and his fields gave way to someone else's fields and those to someone else's. These three, so practiced in ducking between barbed wires, moved over private property as easily and indiscriminately as high water in the spring. They trampled dead cornstalks and spent sorghum. They pushed through bushes and brambles, slid down embankments. Once, after nearly falling in a muddy ditch, Henry caught Ida from behind and held on even after they were standing firmly in the bottom of the draw. Ida stood very still until he let her go.

When they came onto a wet dirt road, tree-lined and lovely in the pure white light, Aunt Ida slowed her pace. She had no choice. She couldn't see where she was walking, with her face turned up to the sky.

"We're lost," said Henry.

"No, no," she whispered, barely moving now.

It was early November and the trees on either side of them were almost naked, black-limbed and throwing down barely shifting shadows, breathing in and slowly out. Henry said they should follow the road until it led them back to civilization. Ida didn't even bother to shake her head. She stood still, her arms pressed hard against her sides, her fingers splayed wide.

When a leaf blew down, Moses chased it. Ida watched him go, then stepped off the road into another ditch. When he returned she was below him, smiling up. "If you know how to go into nowhere, you'll always know how to find your way out," she said.

Minutes later, they stumbled into a backyard, and out on Henry's street. They cheered, then trudged over his curb and up the rickety steps to the storm door that opened into Henry's kitchen.

No one touched the lights. The bright moonlight spilled in through the kitchen's south window, a white rectangle on the old tile floor. Moses heard a mouse scuttle deeper into the shadows and disappear.

Ida ducked left, into the dark bathroom. Henry took his shoulders and pulled him through the middle room, with its howling man and slanting wooden floor, through one end of the TV room and to the side room where Henry painted. He threw a switch and the overhead light snapped on. After the initial shock, Moses saw it hardly touched the corner shadows. One of the bulbs was burnt out. Above the ceiling fixture, the single dingy bulb that still burned illuminated dozens of small, dead bugs.

Henry pointed at the easel in the center of the room. "There she is," he said.

Moses turned to see the painting. He knew what it was supposed to be. And though the scene on the canvas didn't look the way Moses remembered the field that night—it wasn't even dark—still, he liked it better than any other painting Henry had done.

"Why don't you put it up?" Moses asked. He stepped to the doorway and angled his arm behind him, so that he could point at the howling man without actually facing him. "Where that one is?"

"This one's going out," said Henry. "Into the world."

"To know the world, one must travel," Moses said.

Henry snorted. "Whoever said that never stayed in one place long enough."

Ida appeared in the doorway.

"There she is," Henry repeated.

Ida drew her hands behind her and shyly stepped into the room.

"The magician of horses," said Henry, moving past her. "I need a smoke."

Moses followed him back through the dark middle room. In the bathroom, he turned on the light and checked the toilet bowl for mice. Then he turned out the light again. He didn't need it, and he wasn't afraid of the dark. He had moved through it so many times, camping without a flashlight.

He found the toilet handle and flushed. Afterwards he tiptoed back through the kitchen (so as not to scare the mice), past the scary painting (he averted his eyes), through the main room and back to Ida, who stood in front of her painting, just as he had left her, but not alone. There behind her, with his arms wrapped around her again, stood Henry.

Moses retreated, one silent sneaker at a time. In the TV room, he climbed into the big armchair to wait. When Henry spoke from the next room, Moses heard him fine.

"Why don't you stay the night?" Henry asked.

Moses had heard this question before, even watched the scene played out between his mother and other men. So he was not surprised when Ida emerged alone from the next room, but unlike his mom she wasn't grinning. She didn't roll her eyes at him. She didn't say a word. It was a moment before she even saw Moses sitting there, then moved toward him with a strange, stricken smile. She sank beside him, onto one arm of the chair. Moses saw that his aunt's nose was red and shiny. When Henry emerged a moment later, she didn't look.

"Let's have some ice cream," Henry said, and Moses

nodded, even though he was still chilled from their walk. They followed Henry into the kitchen. Somebody turned on the lights.

The following day, Ida met Moses outside his classroom. Together they walked to the cemetery, where they would remove the tea towels they'd placed on the flowers the evening before, and have a little picnic. On the way, Moses asked his aunt if Henry was in love with her.

Her face, which had been laughing moments before, lost its brightness. She looked almost angry. "No," she said.

"Why not?"

Ida took a deep breath and let it go. "Most people don't love most other people. That's the usual state of affairs. Love's the unusual thing. And even when it happens, people don't always know the reason."

"Do you know the reason?"

"I might if it happened. But I'm not in love with anyone. And once I am, if I don't know why, that'll be okay."

"How do you know?"

"How do I know what? That it'll be okay?"

Moses shook his head.

"How do I know I'll fall in love?"

Moses nodded. "That one," he said.

"Because other people do. So I know I will too."

"But how do you know?"

"Because I'm human. Why shouldn't I fall in love?"

"And I'll fall in love."

"Yes, you will."

"I'm in love already," Moses said. "I'm in love with you."

Ida smiled and poked him in the stomach. "Me too," she said.

"But you said you weren't in love with anybody."

"I was wrong."

"Why are you in love with me and not with Henry?"

His aunt smiled at one side of her mouth, a funny, lopsided smile like his mom's and Uncle Johnny's. He had never seen his aunt smile this way before, but he knew it meant she wasn't going to answer the question. So he posed another.

"What if nobody ever is in love with Henry?"

"Then he might remain a bachelor."

"What's a bachelor?"

"A bachelor is a man who doesn't marry anybody."

"How old do you have to be before you're a bachelor?"

His aunt cocked her head to one side. "That's an excellent question," she said.

"Are you a bachelor when you become a man?"

"No," she said. "Not just yet."

"So how long after?"

"That's tough," said Ida. "It depends on the man. With some men, you never know for sure. Some men could be seventy and still not seem like bachelors. They seem like they might get married any day. Other men, maybe by thirty-five, you suspect they're already bachelors for life."

"So once you are a bachelor, you're a bachelor forever?"

"If you really are a bachelor, yes."

"And Henry is a bachelor?"

Ida shook her head. "I don't know. I think he might be."

"But somebody might fall in love with him. Somebody besides you."

"That's true. I hope they do."

"And what do they call a woman bachelor?"

"They call her an old maid. Or a spinster."

"What's the difference?"

"No difference."

"Was my mom an old maid?"

"No."

"Are you?"

"Not yet."

"When will you be?"

"I won't," she said. "I'm going to fall in love."

"And Mom will never be because she died."

"Your mother never could've been a spinster."

"Why not?"

His aunt was silent again, but this time Moses could tell that she was going to answer his question in good time and so he waited.

"For lots of reasons," she said finally. "But the best reason is you."

Moses did not question this, although it didn't make obvious sense: He hadn't been his mother's husband, after all, but her son.

"And I can marry you," he said.

"Nothing would make me happier."

They'd reached the cemetery gate. Before they turned in, she took his head between her two delicate hands, leaned down, and dropped one hard kiss into a spot just between his ears. He lost it somewhere in his hair.

From the cemetery, it was an easy walk up the hill to visit Henry, but Ida said they wouldn't go that way today. When they arrived home, though, Henry was waiting on their front porch, holding flowers.

Moses didn't tell him it was no good, courting her. He didn't want to hurt Henry's feelings, and besides, it wasn't as if Henry was any threat: Ida had said she loved him. When he became a man, before he could ever become a bachelor, he would marry her himself. Henry would always be their friend and always have them over to his house for dinner and paint paintings of them and they would catch gray mice. They would always run laughing through the woods, the three of them, and even after he became a man he wouldn't really be any different from who he was right now, the same way, he could tell, that his aunt hadn't changed since the black-and-white photographs she'd shown him of herself when she was six years old.

Ida had said Henry didn't love her, but Moses was not so sure. He couldn't help but feel a little bit sorry for Henry. When Ida took the flowers from him, she bent her head into the blooms and smiled and thanked him nicely enough, but it was not all that it could have been, and Moses knew he was beginning to understand about love. Back in September, when the flowers were still blooming in the fields, Moses had brought her bunches which she'd gathered up into her arms, and she had closed her eyes and almost seemed to swoon.

No, she was not in love with Henry. And for that reason, Henry would never know his aunt quite as well as Moses did. It was a funny thing, Moses thought, because he knew it was his aunt's love that enabled him to see her better, and the better he saw, the more he loved, yet Henry loved without being shown all these things.

Maybe it's because he's older than I am, Moses thought. There's less for him to see, but what he does see, he understands better. Still, if that were the case, then all the bachelors should be in love with Ida, shouldn't they? Ida said there was no reason people didn't love, but in her case he knew it was because none of the others could see what Henry saw. Maybe his aunt had ways to keep the other bachelors from seeing. Maybe it was as Henry had said, and she was a magician, after all, not of horses but of bachelors. Most magicians could make people see things that were not there, but wasn't it just as amazing to keep them from seeing things that were? Like being invisible, thought Moses. Like throwing on a magic cloak!

He narrowed his eyes on his aunt's face, poised over the pink carnations—pink was not, he knew, her favorite color—and for one moment, their eyes met. Moses winked.

Ida looked away, but it was too late. Moses was on to her. And it's a good thing I love her, he thought. Otherwise I could tell all the bachelors she's played for fools.

CHAPTER FIVE

Because Shoe had several of her sister's paintings and no good place to hang them all, each month she rotated a different painting onto her bedroom wall, and stored the others in her closet. When December rolled around, she put up the sidewalk painting. Ida called this particular painting Lessons in Self-Defense, and for once, Shoe knew what the title meant, because Shoe was in the painting.

It was nothing complicated, just a view along a sidewalk, with a few thick tree trunks and long green grass on either side. Far down the walk, maybe a half-block off, was Shoe's retreating figure, carrying a big black bundle under one arm. All along the sidewalk behind her snaked a trail of gold dust.

The first time he saw it, Max stared at the painting. "Where is this?" he asked.

Shoe was a little surprised at the question, and a little disappointed. She had thought he might ask who it was.

"That's my hometown," she said. "That's the sidewalk

leading from our house."

Max tapped his foot. "I want to go there," he said suddenly.

"Well, you're in luck. The sidewalk's still there. Not the dust, though."

"And not the girl," Max said.

"No." Shoe went to her closet and rummaged around for her ski boots, which she would need the following morning. "Not the girl."

The girl in the painting was sixteen years old. The month was September, the same month a young woman was raped in Hueston Woods, the state park a few miles from their house. One night at dinner, Professor Tumarkin announced that none of the children could go to the woods alone anymore. Everyone looked at Ida.

"You mean Hueston Woods," she said.

"Yes," said her father.

She reached for her milk glass and swallowed serenely. "Okay," she said.

Her parents looked at one another. Her father frowned.

"All the woods, Ida," he said. "Wherever it is you go."

Ida raised her chin. "If you don't know where I go, you can't very well forbid me. You don't even know what you're forbidding."

"Ida," he said. "You're old enough to distinguish between the letter of the law and the spirit of the law. The point is that we don't want you alone in a secluded place."

"Fine," she said. "I'll take Johnny with me."

Johnny looked up from his green beans in surprise.

"Johnny is ten years old," her father said.

Ida stared down at the table. Her dark eyes grew darker. "Seclusion is safer," she said.

Her father shook his head.

"I'm not afraid for my body," she said.

"Then we're afraid for you," said Mrs. Tumarkin.

"They'll never find me," Ida pleaded.

Professor Tumarkin went on shaking his head.

"Honey," Mrs. Tumarkin said, "we're not saying you can't go. We're saying you can't go alone. We'll make an excursion out there soon with the whole family. And maybe you can organize a picnic with some of your classmates. Aren't there some nice girls in your class you could invite out there with you? You know the park so well, I'm sure they'd be honored to have you as a guide."

Ida rose miserably from the table and disappeared upstairs, into the bedroom she and Shoe had always shared. When Shoe came in later, she turned out the lamp and started undressing in the dark.

Ida had crept under her covers, but she wasn't asleep. She blew her nose, sat up in bed, and arranged her flannel nightgown around her calves. Her face was blotched and puffy.

"I need the woods," she said.

"Don't worry." Shoe's voice was low, conspiratorial, and utterly assured. She yanked off one boot and then the other, letting each drop on the pink carpet with a thud. "We can get around this one."

A week later, Shoe brought a narrow white box with her to the dinner table. The box sat quietly at her elbow all through the meal. After they'd cleared the plates, while Mrs. Tumarkin was dishing up the chocolate cake, Shoe removed the lid, tossed it over her shoulder, lifted the box, and displayed the contents for everyone to see.

It was a knife. The handle was wrapped in rawhide, the blade eight inches long. Shoe lifted the weapon from its bed of tissue paper. Turning the point toward herself, she handed the knife to her little sister. The moment Ida gripped the handle, Shoe broke out in a grin.

"That is a dagger," Professor Tumarkin observed.

Shoe raised her eyebrows in agreement. Johnny held out his hand for the knife. Ida proffered it carefully. Professor Tumarkin leaned around the corner of the table for a better look.

"Where did you get it?" Mrs. Tumarkin asked Shoe.

Shoe surveyed the knife's circuit around the table. She had to bite her lower lip to hide her excitement. "I made it in shop," she said.

Her parents looked at one another. Shoe was supposed to be on the college preparatory track. Was shop college prep?

"Tomorrow after school," Shoe announced, "I'm gonna teach Ida how to use it. Once she knows how to protect herself, she can go anywhere."

But the following day when Shoe took her out in the backyard, Ida didn't seem to take the training seriously. She stood off and watched Shoe and Johnny aim the knife at different objects, laughing just as hard when the knife struck home as when it missed its target. Only when Shoe began throwing the dagger into the smooth white trunk of one of the sycamores did Ida sober up. She asked them to stop. When they ignored her, she stepped in front of the tree, arms thrown wide.

"Not the sycamores," she said.

"Oh well," Shoe said. "That was just James Bond stuff anyway."

The next day Shoe brought home a dressmaker's dummy from school. She set up the model at the side of the house, in a spot out of easy view from any of the windows. Then she licked her lips.

"Today we stab," she announced.

Shoe crooked her arm, poised the dagger, and made the first cut with impressive swiftness. Their dummy was old but still offered considerable resistance. Each time the blade went in, a little of the dry yellow foam crumbled into the grass.

"Stuffing would've been better," Shoe said. But at least Ida paid attention.

On Monday, Shoe was called to the principal's office on suspicion of stealing a dressmaker's dummy from the home ec room. There were witnesses, the principal said, who had seen the missing model in her possession. Shoe asked to know who these witnesses were. Your father, for one, the principal said.

Shoe was unapologetic. That night at dinner, she explained that appropriating the dummy was done in the best interests of her little sister. With the knife and a few martial arts skills, she said, Ida could roam freely through the world and do pretty much as she pleased.

"Like stealing and vandalizing property?" asked

Professor Tumarkin.

"Not necessarily," said Shoe. "But those activities wouldn't be precluded, no. This family is too nice for its own good. I say we give up the pansy routine."

"Well, maybe I like being a pansy," Mrs. Tumarkin said.

Shoe gave her mother a narrow, discerning look. "Maybe. But a little experimentation never hurt anyone."

Tuesday morning, Shoe was forced to return the dummy to school. Her mother wrapped it in trash bags, thinking the dummy would draw less attention that way, and since it was now leaking dry yellow foam from more than a dozen places. But the plastic made the bundle slippery and hard to carry.

"I'll drive you to school," her father offered.

"Oh, no, sir," Shoe said. "Sorry, sir, no."

Her mother suggested that she and Ida carry it back together, one girl at the prow and one at the helm, but Ida was only halfway through her Rice Krispies when Shoe slipped away with the thing. Walking alone ten minutes later, Ida followed a faint trail of yellow dust all the way to school.

After the dummy decamped, Shoe was forced to leap to the final stage of training: a little wrestling, a little kicking, the art of the punch. Johnny practiced eagerly, but Ida seemed to have no interest at all. Shoe let Ida climb her beloved trees and turn cartwheels on the lawn, but that night when they were alone in their bedroom, she finally confronted her.

"Why won't you learn?"

"He who lives by the sword shall die by the sword,"

Ida replied. "Anyway, I'll be fine."

"I don't know why you keep saying that. Do you think God's going to protect you?"

"No," Ida said. "That wouldn't be fair."

"Then you've got some weird kind of faith in your own luck."

"No, I don't," Ida said. "But I don't want to be afraid."

Like you, was the implication, but this was a thing they never would discuss, never would say aloud. It just hung between them in the dark.

"Let me tell you something, kid," Shoe said finally, before her sister could drift off to sleep. "You got an interesting strategy there. You're an original thinker, and you know I like that. But admitting a bad thing exists isn't what brings the bad thing into being. And turning your back on a bad thing won't make it go away."

Next door to their room, someone flushed the toilet. Instead of filling and shutting off, the water continued to run. Ida rolled out of bed, moved to the bathroom, jiggled the toilet handle several times. The toilet tank filled, the noise faded, and the house settled down again. When she returned to their room, Shoe was sitting on her bed.

"Look," said Shoe. "Mom and Dad have a point. Disobey them all you want, but if you're going to go out in the big wide world, you have to know how to defend yourself."

"I'm not afraid."

"So you keep telling me," Shoe said. "If you don't want the knife, give it back. I'll use it. And from now on, just do what you want and don't talk about it. There are ways to live life without working everyone else into a snit."

Ida kept the knife. After a few weeks, Shoe was nearly certain Ida began to slip back to the woods. But their parents never asked her flat-out where she went, and Ida never told them. Or Shoe.

Max didn't solicit the story, and Shoe didn't volunteer it. She seldom told stories of home, and certainly not to him. But he drew his own conclusions.

"So that's how it is with you and her," he said. "You're the inspiration, and she uses you to make her art."

"No," Shoe said. "Ida doesn't need me for inspiration. She doesn't need anyone."

"It's strange," Max said, "the way you talk about your sister. She's living this cooped up little life, yet you don't seem sad."

"I'm not sad," Shoe said. Not for Ida.

They'd been sisters for nearly twenty-six years. Like most sisters, they had their disagreements and sometimes fought in the liberating way that sisters fight, free of courtesy, without mincing words or else by mincing so many that they ignored each other. Both were dark-haired, slender, both a little zealous. In every other respect, most people thought they were diametrically opposed. They were, but in the way heads and tails are: The two sides still make up one coin.

Shoe left Ohio at seventeen; Ida never even left home. In that way, Ida managed to avoid her fears of the larger world and so grow older seamlessly, dreamily, which suited her fine. Her sister understood this better than anyone.

"She's living the life she wanted," Shoe said. "How many people can say that?"

"But you don't respect her."

"I don't disrespect her. My sister isn't someone you respect or disrespect. Her life isn't about that."

To Shoe, Ida's life was a grand experiment. So was her own. And Shoe wanted to find out whose experiment would turn out better.

"But you're closer to your brother."

"In a way," she said. "It's different. I love Johnny because he tries to protect me. I'm the one protecting Ida."

Max turned from the shimmering sidewalk back to her. "How?" he asked.

"I told you before. She'll never have to change."

Max blinked slowly. She could see he didn't understand, though it shouldn't have been so hard. She and Ida were simple enough, Shoe thought. Their motives were practically transparent. Not like his.

He cast a final glance at the painting, then stepped out of his pants and toward her. "I'd like to meet her someday," he said.

But this, Shoe already knew, was out of the question.

CHAPTER SIX

The morning of the opening, Ida went to her bedroom, opened her closet door, and considered how she might approach the event.

First off, there was the question of whether to go looking like herself or like everybody else. She had practiced in front of her mirror before: Everybody was a look she knew how to do. It was not for lack of wherewithal that she refrained, as a rule, from normalcy. Over the years she had tried on so many disguises that she had them all at her disposal.

She had, for instance, a lipstick. And she knew the way some women now were wearing their hair on their shoulders, while others wore it all fastened on top. She could do either if she chose, and she even had normal clothes she could wear, a pair of jeans, loafers, and a plain white shirt. She had four winter coats and she knew the right one—not the warm one and not the ones Moses loved to pet but a wool peacoat, neatly tailored, that she had bought on a day when she was feeling mischievous, bought for an event like this, should it ever arise.

So looking normal was within easy reach. She could rest assured on that score. But Ida knew if she went in looking like everybody else that people, men and women, would assume she was. That would be unnerving. She chose instead her common daytime option, to go incognito.

That afternoon she and Moses drove to Hamilton, the county seat, to look at wigs. She parked the car near the shop but they didn't go in right away. Instead they stood out on the sidewalk, where the storefront windows faced north and west. There were probably two dozen wigs set up for street display, all for women, all on white plastic heads with identical, highly feminine features. Ida realized that if the heads belonged to real women, they would all be younger—slightly—than she was. Yet they looked so grown-up. She had seen real women like these in magazines and never understood them.

"I like that one," Moses said, pointing to a wig of red hair in long, loose coils.

"I do too," Ida said, though she was afraid she liked it too much, that she might wear it all the time.

Inside, they discovered the wigs in the window were all new, many of them made with the hair of women from some remote part of Russia.

"The women whose hair went into these wigs have never even used shampoo," the saleswoman marveled.

Ida examined several price tags, then turned and wandered over to a pile of used wigs on a corner table. Unlike the wigs in the window, a lot of these were gray. She tried one on but Moses shook his head. Ida set the wig on his head instead, then turned him around to face a mirror.

"Too bad Halloween's over," she said.

The saleswoman gave her a nasty look.

"I liked my costume," Moses said. He'd gone as Frankenstein, with green skin, fake stitches, and knobs his aunt had glued onto his neck.

Ida bought a chin-length blond wig for six dollars and they left the shop, in search of a diner selling pie. After several blocks they found the sort of place they had in mind, but it had closed up for the day. They stood together with their faces pressed against the glass, gazing at the bright blue booths inside.

"Did your mom ever work in a place like this?" she asked.

Moses shook his head.

"No pie?" she asked.

"Nope."

"Did she bring stuff home, though? To eat, I mean?"

Moses nodded.

"Did you like it?"

"Sometimes."

Ida turned and studied his profile. Moses kept staring through the glass into the restaurant's shadowy insides.

"You can talk about your mom, you know. Anytime you want."

"I know," Moses said. "So can you."

Ida had not known this. Or rather, she hadn't known what to say, and didn't still.

On the way home, she stopped for gas and bought a

box of Cracker Jacks. She opened the box in the car and passed it to him.

"When you're really good, they call you Cracker Jack," she said.

"Good at what?" Moses asked.

"Doesn't matter," Ida said. "Take your pick."

She rolled crepes for dinner, then picked at one through the meal, barely following her parents' conversation as to why Johnny couldn't make it home from Utah for Christmas. She sat knowing that wig or no wig, if she got to the art opening before Henry, she would die.

So she made a point of being late. She put on the blond wig, red lipstick, her purple velveteen coat, then sat very still on her bed and watched with a baleful, made-up gaze the slow forward flip of the numbers on the nightstand clock. Tardiness was discourteous, intentional tardiness was worse, and worse still was keeping someone waiting in a public situation where they had nothing to do and no friends to talk to. She loathed herself in a way that she hadn't in years, in a way that had grown blessedly unfamiliar to her, a loathing that only surfaced in uncomfortable situations like this one, situations she had managed to avoid most of her adult life. But still she waited.

When she was ten minutes late, she slipped out of the house and started the walk toward the art building, her fists balled in her pockets, sweaty and tight. Each time somebody passed her on that short walk, she nearly turned and started back for home, where there was gentle light and quiet and people who knew her. The soles of her boots were thin and the balls of her feet, pressing against the pavement, already ached with cold.

But she used the cold to her advantage. She marched across campus like one of her ancestors traversing Siberia, a thousand miles from home. When she reached the building, she had enough momentum to make it up the stairs. She fell against a door and nearly mowed down somebody on the other side. Then that person was out and she was in—a neat exchange—a burst of human voices crashed upon her and people looked up but she made it past and then she saw Henry, holding a plastic cup and sitting alone on a padded bench against the one wall free of art.

"Hello," she said.

"Hello, Marilyn."

Henry was used to her disguises. She sighed in relief and even unbuttoned her coat, but soon one of the other artists approached with some minor calamity, and Henry was whisked away from her. Then she was stranded on a black leather cushion in her wig and her cheap go-go boots, alone. Wine and cheese and fancy crackers were laid out on a card table, but she was too mortified to leave her seat and walk the twenty feet to get any.

This was a common predicament. Sometimes when she had to use the restroom in public forums—at a play, say, where everyone would look at you as you passed—she held it in for hours. She didn't have to use the restroom now—she was careful to go just before she left home—but it was the same essential problem. The problem of other people's observation. Of someone taking note.

Instead she dug out the menthol cigarettes she saved for awkward occasions. She had known that at some point in the evening she would be left alone with no one to talk to and she would need something to do, at least until Henry returned. She just hadn't expected it quite so soon. She struck a match, shakily, then inhaled with all her might. After that things improved.

Both Henry and Ida had paintings in the show and she watched cagily, cringing inside but also curious when people stopped at hers. Like most of her paintings, this one had come from a dream.

Sometimes Ida dreamed of a hall in a house where she had never been. It was a large old house in a golden meadow, with all its doors and windows thrown open to summer and long lines of misty morning light. Whenever Ida dreamed it, she found herself in that hall, just beyond the reach of the sunlight, with no one else around. She stood at a door always pulled shut and put the flat of her hand to its gray wood. Each time was the same: She felt a strange warmth from inside, not terribly hot but dangerous because it was somehow wrong—evil, or supernatural. Once this warmth traveled inside her skin, it translated into a kind of fear. She would remove her hand, stand for another moment at the mute door, then turn and walk toward the summer sun.

The dream never crossed the line into nightmare, because the threat never reached beyond the door, and Ida never chose to open it. She figured she never would: For all the times she'd had this dream, her curiosity didn't mount.

So it was with life. If she came to a door, a threshold, any demarcation, and felt fear, Ida walked away.

When the tall stranger materialized in front of the hallway painting, he studied it longer than most before he turned and scanned the room. His eyes passed over her several times, but never stopped.

She recognized him because of his great height and slightly stooped posture, the way he ducked his head forward, but soon realized he probably wouldn't recognize her. It had been dark when they first met. She had been sitting. Unlike him, she wasn't short or tall. And the hair coming out of her wig was nothing like her real hair; it was much shorter, pale and wispy, soft curls floating around her face. She turned away and blew smoke into the corner. When she turned back, he'd crossed the room and sat down a few feet from her. He addressed her right away.

"Are those menthols you're smoking?"

Ida nodded.

"Can I buy one off you?" He dug into his pocket for some change.

"They're really stale," Ida said. "You can have one, if you dare."

"Oh, I dare." He looked her in the eye and started laughing. Ida laughed as well, and handed him the pack. He concentrated when he lit up, squinting like men in old movies. When he had smoked half his cigarette, he turned back to her.

"These are stale," he said.

Ida nodded a second time.

"Why do you smoke them?"

"I don't want them to go to waste."

His eyes were a pale brown and though it was November, his face was tanned to almost the same shade. Only in the creases around his eyes was the skin almost white, and his teeth were as white as could be. It was a funny face, she thought, almost a goofy face, though probably handsome if you got past those two expressions—the blinding smile, alternating with the frown of absolute concentration. The smile without the frown would have been onerous, she thought. The goofiness she liked.

He watched as she reached for another cigarette, then leaned in toward her with a light. The closeness made her uneasy. His right hand—long and brown and beautiful, with two silver rings—made her more uneasy still. But she bent her head over it to get to the flame.

"They wouldn't go stale if you smoked every day," he observed.

"That's true." Ida straightened and edged away. "I'm a recreational smoker."

"And an artist?"

"You are correct, sir." Ida inhaled and felt a little sick from her fourth cigarette in a row. But with it smoldering between her fingers, she was ready to play. She tipped back her chin and exhaled. "You're batting a hundred so far."

He threw back his head and laughed a wonderful, throaty laugh. The sound alone made her smile.

"That isn't very good," he said.

"It isn't?"

"That's one in ten."

"It is?" Ida was stunned. "I thought one hundred was perfect."

"A thousand is perfect." He laughed again. "I can see you're not a baseball fan."

"I love the idea of baseball," Ida said. "But I don't care for sports."

The tall man scanned her face with something like a rapt expression. His eyes were slightly wild. Ida blushed.

"Would you care for some cheese?" he asked.

"Very much."

"I'll get us some," he said, and stalked away. She was relieved to have somebody else make the trip across the room, and relieved he didn't ask her why she hadn't gotten some cheese herself. Her brother and sister would've asked. They never let her get away with anything.

Henry returned and stole the tall man's seat—Henry's seat first, Ida reminded herself. When the tall man returned he hesitated an instant, then sat down on her other side, right at the bench's edge. His long legs jutted out at odd angles. She had an urge to place her hands on his knees and realign them.

"Name's Frost," the tall man said. He shifted the plate to his left hand and held out his right.

"Tumarkin," she said, and shook it. Then she leaned back and introduced Henry.

Frost gestured across the room toward her painting. "Yours?"

Ida nodded.

"I didn't know you were blond," he said.

"I'm not," Ida said.

"How would you know?" added Henry. His voice was hostile.

Ida knew how. The man recognized her from the stoop after all.

But the man called Frost merely blinked and changed the subject. "Have some cheese," he urged, and held out the plate. "The green stuff is delicious!"

Ida selected a slab of the green and some Swiss cubes as well, then handed the plate along to Henry. But Henry just smoked his cigarette and stared at the far wall.

"It is delicious," she agreed.

Frost sprang to his feet. Before she could stop him, he'd rushed off again. Ida was delighted, but Henry made a face.

"You should try this cheese," she said guiltily.

"I don't eat anything green," Henry said.

"Green foods are good for you." Ida felt inane, then realized she didn't care. She was suddenly glad she'd come.

"Who is that guy?" Henry asked.

"I don't know," Ida said. "But I've seen him before."

Frost was back before she could say more. He sank onto the cushion, balanced the replenished plate on his left thigh, and extended it toward her. No one spoke for several minutes while the two of them attacked the green cheese. When it was gone, Frost leaned against the wall and smiled. Ida sighed in contentment. Henry stubbed out his cigarette.

"I'm heading home," he announced, and rose to his feet. "Ida, do you need a ride?"

"Oh, no thank you." Ida loved walking in the dark, any time of year. She pulled on her purple coat and looked at Frost, who looked back. She was surprised but pleased when her hand rose and beckoned for him to follow. She trailed Henry down the stairs, letting herself fall behind. At the bottom she waited. By the time Frost reached her, Henry was driving away in his gray Toyota. She supposed he was angry. It was not like him to leave her behind.

Frost held open the door. They passed outside, took a few halting steps along the sidewalk, stopped and faced one another.

"What are you doing tonight?" he asked.

"Tonight." Ida frowned and looked away. It was after nine o'clock. She had thought the night pretty much finished. Plus her head was starting to itch from the wig.

"How about a drink?"

Ida balled up her hands in her mittens and looked desperately out across the parking lot. Bars were places where men went to pick up women, and women sometimes went to be picked up. She didn't belong in them. But she wanted to go with Frost, somewhere.

"I can drive," he offered. "Unless you'd rather."

"Let's walk," she said.

It took ten minutes to cut across campus on foot, five more to reach the bar. Inside, lamps hung down from the ceiling, one for each booth, and hovered above each table.

Each circle of light was warm and small and far removed. Between booths it was dark, so the effect was of small, isolated tribes, huddling around their campfires. Ida liked that.

Even better, near the bathroom was a fish tank, glowing softly, with two overgrown fish inside. One was bright orange, the other pale blue. Ida wandered over to them. She clasped her hands behind her back so she wouldn't touch the glass. Frost fetched two beers and walked over to her.

"I came here a few years ago," she said. "At Christmastime, with my sister and brother. There was a group of people at the next table. Some of them were drunk and one crawled under the table with a camera and then the flash went off and there was screaming. Shoe—that was my sister—said one of the guys at the table pulled his pants down just before the photographer snapped the shot."

"Was your sister," Frost repeated.

"Yes. She died this summer. She was killed."

"I'm sorry," he said.

"Murdered, actually." Ida looked at him. "What kind of a name is Frost, anyway?"

"Last name."

He turned and carried both beers over to an empty booth. Ida followed. Once they were seated he turned back to her.

"Tell me about her," he said.

"What do you want to know?"

"Was she married? Did she have any kids?"

"One kid," said Ida. "He lives with us now."

"Who is 'us'?"

"My parents and me."

"What about his dad?"

"We don't know anything about him. We never met him."

"You don't even know his name?"

"She never told us his name. We couldn't get in touch with him now if we wanted to."

"Do you want to?"

"I don't know. She made me Moses' guardian for some reason. But maybe she was just afraid I'd never have kids of my own."

"And you want kids."

Ida nodded.

"What was she like?"

"Oh…" She tipped her head back and considered. "She looked a little like me—except different." Ida laughed. "She moved around a lot, all over the West. She loved the mountains and she loved to be outside. She worked a lot of different jobs, but never made much money. She was a good mom, though. And determined. She had a strong will."

"Stubborn?"

"Not exactly. She could make herself do anything."

"You mean she could do anything?"

"No. She could make herself do things she didn't want to do."

"Why would she do that?"

"She didn't want to be at the mercy of anything."

"We're all at the mercy of something."

Ida wasn't, but she didn't tell him this.

Frost studied her beer. "Try it," he said. "They just got it on tap this week."

Ida tried it and put it down.

"Well?" he said.

"I'm sorry," Ida said. "I've never liked beer."

"A mixed drink, then?"

She shook her head. "I don't like alcohol."

Frost shrugged and changed the subject.

"I want to buy your painting," he announced. "Or at least sell it for you."

Ida hesitated. No one had ever bought one of her paintings before. She supposed she ought to be excited, but then again, it didn't sound like he cared if he ended up with the painting or not.

"I'm an art dealer."

Of course. Ida nodded to hide her disappointment. Until that moment she had thought they were having a flirtation, even a date. She had thought he was interested in her.

"Is that what you were doing last week?"

Frost frowned in confusion.

"You came by our house," she said. "I was sitting with my nephew on the stoop and you stopped and talked to us. Our neighbor wasn't home."

He looked surprised. "That was you?"

Ida nodded.

"I did not know that," he said.

"You knew I wasn't blond."

"No," said Frost. "I asked if you were a blond."

"You didn't ask."

"I did. Because your eyebrows—" he reached up with his forefinger and traced the length of one "—are sable."

Ida snickered.

"They are!" He tossed his hands into the air, then slapped them on the table. "Will I see you without your wig?"

"You already have."

Frost shook his head, laughing, then stopped and pushed aside his beer. They looked at each other without speaking. She thought something momentous was about to occur.

"Look," he said. "If I ordered you a cocktail, would you try it?"

"Sure," she said. "Maybe."

He ambled over to the bar. Two minutes later, the waitress brought something clear and pale brown, with a cherry suspended in the ice. Ida ducked and took a sip, then raised her head and smiled.

He ordered her another drink, different from the first, but just as delicious. Ida went back and forth between the two, sampling one and then the other, fascinated by the delicate taste of each but also thankful to have something to do besides look at Frost, who never took his eyes off her.

"What about your painting?" he asked. "Are there others? Are there lots?"

She nodded and took another sip, pinching the tiny red straw between two fingers. He lowered his head, so high up there on his shoulders, to tell her in his low, rumbling voice that this second drink had been made with vodka. Ida raised her sable eyebrows, pretending to be impressed. She was not impressed, but she could see he wanted her to be and besides, she'd been pretending all night. She was wearing a wig, for Pete's sake. Their encounter had been fun, but not truly romantic because he didn't know her. He hadn't even recalled the first time they'd met. Either that or he was a liar. Ida did not expect she'd see him again.

"I could make you a lot of money. You and me both."

"Oh, please."

"I'm serious," Frost said. "Tell me more about your paintings. Tell me where you get your ideas."

Ida cheered up. After all, her paintings were far more personal than her red lipstick and her blond wig. He had seen past her disguise. He knew what mattered. But that didn't mean she could discuss her art with him. At least not yet.

"I paint my dreams," she said. "That's all."

He waited for more, but Ida was done talking. So he ordered her another drink and talked instead. He told her stories and offered up opinions, not facts, and that was as Ida would have wished it. Facts were almost always tiresome; it was how a person thought—and why—that told you what you needed to know. After a while he helped her on with her coat, then watched with a reverent expression as she pulled on her red wool mittens. On the way out, he offered to walk her home.

"No, thanks," Ida said.

He shrugged. "Suit yourself."

Ida thought he might be irritated, so when they reached the sidewalk, she extended her mittened hand. "Thank you," she said. "I had a lovely time."

He took her hand and lifted it to his lips. When he let it go, Ida turned and started down the sidewalk away from him, a little tipsy from her third sweet drink. She turned once to look and saw him still standing there. He snapped his bare hand into a salute, then disappeared back inside the bar.

Ida had not met many men, living as she did. It had never bothered her. She knew that in the late twentieth century she was an anomaly, an antiquated maiden artist freak. It was a lot of fun, knowing where the truth lay, knowing precisely what hoax was being perpetrated. After all, she wouldn't be alone much longer. She would find true love, and that would change everything. Until then her life was, in a way, a trick she played on other people, letting them think one thing about her when they really should be thinking another. It made her the center of the game, the real, if secret, source of fascination, and she'd never been curious about the other players, all those strangers out there. But she was curious about him.

CHAPTER SEVEN

Six weeks went by and Shoe and Max were going strong. True, some of what went on in the bedroom she suspected another woman might find undignified. But sex didn't signify much to her. She had slept with lots of men out of boredom. She slept with Max because he never bored her, and that seemed like progress. Then one morning, ten days before Christmas, they were lying in bed together, eating chocolate Santas while the sun rose, when Max began to talk about her feet.

Shoe liked to put on her slippers in bed, before she rolled out and landed on the freezing wood floor. She always began with her right foot and ended with her left. That morning when she brought out her left foot Max grabbed the arch and started talking. At first the talk seemed tender. He imagined her as a child, running barefoot down the sidewalk in Ida's painting, skipping through hot sand on a beach, kicking her shoes off at a party and dancing on someone's ping-pong table until it collapsed. He imagined a dozen things her feet had done, and he imagined well.

At first his talk sounded like a celebration of her feet, and of her, and Shoe was happy, because her body had indeed lived well. Her body, of all parts of her, had lived best. But as he went on talking, she began to sense something else creeping in. If it had been a sadness for the rest of her, for the parts that had not lived so well, she would have adored him more than ever. Instead it was regret, which Shoe knew was not the same as sadness, regret bleeding into disapproval.

As if she had ill-used her feet. As if they had suffered at her whimsy. As if a smarter woman would have used her feet less and in so doing preserved them, so that one day a man might be more moved to suck on the tender toes Shoe didn't have, and hadn't had for years. Shoe wrestled her left foot away from him and toward their two heads, together on one pillow.

"Love me, love my foot," she said.

"But of course," Max said. "What do you think I—"

"Love me, love my foot," Shoe repeated. Then she waggled her mashed-up toes through the air.

"Put that thing down," Max said.

She let go, turned on her bare hip, and kicked him lightly in the stomach.

"Darling," Max said. "I made you an appointment for a pedicure. I was going to wait and surprise you."

Shoe's left foot fell back to the bed, where it burrowed under the covers.

"They'll massage your feet and cut your nails and polish them."

Shoe shook her head. She didn't like to warn people—they seldom deserved it—but because it was Max, she did. "Do not attempt reform," she said.

"What do you mean?" Max said. "Your feet aren't beyond repair."

"We aren't talking about my feet."

"I am. Christ, Susan, what's wrong with a little self-improvement?"

"That depends on your definition of self."

Shoe rolled out of bed, grabbed her left slipper, and shuffled down the dark hall to the bathroom. She was deliberating all the way, though over just what, she couldn't yet discern.

She shared the bathroom with two housemates on the second floor. It was warmer than her room, and all the plumbing fixtures were a vibrant green. She tried to find odd times of day to spend in there when no one else was around. At one point she even tried hanging one of Ida's paintings next to the medicine cabinet to make herself feel really at home, but the heavy condensation on the canvas concerned her. After she took the painting down, she occasionally stood before the full-length mirror mounted on the back of the bathroom door and flashed herself. She wore the gold dressing gown she'd won in a poker game off a man who smoked cheroots and entertained herself, sometimes for five-minute stretches, tearing open the lapels then closing them, on and off like a traffic signal.

That morning she went straight to one of the bathroom shelves, and to a shoebox there filled with her personal effects. In the box, buried under cold medicine, bubble bath and razor blades, was a pregnancy test she'd bought a couple years back, the second half of a two-for-one special. The expiration date had passed a month before, but she went ahead anyway, gathering her first-morning sample and dribbling a bit of it into the hole. Almost immediately, the test window changed to a deep, definitive blue.

That she was pregnant with Max's child came as no great surprise to her and so, while the discovery was a moment of sorts, it was not the defining moment of this particular crisis. For Shoe, life had never been about the things that happen to people, but about the things they did as a result. It was the choices that followed events, if you could call them choices, that really made up a life. The rest, whatever held that mosaic of choices together, was just paste.

She was about to make one choice, to walk down the hall and tell Max the news, when she turned instead and rummaged through her shoebox a second time. She found a bottle of black nail polish left over from Halloween, hitched up a foot on the green toilet tank, leaned forward, and applied a first coat. When it wasn't dark enough to soak up all the light, a second coat did the trick.

Her toes, already winter white, looked macabre against the black nails. They looked defiled. She knew that in choosing this aesthetic she'd created the desired paradox: It was an ugly choice, for Max the worst choice, and therefore the perfect choice. In a moment, she would know if he could ever be a father to their baby. If not, better that he never knew that's who he was.

She placed her hand on the glass doorknob and stopped, as the old rapture swept over her. In the bathroom mirror her fingers spread and lifted from the doorknob. Her toes curled tightly against the tile floor. But with her head thrown back, she couldn't see her reflection, the bared throat or unfocused eyes. She stood like this until the feeling waned, then opened the bathroom door and started down the hallway.

If anyone had seen her in that early-morning light, they would have seen a woman flushed with a kind of ecstasy. It was a surge, a swell that sometimes overtook Shoe just before she acted against a fear, sometimes just before she knew what the act would be. For Shoe, it was the most delicious sensation in the world.

When she returned to the bedroom, Max was getting dressed. She stopped him just as he was about to cover up his broad, beautiful chest and placed her hand there.

Max smiled at her. "Cold hands, warm heart."

"Warm hands, cold feet," she said.

He laughed the deep, wonderful, wicked laugh she would always love. "Well, you wouldn't know about cold feet," he said. Then, as if to give them their due, his gaze dropped from her face down to her feet.

Max had found a tanning salon somewhere in town, and was going twice a week. Now Shoe watched, sad but also fascinated, as the surface tan remained but, just beneath, the living color vanished. He fell away from her like someone in a swoon.

When he finally met her eyes again, he shook his head. She watched him struggle for the words.

"Bitch," was all he managed.

"Darling," she answered.

She reached around him to pluck another Santa from the plastic wrap, one with marshmallow insides. She bit off Santa's head, reached up, and pushed the rest into his mouth. That was her final gift to him: Max loved marshmallow almost as much as she did.

CHAPTER EIGHT

When Frost surfaced again, they were in the side yard plugging the gooseberry bush with popcorn. It was not for any mild, domestic effect. They were fostering an illusion.

Sometimes Ida saw a thing wrong. Or rather, she saw it right, but unfettered by human explanations. She saw the way an animal would: the pure form, free of any name or function. In time, she'd come to understand that when you look at something and you don't quite know what it is, you see it better. Once a thing became familiar, comprehensible, Ida was inevitably disappointed.

It was the same when she overheard snippets of strangers' conversations. Out of context, their words could become enigmatic, even dangerous. She might think the strangers were plotting murder, revolution, any manner of things, before she remembered people, even strangers, didn't say any manner of things. Most only said very particular things, chosen from a limited menu of mundane concerns: How are you? Did you catch that game? I am so tired. I am so busy! I am so broke. Who does she think she is? How about this weather?

Ida's disappointment in the mundane was an everyday occurrence, but so were her discoveries of something better, something charming or mysterious or magical. What scared her most was the prospect of living a life that had once been tinged with wonder, and wasn't any longer. That sort of living didn't interest her. It was why she'd never left her parents' house. Out in the world, she knew, she wasn't welcome. Out there, people had to be practical, hard-headed. They couldn't let their guard down or afford to look at things more than one way. Out there, you couldn't live as she did and survive.

Of course, when she mis-heard or mis-saw, it was disorienting. But it also reminded her of the possibilities of an unfettered world. So one day she thought she saw a bush growing popcorn, and then when she reminded herself such things do not exist, she had to make one herself, a popcorn bush growing full-blown milky white kernels.

This bush, of course, was just a modest project. Many of the things she mis-heard or mis-saw were nearly impossible to execute. But the gooseberry sported thorns long enough to hold kernels even in the afternoon's unfriendly gusts. Moses attended to the lower thorns, the ones on the periphery. Ida slipped her gloved hands deeper into the bush, up to the elbows for a deep, dense effect. Most of the kernels stayed on. The problem ones they ate.

There was only a weak show of sunlight, the wind was from the north, and it was cold. They were about to head inside when Frost's car pulled up across the street. Moses noticed, as he noticed most things.

"Look," he said.

But she had already.

It had been three days since she'd seen him, and while Ida had plenty to occupy her—ice-skating and the library with Moses, the grocery store, a trip with Henry for pie— she had grown restless by the third day, and distracted. She wandered from room to room, tapping at walls with her knuckles. Now that he'd reappeared, Ida was so weak with relief she couldn't think straight.

"Look," Moses said again.

"I saw," she said.

Frost slouched in his too-small car, watching while they worked maybe five minutes more. Ida could not think what to do, so she ignored him.

"Come inside," she finally said to Moses.

With a backward glance, he did.

Ida had put some cookie dough in the refrigerator to chill while they worked outside, and now it took no time to roll it out, cut it into crescents, and set the crescents out on trays. From the kitchen, she couldn't keep an eye on Frost or his car, but she could feel him watching the house, could feel it through the walls, so when he suddenly loomed outside the kitchen door, Ida was not surprised.

He knocked lightly. Because her hands were covered in sugar, she sent Moses to let him in. Moses tugged on the storm door, which swung inward, and a cold gust of late autumn wind swept in.

"Hi!" he shouted down to Moses.

Ida marveled at that shout, so fine and loud and happy, so unapologetic. What if everybody went around shouting their greetings like that?

"Come on in," Moses said. Ida watched him haul back on his arm the way his mother used to. He'd learned that loose, lovable hospitality early on.

When Frost had set his big feet inside their kitchen, he crouched down so that he was operating at Moses' eye level, and Ida thought: Here is a man who knows how to be himself in this world and get away with it. It was a thing she'd never known how to do. She was drawn to him, as she imagined many people must be. But she had never intended to want someone everybody wanted.

Still in his crouch, Frost reached out and set his beautiful hands on Moses' shoulders. Ida went on sprinkling sugar across a row of blue crescent moons. He looked—Ida would remember this for years to come—from her to Moses and back again, as if he were making up his mind. She could see little wheels turning inside his head, the cogs of deliberation. She saw the wheels roll one way, then come to a stop and roll back the other, the way she backpedaled on her old bicycle when she wanted to stop. But she didn't know what he was deliberating on at the time, and so it didn't help her.

Then he rose, and as he did, his hands slowly lifted from Moses' shoulders. He took several steps into the kitchen. Ida could feel him filling the space between them. And with that alone, she could feel the world outside shift just enough to offer her admittance.

"What are you making?" he asked.

Ida lowered her eyes to the tray again. "Sugar cookies," she said.

"These aren't sugar cookies." He leaned his long body over the counter. "I know sugar cookies. These are better!"

"They're blue moons." Ida studied the shapes under the cutter. "I haven't figured out yet how to keep that pure aquamarine. If you cook them at the proper temperature they brown up and the blue is marrred. But if you cook them more slowly, they just come out hard."

"Like rocks," Moses added, following Frost across the room.

Frost nodded seriously. "You're forced to choose between something that's beautiful on the inside and something that's beautiful on the outside."

"That's true," Ida said.

"That's a tough call," he said.

"It's a call we shouldn't always have to make," Ida said.

"You won't," he said.

She smiled, though not at him.

"I'm serious," he said.

"I know."

"But you're smiling."

"That's why I'm smiling."

"Look at me."

Ida looked. He was searching her face again, intent on something. No man had ever searched her face like this. The force of his attention made her swallow. It made her heart pound in her head.

"Is that your real color?" he asked.

"What do you mean?" She thought he might be speaking in code.

"Your hair," he said. "Is that yours?"

Ida nodded, relieved when Moses climbed up on the stool and tapped him on the shoulder. "What's your name?"

He told Moses his name was Max.

"May I see your studio?" asked Max.

"What for?" said Ida.

"I told you. I'm going to make you a lot of money."

"You're right. You did tell me that."

"I'll show you," Moses offered.

Max held out his hand and Moses took it. Together, they left the kitchen. Ida followed them downstairs, into the room she called her studio. She watched as Moses escorted Max from painting to painting, silently pointing with his free hand as they went. Max still held his other hand. Suddenly Max turned his head and saw her there. A look came over his face, so full of tenderness she turned away.

"Another masterpiece," he said, gesturing at one of her favorites.

"That's for my sister."

Ida walked closer and surveyed it, finished now and hung up on the wall. The painting was of the inside of a barn, its cavernous interior lit by a single shaft of light. It was a peaceful scene, the light almost heavenly. But lurking in the shadows of the barn were the dim outlines of half a dozen children.

"I was working on something else when she was

killed. And then I painted over it."

"The way you loved your sister," he said. "It's a beautiful thing to see."

Ida smiled down at the tiles in the floor. After they marched back upstairs, Max leaned against a wall and looked around.

"You don't have any photos on your refrigerator," he observed.

"We're not much of a photo family."

"Oh?"

"We're not photogenic."

"That's impossible," said Max. "I'll bring a camera some time, if you'll invite me back, and I'll take some photos."

"When?" Moses asked.

"Whenever you say," Max said. Then he was at the door.

"Don't you want a cookie?" Moses asked.

"More than anything," said Max. "But I have to go."

He snapped his hand into another salute for Moses, turned the salute on Ida, then asked if she'd walk him to his car. Moses ran off to watch the four o'clock cartoons. Ida pulled on her leopard-print coat and followed him out to the curb.

"Get in the car," he barked, but Ida could see he was trying not to laugh.

"What for?" Ida asked, secretly thrilled.

"I want to talk to you."

He opened the passenger-side door and Ida climbed in. When she was settled, he closed her door and circled around to the driver's side. It took a little time for him to fit his knees in under the steering wheel. When he had eased into position, he shut his door and turned to her.

"Where are your mittens? Are you cold? I'll run the heater if you're cold."

Ida shook her head.

"Me neither."

He threw back his head and tried staring upward, but his face came within inches of the car's ceiling. He scanned the dashboard, studied her feet, gazed outside at the popcorn bush. Ida wanted to watch him, but didn't want to make him uncomfortable. She played with her thumbs instead.

"I like your sneakers," he announced suddenly.

Ida studied them but said nothing.

"Have you ever been engaged?"

"No."

"Why not?"

"I've never been in love."

He rubbed his hands in delight. Ida burst out laughing, but he didn't seem to care. When she laughed, he just rubbed them harder.

"Are you happy being single?"

"Yes," Ida said. "But I don't consider it a permanent condition."

"Why not?"

"I know someday he'll find me."

"So you've been holding out for the right man," he said.

"Yes." It was Ida's turn to look away. She studied the popcorn bush critically. It looked crafty, not magical. A starling swooped in and carried one kernel away. Another bird followed. "I mean, what else am I going to do. Not hold out?"

Max gazed at her. "You may be the best thing that's ever happened to me."

Ida didn't know what to say to that. After all, she hadn't happened to him yet. And she was a private person. It took a long time to get to know her. How could he already want her, this shouting, happy man?

"Wait till you get to know me," she said.

"I know you."

This could not be. The way he talked to her was like a person who, even in the midst of conversation, looks just past your shoulder or at the space between your eyes. Yet he was looking right at her. He refused to look away.

"Get out of the car," he said.

"No."

"You don't want to talk about this," he said. "And I'm not going to make you."

"You're not?"

Max stared at her in surprise. "Don't laugh at me. I beg you."

"I beg you not to be so funny."

He threw open his door and leapt out with unexpected speed. The next thing she knew he had rounded the car and thrown open her door as well. He grabbed Ida by the furry arms of her coat, wrested her from the car, and swung her into the air. For one delirious moment she saw nothing but cold blue sky. Then he'd set her down, gently, on her family's lawn.

"I must see you again."

"You just saw me," she said. But she was out of breath when she said it, and wildly happy.

"Again," he said. "And next time I want to meet your parents."

"Sure," Ida said. "Okay."

"I'll take you out to dinner," he said. "I know just the place."

CHAPTER NINE

Missoula is due north of Ketchum, six hours of officially designated scenic highway. The day she discovered she was pregnant, Shoe packed her truck and hit that road by sundown. At ten she crossed state lines, stopped for gas soon after, and picked up two sacks of Halloween candy, marked down once and then again for postseason clearance. By the time she reached Johnny's place at midnight, there were a dozen fun-size Snickers wrappers on the floor of her truck.

She took the fire escape two steps at a time to the top floor of the house, where a light still burned, set down her candy on the landing, and knocked. The heavy inside door opened almost immediately, light spilled out, Johnny saw her standing in it, and smiled. When he went to open the storm door, though, it gave two or three inches and stuck.

Shoe stood by while he wiggled the frame this way and that.

"Stand back," she said, and attacked the door with her

boot. When it swung open, she threw herself into Johnny's arms.

"Shoe," he said, unsurprised as ever, and patted her back. "I thought it might be you."

She followed him inside, presenting him with what was left of her candy.

"There's a message for you on my machine," Johnny said.

"Who from?" she asked.

"A guy. He said to call him when you get in. He wants to know you got here safely."

Shoe felt that combination of relief and despair one sometimes feels when things are finally taken out of their control. She sank onto a nearby couch, the only piece of furniture in the room.

Johnny watched her. "Want to call him?" he asked. "Just to tell him you got in?"

Shoe got up, filled a glass with water from the tap, and drank for a spell. She touched her stomach, just as an experiment, then snatched away her hand.

"Shoe?"

She shook her head.

"He sounded worried."

"He may be," she said. "But he isn't worried about me. He was sending me a message. He wants me to know that he's on to me. But he isn't on to me."

Johnny looked skeptical.

"He's trouble. With a capital T."

"Go to sleep," Johnny said. "We'll talk in the morning."

She sat up on the couch, took his arm, and pulled his

face down next to hers so she could kiss his pretty cheek. "He'll still be trouble then," she said. "Sweet dreams."

She woke to sunlight and the smell of bacon cooking. Excellent, she thought, but in the bathroom five minutes later, she quietly vomited up her quota of candy bars from the evening before. Pregnancy would be an adventure, this she could tell already. But who could she ever tell about the father? When it came to Max, who would believe the truth? She had no reputable evidence of Max's evil, not the sort anyone would understand. Shoe trusted her little brother above anyone, but feared the fact of the pregnancy might confuse him, and that if Max called again, Johnny might be tempted to tell him where she was, and why. Max must never learn the truth.

Shoe wiped her face with a wet tissue and staggered out to the kitchen, where Johnny stood at the stove, just finishing up the eggs. He lifted the pan from the burner, turned toward the table and saw her.

"Johnny," she started, "if he calls again—"

"He already called." Johnny moved to the table and set down the pan. "I told him you were fine."

She sank into a chair.

"I told him you'd called me from somewhere around Spokane. That you were headed for Seattle."

Shoe took this in with silent gratitude.

"That's our story, then," she said.

"Sure."

"For now," she said.

"For forever, as far as I'm concerned."

The toast popped up. Shoe recognized the toaster. They'd had it in the kitchen at home when they were kids.

"That thing still works," she said, impressed.

"In a manner of speaking." Johnny buttered the toast with careful attention, like a boy who hasn't been buttering his own toast for long and needs to think about it. He was still a boy of sorts in those days. But with only a semester to go, he would be the first Tumarkin child to finish college.

Shoe left the room to vomit again. When she returned to the table, Johnny addressed her from behind his morning paper.

"I'd make you some coffee, but you don't seem like you need it."

She grabbed a paper napkin and mopped her forehead. Her whole body was damp with sweat. "No," she said. "No, it wouldn't be considerate."

Johnny lowered his paper and looked at her.

Shoe patted her stomach. When Johnny didn't react, she patted it more vigorously and flapped her eyebrows.

"What?" Johnny said. "It upsets your stomach?"

She didn't tell him that day, or the next. A week later the two of them flew back to Ohio for Christmas. All during the flight she wanted to tell him, but the time was never right. In the end, she didn't tell him until after she told Ida, whom she hadn't meant to tell at all.

Ida was not a sympathetic audience, as far as Shoe was concerned. She always asked why, but never approved of the answer. In order to keep her from asking, Shoe often tried to outsmart her.

On this occasion, she brought huckleberries back with her on the plane, hoping they might distract her sister. Shoe had picked them the summer before on a backpacking trip. They had sat in her freezer in Ketchum for months. She took them with her when she fled Idaho for Montana, and two days before Christmas, presented them to her sister in Ohio.

The following morning, when Shoe went downstairs to ask if she could borrow some underwear, she found Ida in the kitchen, already working the berries up into a pie. Ida had the dough rolled out on the counter. She was cutting it into the shapes of leaves, then using the knife tip on those leaves to trace delicate veins. The rumpled recipe she was consulting included an early photo of household maven Martha Stewart.

"Fancy-foo," Shoe said. She propped her elbows on the counter and watched. Ida paid her no mind.

"Real butter?" Shoe asked.

Ida barely nodded.

Shoe congratulated herself on her tricky ploy: At this rate, there would be no pesky questions from her little sister. Self-satisfied, Shoe watched in silence.

"This is the fun part," Ida announced.

Her tongue poked out shyly between her teeth. Shoe knew that this look of concentration meant her sister was, indeed, having fun. Ida kept her good times largely to herself, so Shoe found this sort of sign reassuring. After all, she wanted Ida to enjoy her life.

"Looks good enough to eat," Shoe said. She settled

the underwear question with her sister, popped a dough scrap in her mouth, and headed back upstairs.

Digging through Ida's underwear drawer, she stumbled across a letter. It was handwritten, addressed to Ida, with a return address in Lincoln, Nebraska. Shoe had driven past signs for the town a couple times on cross-country treks, but had never stopped. Ida had never been there. Shoe was certain of that.

She sifted through the colossal cotton underwear—grannywear, Shoe called it—that made up her sister's collection, settling on a white pair. The only other choice was a disturbing buff shade, not a color Shoe approved of for anyone, let alone a painter. She pulled on the briefs and closed the drawer, but she didn't forget the letter.

The night after Christmas, Johnny and Shoe went out to the bars—Ida, as usual, refused to come along—but since Shoe had stopped drinking eleven days before, the bars were not quite the pleasure she generally found them to be. Johnny was doing okay without her, getting hit on by a couple of girls from his high school class, so she headed home alone, fixed herself some warm milk with cinnamon, and was in her flannels by eleven.

The bedroom hadn't changed much since they were kids. The pink carpet was gone, and the twin beds—their parents had moved in the old double from their room for Ida. When Shoe was home, three or four days a year, they shared. Eyelet curtains, sashed at the sides, still hung at the windows. Ida's kiddy desk still sat in the corner, with one of her early paintings hung above it.

Shoe climbed into the vacant side of the bed, propped herself against the wall, and sipped her warm milk. She'd been self-sufficient for years, but never felt more safe and sound than here, in this room. When her mother called twice a week to glean the details of her life, Shoe could tell she found something glamorous there, but that wasn't how Shoe viewed her own life. For glamour you needed many things, including money, of which Shoe had none. The home she made for her child wouldn't be as comfortable as this one. But she'd be damned if it wasn't just as cozy.

Beside her, Ida lay on her back, reading a hardback novel.

"Library book?" Shoe asked.

"Yes," Ida said.

"I noticed that letter in your underwear drawer."

Ida's eyes flickered, but she said nothing.

"Who's it from?"

"A stranger," Ida said. Then, as if for clarity, she added, "I don't know her."

"What's the letter about?"

"One of my paintings."

"Which one?"

"An old one," Ida said.

"Where'd she see it?"

"She found it in a thrift store." Ida pretended to read for a moment. "She bought it. And then she got evicted and lost it."

"No way." Shoe threw back the covers, turned, and looked at Ida. "Mind if I read the letter?"

"Nope." Ida turned her back to her sister.

Shoe got out of bed and went over to the dresser, which had seen a few paint jobs in its day. There was an old layer of purple showing through in a couple spots from when Shoe was nine, Ida seven. Yellow from their early childhood. White from high school. Now it was scarlet. Shoe fingered the chips and scratches where layers of her past showed through, then pulled out the top drawer. "How come you keep it in here?" she asked.

"I don't know," Ida said. "I didn't know where to keep it."

It was the fact that she kept it, more than the place, that snagged Shoe's interest, but she didn't mention this. She carried the letter back to the bed and dangled it in front of her sister. Ida wrinkled her nose. Shoe pulled the letter from its envelope and read it. When she had finished, she gazed at the ceiling, fanned herself with the letter a few times, and read it again. Then she slipped it back into its envelope, crossed the room, and buried it once again in Ida's underwear drawer. When Shoe climbed back in the bed, Ida turned off the lamp.

Shoe couldn't remember ever having seen the painting in question, but Ida had done a hundred paintings, easy. That one had snuck out of the house and gravitated to a thrift store in Lincoln, Nebraska, was a curious thing, but more extraordinary, Shoe thought, was this stranger's response to her sister's work. For some reason, this woman, Emily, needed that painting. She needed to visit a world transformed by Ida's imagination. As did Shoe. As, Shoe had believed for a brief time, did

Max. She recalled the look of longing she'd seen on his face just a few weeks before, looking at Ida's sidewalk. She'd offered him that painting the next day and he took it, the bastard, but Ida had cornered the market on other worlds. All her paintings had that in common.

Shoe sometimes thought that Ida had chosen the better path. She didn't have to settle for visits, as they did. She could live in those worlds all the time. Shoe had to remind herself she wasn't jealous.

"So you answered it," she said into the dark.

"No, I didn't answer it."

"What? Why not?"

"I couldn't think of anything to say."

"Say, thank you. Say, as a matter of fact, I've got a hundred paintings I've done since that one. Do you remember the painting she's talking about?"

"Yes," Ida said.

"Do you remember how old you were when you did it?"

"Fifteen."

"And ten years later it shows up in a thrift store a thousand miles away. That is fucking cool, Ida. That is fucking amazing, I think. Don't you think?"

"Actually," said Ida, "eight years later and eight hundred miles. She found it three years ago. How do you think it got to Nebraska?"

"I don't know," Shoe said, "but you've got to write her back."

"I've got nothing to say to her."

"Oh, but you will. You will. This is a girl after your

own heart."

"I doubt that," Ida said.

The two of them lay side by side, flat on their backs, wide awake and staring at the ceiling. Shoe wanted to reach over in the dark and shake her sister.

"What have you got against her?" she asked finally. "That's what I'd like to know."

"She's overly demonstrative," Ida said. "She probably majored in drama. Or she's some other kind of exhibitionist."

Shoe snorted with laughter.

"I'm serious," Ida said stiffly.

"I'll tell you something, Ida Tumarkin. I think this girl has been through the wringer. I think you don't know emotional distress when you see it. Or that once in a while you can do something about it."

Ida said nothing. Shoe thought about stopping there, but something had gotten hold of her.

"And another thing. I've thought on occasion that it might do you some good to suffer a little more. You know, there's a whole spectrum of experience out there. I think it might help your art."

Now she was moving into dangerous waters. Ida's art was her stronghold. Shoe knew that. When Ida finally answered, her voice was muffled. "I don't see why," she said.

"Well, of course you don't see it now," Shoe said. "You're not going to see it until after you've suffered. If you could see it before you suffered, you could just bypass the suffering. Very neat and tidy."

"I don't want to suffer," Ida said.

"Join the club."

"You want to suffer."

"I never wanted to suffer," Shoe said. "I wanted to live. If I had to suffer to live, then I'd suffer. Sometimes the only way I knew how to live well was to suffer. It was different with you."

"Yes."

"Anyway," Shoe said. "I've changed."

"Why?"

So like Ida, Shoe thought, to ask that.

"That's immaterial," Shoe said. "The question is how have I changed."

"Liar."

For a moment there was silence. Then they both burst out laughing.

"Ida," Shoe said. "I know you like children."

"I love them."

"But what if you didn't get married in time to have them?"

"I will."

"But what if you don't meet someone. What if you don't meet Mr. Right in time?"

"I will."

"But say that you met Mr. Right, and then Mr. Right died, what then?"

"It won't be like that," Ida said. "Not for me. Why, are you pregnant?"

"Yes," Shoe said. "Absolutely."

So Ida was the first to know. In the weeks and months that followed, when Shoe was carrying Moses but before he was born and the fact of him could reproach such prying questions, there were those who asked her how she'd let herself get pregnant, and why she was carrying her pregnancy to term. She had a few answers.

One was that she was afraid of raising a baby. She knew that for this reason, sooner or later she would.

Two was that she didn't want to end her life, though she had long thought that if done right, the ending could be exciting. Instead, she found herself an earthly commitment. She had a child to keep herself from dying young.

Three was a promise she made to herself early on, in her first week with Max, that if she got pregnant by him she would see it through. With other guys she'd made no such pledge, and been more careful, besides. Once she knew the truth about him, she supposed that promise should have changed, but it didn't. Max had some glorious qualities. She believed his child could be endowed with those qualities and spared the others. She was right.

What all those reasons failed to anticipate was the thing one seldom can anticipate—that she would change. Motherhood changed her reason for living. From that morning in the bathroom forward, she didn't live for fear, but despite it, because she felt it not for herself, but for her child.

In the end, she had no convoluted psychological motivations for keeping the baby. She kept it because she wanted it. Because from the beginning, what she felt for this creature felt like love. But real love wasn't selfish; keeping her baby was. So when people asked she didn't call it love, but hunger, or desire. By the time her son was born, she didn't care what she should call it. The feeling was still hers, regardless. So was Moses.

CHAPTER TEN

Max rang the doorbell at five-thirty. Ida ushered him into the living room and invited him to sit down. When he sank onto the loveseat, she took a chair a few feet away, leaned forward, and settled her hands in her lap. Max slapped his hands onto his knees and leaned forward too.

"You look terrific!" he shouted.

"Thanks," Ida said.

"How are you?"

"All right," she said.

"Me too, now that you're here. Look at you!"

Professor Tumarkin appeared. He shook Max's hand and offered him a beer. Moses came next and sat down beside Max on the loveseat. When Max removed his coat, Ida carried it across to the piano bench, feeling his eyes on her the whole time. She waited until her father asked Max a question to finally look back at him, but that's when she saw Max's sweater.

It was a cotton crewneck, earth-toned and perfectly nice. The effect was supposed to be casual and that was the trouble, somehow. The sweater tried too hard. She reproached herself, recalling her own sometimes-elaborate attempts to look normal. What, after all, was the difference? Casual and normal were practically the same. But each time she looked at the sweater she felt queasy and the queasiness, in turn, made her feel judgmental. She hurried away to fetch the tray of snacks she'd fixed earlier, when she'd been too nervous to paint.

Inside a ring of Ritz crackers she had piled olives and cubes of cheese. She returned with the plate of snacks and set them safely down, though her hands were shaking. Mrs. Tumarkin had taken a seat beside her husband, looking livelier than she had since Shoe's murder. And then Professor Tumarkin took a cube of cheese and the rest began to topple, causing one of the olives to catapult off the tray and roll across the living room rug. Moses leapt off the loveseat, plucked up the olive, blew on it several times, and popped it in his mouth. Everybody laughed, then settled back nervously.

Max was supposed to drive Ida down to Cincinnati for dinner. Snow was forecast, but it hadn't started yet.

"Boy, maybe you shouldn't go tonight," said the professor.

"Of course they should," Mrs. Tumarkin said. "This is Ida's chance to see the city. Then when Max brings her back, if the weather's bad, he can spend the night here."

There was the snow, and there was the unspoken hesitation about sending Ida so far out into the world with this man they'd just met. But they figured it was probably all right.

Max and Moses sat together, both curly-haired, both laughing, and when she tried Max's beer, both looking up at her at the same instant to see the face she made, smiling on her with the same light in their eyes, that strange, almost golden brown.

Uncanny, Ida thought.

"We'll see how it goes," she said.

Ida hadn't been to Cincinnati for years, not since the Christmas she'd ridden down with her parents to pick up Shoe and Johnny at the airport. They'd all gone downtown for dinner, but she hadn't liked the city back then. It was too big, too busy. Driving in this time, it felt different. There were lights strung along the bridges and clustered on the hilltops. It had become a pretty city, almost a magical one. Even after Max had parked the car and she'd gotten out and walked the sidewalk, once they were no longer suspended above the life of the city but part of it, that feeling remained.

They passed a woman on the streetcorner, ringing a bell for the Salvation Army. Ida dug in her coat pockets for loose change, but all she found was an old throat lozenge. Inside the restaurant, after Max had taken her coat and the maître d' had led them away to a table, Ida found herself still gripping the lozenge in her left hand. She panicked, then set it on her chair and sat on it. Max ordered them both gin and tonics, leaned back, and studied her. Ida tried to smile, but the lipstick made her mouth bunch up and she stopped.

"Are you all right?" Max asked.

"Not really," Ida said. "Crowds make me nervous."

"What for?"

"People look at me."

"Of course they do!" Max slapped his hands on the edge of the table and his elbows jutted out on either side. "You are gorgeous."

When a waitress brought their drinks, Max touched the woman's arm to detain her. She smiled at him.

"Look at her," he said, pointing at Ida. "Is she or is she not the most stunning thing you've ever seen?"

The waitress was still smiling, but as her eyes passed over Ida, it seemed to Ida the smile faltered. Ida wrapped her hands around her drink and yanked it closer. The waitress turned and walked away.

"So anyway," she said.

Max was silent, blinking in surprise. It was a look familiar to her, though not on his face. Ida had seen it years before on the boy she tried to date in college, before she gave up dating and college too. Later on, she'd seen it on the faces of other men, here and there, though she pretended not to. She turned away from him and looked around the room so that she wouldn't have to see it now.

"There was a crowd last week at the bar. You weren't nervous then," he said.

"I was. But it was different."

"Because you were in disguise."

Ida nodded.

"I like you better this way."

"What way?"

"Nervous," he said. "And brunette."

For a moment they drank in silence, though Max drank much faster. As the snow began to fall outside the window, Ida looked out over the other tables and felt part of something she never had before. She knew it was because of him, having him by her side, the most fascinating man she'd ever met. He made the outside world compelling.

Before, her own world had been the only one she wanted. Tonight, with candles on her table in a softly shining city on a river with such a man, she came to understand the allure of the outside world. She longed to do something tonight in this world before returning home to her own.

Max watched her over the top of his glass.

"I can't get you out of my head," he said. "I dream about you all night, and I wake up wondering, does Ida feel for me one-tenth of what I feel for her? Someday, will Ida let me hold her hand? And I have this feeling if Ida did, if Ida fixed me with those eyes of hers and said, Max, will you kiss me, I'd be the happiest man on earth."

"On earth?"

"You're merciless," Max said. "I bring my heart to you, and you trample it in the mud."

Ida laughed and looked up at the ceiling. It had to be twenty feet high, and made of shining squares of copper, pressed into intricate patterns. Ida had never seen such a marvelous thing before, had never even expected to. When she lowered her gaze again, Max was watching her with delight.

"If you loved a man, I'll bet you wouldn't let anything

stand in your way."

"That's true. I would give everything for love."

Max leaned his head back against the booth and closed his eyes. "Keep talking," he said.

"I would give everything for love," Ida repeated. With his eyes closed, she felt safer, almost as if she were talking to herself. "Because nothing matters more. Because the world is lonely, and when you find your true love, it's a once-in-a-lifetime chance. It's the greatest happiness two people can know."

When Max opened his eyes again, the light from them was impossibly pure.

"Are you still happy being single?"

"Yes," she lied.

"Your happiness is contingent on not being single at some point in the future."

"Yes. But I'm also happy now."

"You seem happy," he said.

"I live in hope."

"That's a courageous thing to do," he said. "It sounds as if that was a thing your sister couldn't do."

"It's not about courage. It's about me. For Shoe it was totally different."

"Courage means doing something even if you're afraid to do it. Not because you're afraid."

That was Shoe in a nutshell, but almost no one knew why she did the things she did. Nor did they care. People only witnessed her exploits—the act and not the motive, Ida thought.

"It made everybody think she always did exactly what

she wanted, but I'll bet that wasn't true. I'll bet she almost never did what she wanted."

Ida nodded eagerly, glad someone finally understood. Shoe had done a thousand things she didn't want to do, and with single-minded determination. To Ida, that had always seemed a bad way to live. She wasn't one for testing limits or herself, and she'd never cared to build her character, which had served her well for years. She had simply managed to live her life so that she didn't have to do things she didn't want to do. Those undone things had never troubled her. Ida wanted for little, and what she still lacked in life she had always believed fate would bring her in time.

Instead of relying on force of will, she trusted her instincts. If something made her uncomfortable, she avoided that thing, for in her early experiences, in the old days when she was still forced to go to school and deal with a hundred people every day who didn't understand her, Ida had learned that her misgivings were almost always indicative of something more terrible to come. Apprehension was ripe with meaning and rich with promise, like the growl of an angry dog, or the rumble of an engine before a car full of boys cruised by, rolled down their windows, and shouted out something obscene.

"It's you," Max said. "You do what you want."

Blood rose to the surface of her skin. She lowered her eyes so that he wouldn't see how right he was.

"Sometimes," she said, trying to change the subject back to her sister, "I thought maybe she just didn't know what else to do with herself."

"But you're the opposite."

Ida looked back at the ceiling, then at the flowers on their table. She touched one of the yellow petals to see if it was real. She saw people moving off in the distance, but everything had gotten very quiet. It was as if the people were on television, and someone had come along and turned down the sound. "I always knew what to do, if people would only let me."

"I'll bet that everybody thought it was your sister who did that. I'll bet they thought it was the other way around."

"Yes." Ida tried to smile, but her mouth wouldn't move. She couldn't feel her legs, either. "That's my little secret."

"Your big secret," said Max. "The one that's made you what you are."

Ida set down her drink. Now she felt a tremor, but when she looked down at her hands, they were still. Desperately she looked across the room again and saw a waiter moving toward them, balancing a large tray on one hand.

"Do you want me?" Max asked suddenly.

Ida tried for flippancy. "Doesn't everybody?"

Max laughed. "Everybody but you," he said.

She did her best to laugh along. Sometimes he came off as a very different sort of man, as a conceited man. But then he looked at her and she could see they had an understanding, that Max had perceived a running joke in life and so had she. It was hard to formulate the joke exactly, but that didn't bother Ida. They both knew conceited people were funny.

"And every guy wants you," he added. "Every guy here tonight is gnashing his teeth that he's not sitting here in my place."

The waiter reached their table. He looked from Ida to Max, then silently laid out their dinner. Prime rib for Max. For Ida, tiny ravioli in a sage cream sauce. The moment the waiter had turned his back to walk away, Max leaned his long body across the table. "But I asked if you want me."

Ida nodded.

"Tell me."

She reached for her drink, but discovered she'd already finished it. She looked back at him. Her mouth opened and closed. Finally, she shook her head.

"Someday," he said, "I want you to tell me. When I've undressed you and I'm touching you exactly where you want to be touched and the way you want to be touched—the first time we make love—you tell me then."

He signaled the waitress for more drinks, and Ida left the table to use the restroom. She needed to compose herself. In the mirror over the sink she looked flushed and agitated. She sat in one of the stalls and leaned her cheek against the cool marble wall, but the feeling didn't wane. His boldness not only thrilled but persuaded her. He regarded their future together as inevitable, and she was beginning to as well.

When she returned, she saw the lozenge sitting on the table.

"The waitress found this by your chair," he said. "Is it yours?"

Ida nodded and sat down.

Max looked worried. "Are you sick?"

Ida shook her head.

"Are you sure?"

Ida waved her hand. "It's a long story."

Max laughed. "We've got all night."

Ida took a drink before starting. "It was the Salvation Army lady, out there on the corner. I wanted to put something in her kettle, so I was digging around in my pockets. But all I had was a lozenge."

"That still doesn't explain how it ended up on the floor."

"It was still in my hand when the guy took my coat. My dress doesn't have any pockets. I didn't know what to do. So I sat on it."

"You're adorable," Max said.

"Actually," Ida said, "I wondered if you'd mind lending me a dollar to give her on the way out."

"A dollar?"

Ida shrugged. "I usually give a dollar."

"Do you really think a dollar's going to do anybody any good?"

"Well," Ida said. "I'd give more, but I don't have a job."

"You work," Max said. "You run your family's household. That's a job."

The subject of work mortified Ida, so she changed it.

"There's one charity I give to every Christmas. It's my favorite. For thirty dollars, you can buy kids in a third-world country a goat, or some chickens. And that animal helps feed them for years. You can buy a cow or a pig—all sorts of animals, and other stuff too, to help them be more self-sufficient—but I usually buy a goat."

"You think you're buying them a goat."

"Why? What do you think I'm buying them?"

"You're buying some administrator somewhere a cushy job."

"Less than ten percent of donations in this organization go to administrative costs."

Max snorted. "So you're buying them ninety percent of a goat."

"Yeah," Ida said. "Okay."

Max shook his head. "You are adorable."

His look was adoring. Ida pushed the lozenge behind her plate and tried not to blush.

They finished their meal and somebody brought the bill and Max must have paid it, but Ida was gazing out onto the city street, watching the snow fall in huge, scattered flakes, and didn't notice. She wanted to stay out on the town, to do whatever adults did at night in a city, but Max said if he kept her down there any longer, she'd have to spend the night.

"But that's fine," Ida said. "I'll call my parents and let them know."

Max studied her again.

"Why not?" she said. "It could be fun!"

Max shook his head. "Darling," he said gravely, "I don't think you're ready to spend the night."

They struggled back into their winter coats and through the falling snow toward his car. Several times along the way, Ida wanted to argue but stopped herself, confused. They drove silently through downtown, then out onto the interstate. As she felt the magical lights of the city grow dim, she prepared to ask him just how he knew what she was ready for. When she finally opened her mouth to speak, Max spoke first.

"I saw you that night with the horses."

Ida was so surprised, she forgot her question. This statement rendered her more vulnerable than anything he'd said before. She felt as if he'd come upon her in a state of undress, except that what happened with the horses meant more to her than showing him her naked body.

"Did you follow us?" she asked finally.

"I did," Max said.

He admitted it. But it was more than that. If he had seen her with the horses then he understood her, and all would be well. She would never have to explain herself now: Max could explain her to everyone else. He could translate anything about her that needed translation.

"I'm glad you saw," Ida said, knowing that in those four words, she had told him everything.

"Me too," Max said.

The rest of the way home she watched the snow fall past the headlights, lovely and hypnotic. Ida could not remember ever having been so happy, if the joy she felt now could even be called happiness.

When Max reached the Tumarkins' house, she glanced up at Moses' bedroom window on the second floor. The light was out. He was probably fast asleep. Max shut off the windshield wipers but kept the engine running. They watched the flakes slowly pile on the glass.

"You have faith in strength," Max said. "That's good. Do you know why?"

Ida thought she understood the question, but she wasn't sure. Did she know why she had faith in strength or did she know why that kind of faith was good? She didn't want to break the mood, though, so she just shook her head.

"Because I'm strong." Max turned and looked at her. "And I would never hurt you."

Ida nearly laughed, but stopped herself.

"Do you believe me?"

"I believe every word you say." Even the ones I know aren't true, she thought. That's how I know it's love.

She had harbored a hundred fantasies—some little, modest things, some not—about her true love, the man yet-to-come. She could never make out his face, because his face was both sacred and unimportant. Now he had come for her, and it didn't matter if his face wasn't beautiful, not even, somehow, right for her. It didn't matter if they never waltzed to the "Blue Danube." She realized that all her schemes and movies of the mind were immaterial. In fact, this business of love was nothing like she'd imagined it, but Ida didn't care. If this love was no match for her imagination, that only convinced Ida it was real.

He was waiting for her to get out of the car, she could feel him waiting, but she couldn't move.

"What's wrong?" he asked.

Ida turned and looked at him. Whatever it was he saw

in her face made him swallow.

"Those are the eyes I want to wake up to each morning. But you're going to disappear into that house tonight and never speak to me again."

"That isn't true," she said, although the thought had crossed her mind. Part of her was scared of him. The childish part, she thought, and then her brain turned violent. *I'll kill it. I'm an adult now. There's nothing here to be afraid of. I can kill that part of me. I'll do what I have to do.*

"Ida," he said. "There's something I have to say to you before you leave me. I was going to wait to say it, but I'm laying myself in your hands here."

Ida waited.

"If you were mine, you'd never be alone again. Because everywhere you went, you'd have me with you." He pressed a hand to the buttons of her coat. "Our home would be like a fortress—when we closed its doors at the end of the day, nothing and no one would enter if we didn't let them. I would protect you from everything."

Ida turned away in amazement, all the while knowing that the safety he held out to her wasn't really the kind she sought. She wasn't looking for physical safety, financial security, or whatever it was he thought he could protect her from. Ida just wanted to stay the same.

"Are you crying?"

Her eyes were wet. She could feel tears hanging there, but she wasn't sure why. Was it because she knew that what he promised was impossible? Or was she moved because he went ahead and promised anyway?

She laughed shakily.

"Go ahead," he said. "That's what I do every time I look at you because I can't believe you're real. But here you are."

Ida felt as if she were in a play. Her character was feminine, irresistible. She could steal the show. But for now she was just struggling for her next line.

"You've never been in love before," he said again.

She shook her head.

"Give me your hand."

Ida gave him her hand. Max squeezed it.

"Courage," he said with pale, glowing eyes, "is holding out for what you want. Like I held out for you."

"And I for you," she said.

"Then I am yours," he said.

"And I yours."

"I hope you mean that," Max said.

She meant it—insofar as she knew what it meant.

Light snow veiled the car windows. Nobody passing on the street could have seen inside. Her face turned up to his and they kissed once, a gentle, open-mouthed kiss. His head fell back upon the headrest and she buttoned her coat, opened her car door, and climbed out. Once she had gone inside and up to her room she looked out the window. His car was still there. She got ready for bed and checked again. Still there. In the morning it was gone, the tire tracks just discernible under a fresh layer of snow.

CHAPTER ELEVEN

A few days after reading Emily's letter, Shoe called her up and introduced herself. They met three months later in Shoe's next mountain town, Crested Butte, Colorado.

Shoe was four months pregnant at the time, and staying in a vacant house, one of the town's oldest. The couple who owned it were in the Caribbean until late spring, while two guys she knew did repairs on the interior and the foundation. It was late March, and Shoe had convinced Johnny to fly down from Missoula for his last spring break and work for the week as a lift operator on the same slope where she taught lessons. She and Johnny took advantage of the fireplace, but since they couldn't use the central heat, they often stayed out until bedtime.

So it was that she and Johnny were at a table in the Forest Queen when they first set eyes on Emily. Shoe was eating her way through a heart-shaped box of candies, marked down for quick sale. Johnny was polishing off a hamburger. The next morning he would catch a bus to

Denver, then a plane back to Missoula.

Emily came in bundled in her sensible winter clothes, small and unremarkable, with a face you'd never notice in a crowd, Shoe thought. She watched Emily take in the bar of the old hotel at a glance—the ferns, folksy music and crowd to match—with an expression somewhere between serenity and blankness. Shoe knew the blankness was deceptive, and probably the serenity as well.

Shoe shot up her hand. They watched Emily wend her way between scattered tables, accidentally knocking into a man's chair and placing apologetic fingers on his shoulder. When she reached their corner, Shoe leapt to her feet.

"Emily Barker," she said. "How the hell are you."

Emily pulled off her hat and static crackled in the air. "I'm good," she said. She tried smoothing down her hair, but the static lifted it right back up again. "It's good to be here."

Shoe grabbed her hand and shook it. Johnny reached up his hand and Emily shook it too. He flashed a devilish grin but didn't mean to. It was just the combination of his sunburn and his good looks. None of the Tumarkins knew where he had got them all.

"This is Johnny," Shoe said. "My baby brudda."

He laughed and so did Emily, as if they shared a joke already. Shoe could see his beauty didn't fluster her, and decided this was because Emily was in love with someone else, or believed she was.

"You must drink," Shoe said.

"As must we all," said Emily.

"Yes," Shoe said. "As, in time, we shall."

Outside, more snow had begun to fall. It dropped a lifetime through the dark until it passed the windows of the Forest Queen, caught a moment's light, then sank beyond it, into the creekbed that ran alongside the bar. Parts of the creek were frozen solid, but here the snow fell into the icy water and was carried away.

They talked about her drive, about Johnny's biology classes, about the town.

Emily wasn't much of a skiier, but she told them that the next day she'd try out cross-country on some public land. They talked about avalanches, because there had been several in the last week. One man had only survived because his dog managed to dig him out. By this point in winter, many of the slopes had acquired a slick surface, so when the March snows came, sometimes they didn't stick. This was when most of the avalanches occurred.

When Emily offered to buy a round, Shoe turned her down. Johnny excused himself and left the bar to go buy fortune cookies.

The Tumarkins liked their fortune cookies. It was a family tradition, one Ida had started years before. She saved each of her fortunes and pasted it, in the order she'd received it, into a small red book. She swore that if you followed them closely, you could trace the progression of your life.

It was while Johnny was gone that Shoe told Emily about Max, the black toenails, and the baby on the way.

"It sounds like you're already over him," Emily said.

"That's because I never loved him," Shoe said. "I

loved a man who didn't exist."

Emily nodded sadly, wearily, almost as if she wished she could love such a man.

"I thought love was finding someone who understands you," Emily said. "But the trouble with that is, someone might understand some version of you that you don't want understood. That maybe you're ashamed of."

"Or that they are," Shoe said.

They eyed one another knowingly. Johnny returned with snow in his hair and sat down between them.

"Sometimes," Shoe said, "it's better not to be yourself. I don't think that's why we're here."

"I don't know," said Emily. "It's a while now since I believed we were here for a reason."

"And I don't mean to speak for you," Shoe said. "But I was put here to overcome my basic nature."

Emily studied her.

"You know what I'm talking about?"

Emily nodded.

"I thought so," Shoe said. "See, I never would've done anything if I'd acted like me. I wouldn't be here now. You and I never would've met. It's better this way."

"Did she tell you about the field trip?" Johnny asked.

Emily shook her head.

"I'll tell you about my first-grade field trip," Shoe said. "To the farm." It struck her then that she had never told Max. Not that he needed to know the story—he already understood the moral, which was the important thing, after all—but Shoe liked to tell stories, to a willing audience. Max hadn't been a willing audience, she reflected. Just a willing performer.

The music had stopped, and for a moment there was silence in the room. You could hear the creek outside the window slipping under the ice. Then Shoe told Emily the first real story of her life, the formative story, as Shoe recalled it. She told how the light streamed in through that opening up top, three, four stories above her and the other children on the barn floor. How the inside was filled to the rafters with bales upon bales of hay. About the long yellow rope that hung down for miles from the central beam, and about their teacher, who told them that after lunch they could all return to play until it was time to go home.

"But first she said we all had to take a nap."

Emily bit her lip. She saw it coming.

"So," Shoe said. "I'll cut to the chase. We weren't five minutes into the nap before kids started sneaking off to the hay barn. First it was just the most daring kids—the bad kids, I called them then—slipping away in twos and threes, but by the time the teacher showed up again, there were only a handful of us left. She rounded us up and took us with her to the barn, where we stood in the door and watched the other kids, swinging and leaping through the light, flinging themselves on hay bales, and the smell—" Shoe stopped and shook her head.

"Then she said that since they'd disobeyed, there'd be no playing in the hay that afternoon. For anyone."

Emily sighed, which pleased Shoe to no end.

"That was lesson enough for me. That taught me everything I need to know about this world. I never save the best for last. I never worry about getting caught. And if I'm too chicken to do something, I turn right around and do it anyway."

The bartender announced last call. Emily downed her drink and pushed it aside.

"Anyway," Shoe said, suddenly embarrassed. "Love's not so easy, is it? I thought I loved the father, but I didn't." She settled a protective hand on her belly. "Theoretically we had a lot in common. I mean, we're both working from here." She raised her other hand and tapped her skull.

"Really?" said Emily.

"Oh yes. Oh yes." Shoe nodded grimly. "We both work from the head, but it's a question, see, of motivation. He and I were not working from the same motivation."

Shoe smacked her brother gently on the back of the head. "Johnny keeps my brain in check. If it weren't for him, I'd probably be dead by now."

Johnny looked away.

"Motivation is everything. Helmut and I were not working from the same motivation. Mine may be silly, but his is insupportable. That's why," Shoe ended darkly, "he's not getting hold of the kid."

Johnny dug into his pocket. Seconds later he laid down three fortune cookies on the wooden table. Johnny and Shoe picked up their cookies, still sealed in their plastic wrappers, but Emily made no move toward hers.

"Is something the matter?" Johnny asked.

Emily smiled. "I think that one's mine."

Johnny handed her his cookie. She handed him hers.

"How could you tell?" Shoe asked.

"I always feel one particular cookie calling me." Emily blushed beautifully. "Now let us read our fortunes."

"In bed." Shoe snapped her cookie in half and read aloud. "'Don't be hasty'—in bed. 'Prosperity will knock on your door soon.'"

"'Beware a heavy load,'" read Emily.

"In bed," Shoe added. "That's sound advice. But not exactly a fortune. I'd call that a warning."

"It depends," said Johnny. "I mean, in Oedipus Rex, the oracle tells Oedipus he's fated to murder his father and marry his mother. He treats it like a warning."

"And that is his mistake," Emily agreed.

"Oh, don't encourage him," Shoe said. "Oedipus Rex, my ass."

"What's wrong with Oedipus Rex?" asked Emily.

"Grow up!" Shoe hollered, thoroughly enjoying herself now. "Anyway. I like warnings as much as the next guy. Give me a good warning any day and I'll do what I need to do. Now Johnny has to read his."

Johnny refused to share his fortune. When Shoe tried to snatch it from him, he ate it. Shoe clapped her hands.

It was past midnight, and most of the customers had cleared out of the Forest Queen. She sat back, well-contented with her new friend.

"I'm glad you found us," she said to Emily.

"Yes." Emily smiled at her, and Shoe saw something of Ida there, that Emily was capable of a certain kind of peace that she herself had never been, even if that peace came and went. "Things are looking up."

They stayed a little longer, just to savor the silence and warmth and the fact that they could share these things. Then the three of them walked out into the night.

In the morning, flanking Johnny on either side, Shoe and Emily walked to the bus stop. He already had his ticket, so there was nothing to do but wait under that brilliant mountain sun. They didn't wait long. When the bus approached from Gunnison, Shoe threw her arms around him, then let Johnny go by digging the toe of one boot into the snow.

Johnny turned to Emily. They looked at one another.

"Good luck," she said.

Johnny leaned toward her. A moment later his mouth brushed her cheek, then he was stepping onto the bus. Shoe and Emily watched through the tinted glass as he made his way toward the back. For several minutes the bus just sat there, filling the sharp air with the sound and smell of its idling engine.

"I hate to see him go," Shoe tried to explain, but the words got mangled in her throat, and it wasn't necessary, besides. Emily had already put a mittened hand on her shoulder.

The brake released with a woosh, and as the bus pulled away, Johnny raised his hand to the window. Shoe couldn't wave back, so Emily did it for her.

They all survived: Emily her skiing and Shoe her pregnancy and Johnny college, though it seemed to Shoe he lost something along the way—not his equilibrium, exactly, but his strange, beguiling repose. The more adulthood encroached, the more people began to bother him, as they had always bothered Shoe. It was not a similarity she would have wished for him, but at least Johnny had an excuse. His good looks seemed to garner expectations he was not equipped to deal with. He only wanted to be left alone.

Emily never did return to Nebraska. It was supposed to be a round trip, to Crested Butte and back to Lincoln, but the day Johnny rode out of town was the same day an avalanche sucked her up and spat her out. When it was finished, she kept on driving and didn't stop until she got to Arizona. Shoe was always trying to get her to move wherever she was in the mountains, but Emily got a reporting job down in Tucson and stayed. She said living with the desert plants was tranquil, like living at the bottom of an aquarium.

Johnny never returned to the mountains either. He settled down in southern Utah, red rock country, quietly charting fish and birds. Like Emily, he fell in love with arid wide-open spaces, and after that nothing else really felt like home. The three of them got together when they could, for camping trips with Moses or climbing. Once they met at the bottom of the Grand Canyon. Once in Las Vegas, just for laughs.

Those trips, Johnny lost his deep and, Shoe figured, probably well-founded irritation. When he was with Emily, he was at peace. But Shoe thought maybe he wasn't ready yet for peace. So she left him alone to stumble around with other girls and women who simply liked his looks when he was brooding.

One day, she thought, my brother will get tired of brooding. When he does, my friend will be there. In the meantime, she'll be as lonely as the rest of us.

CHAPTER TWELVE

Henry and Max were both away for Christmas, which would've been all right with Ida if she'd had her siblings there. But for the first time, she had neither one. The only highlights of the holiday were watching Moses open his presents Christmas morning and, of course, the cookies.

When Johnny called on Christmas Day, Ida told him she'd fallen in love, that she was going to be married. She was eager to convince him of her success, to vindicate herself, her life. She had become self-conscious about both, and now she wondered if he and Shoe had been laughing at her all along.

If he was surprised, Johnny didn't let on. "So what's he like," was all he said.

"Johnny—he's the most amazing man I've ever met."

"Amazing how?"

She tried to tell him about Max's sense of humor, his charisma, his way with people. About his extraordinary ability to assess a person's motives, about his shrewd judgment in all things human.

"If he's that amazing, I guess I've got to meet him."

"Oh, yes," Ida said.

"Does Moses like him?"

"Oh, yes." For a moment, Ida was smiling too hard to speak. "Max will be an excellent father."

In the weeks leading up to Christmas, Ida and Moses had seen a lot of Max. He'd pop in, always unannounced, usually just before Moses got home from school. It was a time of day when Ida sometimes liked to paint, but she didn't tell him this. Instead, Moses and Max would sit in the kitchen while she cooked them something, or they'd all go down to the basement rec room to play Operation, Chutes and Ladders, Twister or Crazy Eights.

"He even looks like Moses."

"Oh, yeah?"

"Yeah."

Silence fell between them. It might have been an opportunity for Ida to ask about Johnny's life, but she didn't think of it.

"So what does this guy do?" Johnny asked finally.

"He's an art dealer."

"Really," Johnny said. "I think Moses' dad was too."

"A lot of people deal with art."

"No, they don't."

"Maybe not. Look, why wouldn't I meet an art dealer? I'm an artist. I met him at an art opening." Although this was not entirely true, she thought. She'd met him while sitting on the front porch with Moses, a week before that opening, at dusk. He'd followed them to the field.

"I think you should call Emily."

"What for?"

"She'll know if it's the same guy."

"It's not the same guy."

"What makes you so sure?"

"Because," Ida said. "Why would he wait until now to track us down?"

"Maybe it took him this long," Johnny said. "Or maybe he was waiting until Shoe was out of the picture."

"How would he even know?"

"Maybe he arranged it."

"Oh, please. Anyway, I'm marrying him whether he's Moses' father or not. So it's fine either way."

"Wouldn't you like to know first?"

"What for?"

"So you know why he's marrying you."

Ida felt her heart race, then realized why. Of all the criticisms her siblings had lodged over the years, this was the worst: In order for a man to marry her, he must have an ulterior motive.

"Plus there's Shoe."

"What about her?"

"She didn't want the father to get him. You know that."

"What do you mean, 'get' him?"

"I mean she put her hand across her stomach and she said, 'He isn't getting him.' Well, the baby. She didn't know it was a him yet."

"She could have just been scared."

"Huh?"

"Just scared of her own emotions."

"Oh brother," Johnny said. "Since when? She ran away because the guy was a bastard and she didn't want him to know she was carrying his child."

"But in what way was he a bastard?"

"Who cares? A bastard is a bastard."

"But you have to consider your source," Ida said.

There was a pause. When Johnny responded, his voice was flat. "Shoe is the source," he said.

Ida could not think what to say to that.

"Call Emily," he said.

"You call her, if you're so wound up about it. She's your friend. Or whatever."

"I can't call her," Johnny said.

"Why not?"

"We had a falling-out."

"Well, I'm not going to call her."

And she didn't. If she had, she'd only have been calling because she was angry, because Johnny was impugning Max without ever having met him. Impugning Max because he was dating her.

It was insulting. It was infuriating. But it was also good, Ida told herself. Now she knew who her friends were.

She was relieved when Henry got back from Texas, and took Moses with her to visit him right away. It was a bright, windless January day, and they played outside for hours, until their jeans were soaked through, Henry had bent the frames of his glasses in a snowball fight, one of Ida's braids had come undone, and Moses had wiped his nose a dozen times across his mitten. They didn't climb the rickety steps to Henry's kitchen until the sun had dropped below the treetops. When they did, the phone was ringing.

Henry answered it, looked at Ida, then away. The dark hair from her defective braid unfurled across her cheek and down her sweater.

"It's for you," he said. He relinquished his armchair and Ida perched on the edge of it, holding the phone between her shoulder and chin so she could re-braid her hair. Before she said a word, Max started firing questions.

"Do you want me?"

"Hi!" she said.

"Do you want me?"

"Are you in town?"

"Do you want me?"

Ida secured her new braid, then glanced furtively around the room. Henry had lit a cigarette. She couldn't see it, because she was afraid to look at him, but she could smell the smoke. "Yes," she said.

"Do you know what it means to want a man?"

Ida nodded.

"I can't hear you," Max said.

"Yes." She cleared her throat. "Yes."

"Tell me," he said.

Ida felt her mouth drop open. She shut it again, rose with the phone, and crossed to Henry, leaning in the doorway. She reached for his cigarette and he handed it over. She carried it back with her and sank into the armchair.

"Ida," Max said. "Darling. Please."

"I can't," she said. Around her, the room was silent. Henry lit another cigarette for himself. She took an opening drag on hers, then coughed. Henry did not smoke menthols.

"Is someone there?"

"Yes."

"Who?"

"Moses, for one," she said. "And Henry."

"No," said Max. "I asked if someone was there. He's no one. He let you go first through the fence."

"But I wanted to," Ida said.

"Tell me what it means to want a man. Maybe he'll learn something."

She could feel Henry watching from across the room. When she finally stole a glance at him, his blue eyes narrowed behind his glasses. She watched as he took a slow drag on his cigarette, then watched as he exhaled, already forgetting she held one of her own.

"Has he grown any since the last time I saw him? As I recall, he was standing about three-foot-four."

"Oh, really now."

"Put Moses on."

"What for?"

"I want to talk to him."

Ida gestured Moses over to the phone.

"It's Max," she whispered.

Moses put the receiver to his ear. A moment later a smile spread over his face. He said nothing, just let a steady stream of words pour into him. Suddenly he looked at Henry.

"No," he said.

More words.

"No, you are."

Henry flinched. Ida looked for an ashtray, then set her unsmoked cigarette on the nearest windowsill.

"I like you both," Moses said.

Ida put out her hand for the telephone. Moses looked at her.

"Aunt Ida wants to talk to you again," Moses said.

More words.

"No," Moses said. "But he's in love with her."

"Moses, honey." Ida waved him near. He handed her the phone.

"Goodbye," she said into the receiver.

"Darling," said Max. "I'll be back tomorrow and I'll drive up in the afternoon to see you. Figure out a place where we can go to be alone. I miss you like crazy."

"Okay," she said. "Bye."

Ida hung up the phone. She sighed without realizing it. Within seconds, the phone rang again. Henry wanted to answer it, but Ida wouldn't let him. She helped Moses bundle up again, damp mittens and all. The phone rang eleven times and then stopped.

Ida sent Moses out to play once more. She listened to his boots rush through the next room with its solitary painting, then slow when they reached the kitchen floor. Through all this, her eyes stayed on the faded rug that covered a patch of Henry's sitting-room floor. When the kitchen door closed and Moses clattered down the wooden steps outside, she raised her eyes to her friend.

The phone rang again.

"Who's the asshole?" Henry sprang from his chair and started for the phone. But Ida was closer.

She leaned around and snapped the phone cord from its jack. Henry stopped mid-stride. Both his fists were clenched. His cigarette was clamped between his teeth.

"Henry." Her eyes drifted away from her friend and toward the water stain on the ceiling. She noticed, as she always did, that the brown edges formed the coasts of Africa. "Just forget about it."

"Ida," Henry said. "I saw you blush. Is this guy trying to have his way with you?"

"Well, sure. I guess."

Henry crushed his cigarette underfoot on the sloping wooden floor. As he stooped over to pick up the butt, Ida realized he was shaking.

"Lucky bastard." He reached for the butt, then changed his mind and got to his feet without it, facing Ida with a somber expression. Slowly, he raised his arms.

"Come here," he said.

Ida rose from her chair and stepped into his embrace. Even through their winter clothes, she felt his erection and stepped away again.

"We'll see you later," she said. "You put on some dry clothes."

Henry nodded to himself. He turned away to light another cigarette and let her go.

She trudged down the snowy stairs and around to the backyard, with Moses nowhere in sight. She had just raised a red mitten to wipe at her eyes when a snowball smacked her in the chest—the very place Max had pressed his hand that night in his car—and Moses leapt out from behind the fort, waving his arms. Ida tried to laugh. They set off down their brick path, hidden now beneath the snow, through the bare trees to the highway.

It was inevitable, she thought, as they hiked past the campus toward home. She was not in love with Henry and she could not be. He was lovable, sensitive, maybe even passionate. But he wasn't man enough to make her feel like a woman. And when it came to unrequited love, there was no happy outcome. Now that he understood how it was with her and Max, Henry would let go. Now he could move on to someone new.

Ida realized that although something cruel had just transpired, she was relieved. Maybe Max had planned it this way. He was so canny when it came to people. Why else would he call for her at Henry's house and carry on that way? He knew better than she how to cure someone of a hopeless longing. Strength had the power to be kind where weakness failed: Max was strong enough to deal the blow swiftly. She could not have done it, but now she, too, was free. Henry knew he had no claim on her. Her body recalled his again, coming at her in that way, and shrank in on itself.

She had escaped him. He would not subject her to any more unwelcome advances. Now she had Max. She knew a hundred places they could go to be alone, and all of them were somehow hers. But she would take him to the woods.

CHAPTER THIRTEEN

In childhood, Ida and Shoe had ridden their bikes out to the state park five miles north of town and scouted around in search of adventure. But too often nothing happened, and only Ida could live off the adventures in her head. It was real-life adventure that Shoe fed upon, even if she had to manufacture it. So about the time Shoe started junior high, Ida found herself going to the woods alone.

By that time she knew all the paths to get her there, the highway, the county roads and the back route past the angry dogs, a route that slowly turned to dirt, then offered up its secret entrance. She knew where to hide her bike so no one would find it while she roamed around, visiting her favorite haunts, the clearing in the woods where clover carpeted the ground or the hollow log big enough to conceal a family of skunks—or a girl. She knew how to hide herself because she and Shoe had played hide-and-seek in the state park for hours on end, creeping around on their hands and knees and bellies, tracking one another through the woods.

By the time Shoe quit going, Johnny was old enough for hide-and-seek but not yet old enough to bike that far. So in the woods Ida didn't have anyone to play with. She grew solemn and shy. If she heard someone coming, she still dropped to a crouch, but it wasn't a game anymore. It had become simple instinct. By herself she was singing, smiling, laughing, but she didn't like to be disturbed. To avoid other humans, she crawled behind the fallen trunks of trees, or sometimes climbed standing ones.

The woods never betrayed her. Over the years she saw fox, raccoon, turtles, deer, possum, and once two men, tugging one another's pants down around their ankles, but no harm ever befell her there. When Moses came to live with them, she took him out with her to see the dam, the diving ducks, the little silver fish that worked themselves into a stupor just before they dropped over the spill into the creek far below. Now it was Max's turn, to see and understand. Once he did, Ida believed, nothing could come between them.

When Max and Ida reached the parking lot the next day, she wanted to get out and walk around the lake. If the ducks were out or if the ice was thin by the dam and the fish were visible just underneath, she wanted to show these things to Max, but Max said it was too cold. Instead they sat side by side in the front of his car, holding hands, mute with happiness. Max kept the engine running so they could stay warm.

"Max," she finally said, "why are you here?"

He watched her and waited.

"You're not from here. You don't like Ohio. Why did you come?"

"I came for you."

"You didn't know I'd be here."

"I did."

"How?"

Max grinned broadly.

"Are you the father?"

"What father?"

"Moses' father."

He didn't answer right away. Then he looked at her with apparent surprise. "You didn't know?"

"How would I know?" Ida asked.

Max shrugged. "Isn't it obvious?"

"Yes," Ida said. "In retrospect."

"Are you sorry?"

Ida crossed her arms. Her reaction was beside the point. She didn't know how to react, anyway. She was happy for Moses, of course. But she felt deceived and, maybe worse, jealous. He was the father. She was just the aunt.

"Sweetheart." He laughed. "It was supposed to be good news. Why do you think I brought you out here today?"

"How long have you known?" she asked.

"Known what?"

"Known about Moses."

"Not long. I only found out she had a son after she died. Your sister didn't want me to know."

Ida knew that was true. Shoe had told her that much about Moses' origins and that much was all she knew.

There had been a man and the man had fathered Moses and then Shoe hadn't wanted the man. End of story.

"She never talked about me? Never told you why she left me? Took off with our child?"

Ida shook her head.

"It must have been the challenge of going it alone," he said. "She had a reputation to uphold."

"No," Ida said. "It was never about that."

"Well, whatever it was about, she got what she wanted out of me."

"I don't know," Ida said. No one knew whether Shoe had wanted Moses. Not, at least, before he'd been a fact inside of her. "Shoe didn't use people to get what she wanted."

Max laughed a short, sharp laugh. "Let me tell you something about your sister."

Ida waited.

"You owe her zero."

Ida tapped her foot.

"Without you here, she was nothing. Nothing. Believe me. I saw her in some of her darker moments. I know how precariously she positioned herself against the world."

Ida was silent. Shoe had always been precarious, yes, that much was true. But to say that Ida therefore owed her nothing didn't follow. Ida couldn't begin to fathom what he was driving at. And if Ida did owe her sister something, where was the harm in that?

"Do you know why I didn't tell you I was Moses' father right off the bat?"

Ida shook her head.

"I was afraid," he said. "I was afraid, because I knew your sister. I knew how she shaped—concocted—reality to fit her purposes. I came to see if it could really be my son, and then I saw this woman sitting beside him and I couldn't breathe. I wanted you the first time I saw you. But I knew I had to proceed carefully. I knew that if you knew I was the father, you might have strange ideas. Moses too. That you might have heard her stories, and you wouldn't let me within a hundred feet of either of you."

Ida didn't know what to say. When he talked about Shoe, he was talking about some other woman—not the sister Ida had known.

"No stories," was all she said.

"You were my revelation," Max said. "When I met you, everything about your sister fell into place. Do you know why?"

Ida shook her head again. It seemed she didn't know a lot of things.

"You and your sister always worked in opposition to one another," he said. "It was that opposition that allowed her to define herself. She needed you as an anti-model. Without you here, she wouldn't have known what to react against, where to go or what to do. She wouldn't have known where to start. And she fed off you because you were so strong. You never needed her, Ida; she needed you."

Ida didn't understand what he was driving at. Maybe she had been Shoe's "anti-model," as he put it, but if so, Ida had never minded. If she had been the strong one, that was fine too. But she wasn't sure she had been. She was only sure she wanted to believe him.

"Were you in love with her?"

He squinted. "We weren't together very long."

"That doesn't answer my question."

"What do you want me to say?"

"The truth," Ida said.

Max scowled. "Nobody wants the truth."

"I do," she said. "I want to know why you're here. Why you came."

"I thought I came to see my son. To see him and to make sure he was happy, that he'd found a good home, even if it wasn't with me. But now that I'm here, I can see I came for more than my child. I came for my wife."

This is romantic, Ida told herself. But it didn't feel romantic.

"How many babies do you want to have?" he asked.

Ida put a finger to her lips.

"Don't you want to have kids?"

"More than anything."

"So do I," Max said.

"You've already got one."

"Sweetheart!" He caught her left hand and lifted it, gently, to examine it. "Do you remember the first time I came into your kitchen and you were making those blue moons? Your fingers were covered with sugar. I wanted to take them up one by one and suck it all away."

But Ida shook her head. "You can't just have it all."

"I didn't think so either." Max brushed his lips across her knuckles. "But looking at you, I have to think again."

"You could've told me."

"I couldn't tell you. And there's something else I can't tell you, but I'm going to tell you anyway. I loved you even before I saw you."

Ida stared at him.

"I saw one of your paintings years ago."

"Which one?"

Max didn't hesitate. "The girl on the sidewalk with the golden dust."

Ida felt herself on the verge of tears. She leaned forward and played with the heating controls to hide her face.

"Darling," he said. "I have to go away again for a couple weeks, on business. I'll be gone for a month at most, probably less."

Ida swallowed the lump in her throat. "What sort of business?" she asked.

Max waved his hand. "Clients back East. But I've got something I want to ask you before I go." He sighed. "Can you be faithful to me while I'm gone?"

Ida opened her mouth to protest, but he rushed on.

"If you can, if you don't kiss another man while I'm away, the day I return, I'll come to your house and ask you to marry me."

"But who would I—"

Max raised one hand to silence her. "Doesn't matter," he said. "With a woman like you, there's always someone waiting in the wings. I want you to keep him waiting forever."

This time Max pressed his fingers to her lips. When she took his fingers into her mouth, he moaned and began to kiss her, one kiss tumbling into another.

"Sometimes," he breathed as his lips grazed her ear, "I find it hard to believe you're a virgin."

He bit into her neck. Ida heard her breathing get louder. She watched the windows steam over. Suddenly Max pulled away. He looked around.

"Are we going to be interrupted?" he said. "I don't want to be interrupted."

Ida wasn't worried. Almost nobody came out to the lake in winter. The ones who did parked at the other end, where the ice was safer and where someone always cleared away the snow. But she still hoped the two of them could get out and at least go for a little hike before they left. She was about to suggest this when Max reached around and pulled out a sack from behind his seat.

"I brought you something," he said.

She sat up straight and smoothed her hair. Ida enjoyed getting gifts, and he'd given her several already, small gifts like the ones he gave to Moses. Her favorite was a small plastic crab that squirted water. She used it in the tub.

Out of the sack, Max pulled a glossy magazine. He held it out to Ida, but when she didn't take it, he thumbed through himself, stopping at the centerfold.

"Do you see that?" he asked.

Ida saw.

"See how she's shaved all around there?"

Ida nodded. It had never occurred to her that a woman might shave that part of her anatomy. She leaned over for a closer look. If she thought of the model as a woman, Ida found the photo upsetting. But the woman was so hairless, Ida could almost forget she was human. As some other kind of animal, she was fascinating. Ida studied her while Max studied Ida.

He pushed the controls from heat to defrost. In a moment, two clear circles appeared at the base of the windshield. Max handed her the sack—that way, he said, she could sneak the magazine up to her bedroom—then slipped the car out of park, bent his long frame to peer through the glass, and made a slow swing out of the parking lot and onto the asphalt road.

"You know I'm ready to explode," he said.

Ida looked over at him.

"You know that, don't you, sweetheart?"

Ida turned her face toward the passenger window. "I didn't know that," she said. She made a circle in the frosty glass with the heel of her hand.

"Don't do that, darling," Max said. "It leaves a mark."

They kissed goodbye in front of her house, then Ida got out and watched Max drive away in the car that was too small for him. He rolled down his window and waved until he was gone from view.

Of course they would all live happily ever after, Ida thought. Of course they would. But what if they didn't? What would they do instead?

After he left town this time, Ida was at a loss. It was okay when Moses was home, but when he was at school, she couldn't think how to fill her time. She was too restless to read and too distracted to paint. Every day she thought about driving down to Cincinnati, just to be in the city where Max lived, but she didn't go. She didn't go anywhere. She sat at home and waited for his call.

Each morning she went to the basement and stood before her easel. She hadn't touched her paints in over a month. And for the first time in her life Ida felt apprehension, coming to the canvas, an unfamiliar fear of trying to create something from nothing. She had never felt this kind of fear before. She had never sensed the nothing. Every morning she ended up wrapping a hand around the wooden backbone of her easel—to give comfort, or take it—then walking away.

She was too scared to talk about this to anyone. She was afraid Henry would feel sorry for her, and that was not the nature of their relationship—she was supposed to feel sorry for him. As for Max, when he called her each day, he wanted to talk about sex. More than once she felt herself recoil from his suggestions, lewd antics that had never crossed her mind. Did people do that? And what for?

"That sounds good," she would say, though it didn't. Even the sexual acts she had heard of before, she'd never given much thought. Now she couldn't understand his fascination with them, though she tried.

Max told her that the first time she went down on him, she might be overwhelmed by how much stuff came out. He sounded almost worried. Ida, who knew what it meant to go down on someone, wanted to reassure him.

"That's okay," she said. "It's not like I have to drink the stuff."

A dead silence followed. Then Max burst out laughing.

"You're the greatest," he said.

Maybe because I'm a virgin, she thought, intercourse seems more perilous, more sexy, more exciting. More, maybe, than it is. But that was still what she wanted to do, to do and not talk about—not, at least, in workmen's terms. Any sexual act consisted of more than its anatomical tools, she thought. And one didn't need to describe or inventory those tools in order to use them. In fact, it seemed to her, the less attention paid to the tools, the better.

Some of the terms he used were not in Ida's vocabulary, and it seemed to her this was no accident, since she had never had need of them. Nor did she feel such words had anything to do with her and Max. What troubled her most were the little rituals he'd lined up for their married life, such as, "Each day when I get home from work, you will drop to your knees, take my cock in your mouth, and say, 'Thank you.'"

She thought he might be joking, but it was hard to tell.

When Max phoned her in the mornings or the evenings, she tried to speak this language. She pulled the phone into a closet or the bathroom, shut the door, and tried whispering back to him dirty, detailed vignettes. She tried stringing words together to say anything at all in this alien tongue, but it was like learning a language of lies. Although she understood it when spoken, she lacked all native ability, and disliked it besides. Each time she tried to get around herself she failed, and fell silent. In this language, she was mute.

She needed another woman to talk to. Shoe would

have been the obvious choice. One day, after a particularly strained conversation with Max, Ida approached her mom.

It was hard to know how to broach the subject. She tried telling her mother some of the things Max had said to her, but her mother threw up her hand.

"That's between you lovebirds," she said. "I don't want to know."

"Okay," Ida said, trying to persevere. "But what I guess I'm wondering about, what concerns me, are the more pornographic aspects surrounding sex. How negotiable they are. And how significant. In the relationship as a whole."

Mrs. Tumarkin rolled her eyes, then smiled.

"The secret to being a woman is knowing when not to be too much of a lady."

Her mother had lifted it from a perfume commercial, but Ida was too disappointed to point this out.

It occurred to Ida for the first time that she might be flawed. If this really was how lovers talked, perhaps she was not intended for such happiness. Max said she was just reluctant because she was a virgin; Ida began to suspect she was a prude. Max said he could teach her—all that was needed was her desire to learn. Good, she said, I'm glad, knowing that all she really desired was to please him and that, sooner or later, he would detect the difference.

After several weeks of these conversations, there came a day of sun and thaw. Ida met Moses after school and they walked to the cemetery to visit Shoe's grave. When they reached it, the tips of the daffodils they'd planted in the fall were already two inches above ground, with clods of broken soil all around them. It was February, and as they wandered along the wild edges of the cemetery, where the oldest tombstones had begun to disappear back into the woods, she realized that many of the buds were swelling, the lilac and the maples alike. Another eight weeks and the dogwood would start to bloom.

On the way home, she tripped twice because she couldn't lower her eyes to the pavement long enough to watch where she was going. It was Moses who finally took her hand to lead her safely across the street.

Ida resumed her painting that afternoon, and painted the next ten days. Then Max returned.

CHAPTER FOURTEEN

Tuesday at lunchtime Max called to tell her he was back. He'd gotten a new place in Cinci. He was dying for her to see it.

"When?" she said.

"Now."

"Right now?"

"Right now."

Ida didn't tell her mother she was leaving. She'd been avoiding her for days. Instead she taped a note to the refrigerator, another to the side door just in case, grabbed the keys and made it to Cincinnati before two. She was fine for most of the drive, until she approached the city limits and the traffic began to swell on every side of her. She had to pull over twice to consult the directions he'd given her, but she found the apartment complex, and then the building. When she parked and got out, she felt self-conscious and strange, as if people in other apartments were watching her from their windows. But climbing the stairs to his floor, that feeling changed to pride and once more her secret swelled in her, that this was her life, and she was really living it. She found the number, knocked on the door, and then Max was there, grinning down on her.

"What took you so long?"

He stepped aside, and Ida entered. She had imagined that coming to Max's place would be like coming home, but as she looked around, she felt nothing. His apartment reminded her of a motel suite. It was that clean and that bare.

"Are you still unpacking?" she asked him.

"Nope," Max said. "This is it."

They went through the apartment hand in hand. He showed her two paintings he'd put up on his walls. The third, on the landing below the bedroom, was hers. Ida traced the trail of gold with her finger. She hadn't seen *Lessons in Self-Defense* for years.

"Hello," she whispered.

"I want one of yours to go here," he said on the landing below the bedroom.

Max led her slowly up the stairs. They reached the bed and sank down on it. When they had shed their clothes, Ida lay still and peaceful, hands folded across her stomach, eyes on the clean white ceiling. Max raised himself on one elbow and looked at her.

"My God," he said.

"I didn't kiss anyone," she announced.

Max lay back down. "Neither did I," he said.

Ida rolled on top of him. For a moment they lay there, chest to chest, Ida relaxed and laughing. She rose up on her arms and put her mouth to his skin, dragging her tongue across his ribs, feeling the ridge of each bone, then dropping into the sink hole of his belly button. Another laugh was welling up in her when Max's hands took hold of her head. Once he had her in position, Max began to move, pushing against the space in her head until she felt it all disappearing.

Ida shook away his hands, lifted her head and looked at him. "Hold still," she whispered.

"What did you say?" Max was propped up on his elbows again, staring at her.

"Relax," she said. "Just let me touch you."

Max stared at her a moment longer, then dropped off the bed and disappeared into the next room. Ida crawled under the covers. She pulled the white comforter over her head and tried not to think. When she heard him come back into the room, she didn't look. She watched the light rain through the cloth and used it to make her mind a blank.

Max pulled back the comforter and sat down beside her on the bed. He was fully clothed.

"Do you have time to watch a video before you go?" he asked.

"Okay." She hadn't known she was in a hurry.

Ida sat up. With the comforter bunched around her, she reached for her clothes. When she couldn't reach her underpants, she had to ask Max to retrieve them. He laughed. Fully clothed, she climbed out of the bed, sat down on the floor and put on her tennis shoes, fumbling a little with the laces when she heard Max sigh. Then Ida pushed her heavy hair behind her ears and followed him downstairs. Max threw himself down on the long couch, and since there was nowhere else to sit, Ida did too, not beside him but a few feet away.

"There are half a dozen theaters showing stuff in Covington," said Max, "but this is animated so there are more creative possibilities."

Covington was the Kentucky town just across the Ohio River, commonly referred to as Cincinnati's red light district because of its prostitutes, strip bars, and X-rated movies. Suddenly Ida realized the kind of video Max was about to show her.

"Oh," she said. "No. I don't want to."

Max had already popped in the tape. Images formed on the screen. He turned from the VCR and finally looked at her. When Ida shook her head, Max came over and sat down, beside her this time, taking one of her hands between his. He tried to look concerned, but Ida only saw the creases of his forehead deepen, and did not know what that meant.

"What's the matter?" he asked.

"I don't want to see this."

"I thought it might help."

"It won't." The video was starting. Ida saw a cartoon woman sitting in some cartoon rubble, a junkyard or a city dump, skyscrapers in the background. Everything was in blue and gray except the woman, who had her dress hitched up, her hand between her legs. Ida yanked her own hand from between his and rushed toward the TV. She punched buttons until the frame froze, a close-up on the woman's spread legs, bent knees, head thrown back, red mouth half open.

Ida put her back to the screen. "Don't try to train me," she said.

Max blinked once, as if in slow motion. She watched as his great head fell to one side. Then he shouted.

"WHAT?"

"You're trying to train me like a dog." Ida scooped her bag off his carpet and started for the door.

"If you walk out that door now, don't come back."

She stopped in her tracks.

Max swung himself over the back of the couch and dropped onto the carpet, so close to Ida that she had to keep herself from taking a step back.

"I've never seen you like this. Throwing a fit. What's gotten into you?"

"It must be natural," she said. "It can't be forced."

They stared at one another. Max began to blink again, not in slow motion this time but rapidly, over and over.

"I don't understand," he said. "There isn't anything that you and I can do together that isn't natural. So that's not it."

He stared so hard that Ida thought he might be seeing something she couldn't, that flaw again, or some other defect she was still blessedly unaware of.

"Don't you want me?" he said.

Ida nodded.

"How much?"

Ida's mouth opened and shut, like the mouth of a fish

rudely pulled from its element.

"Say it."

"Very much," she mumbled.

"That's not good enough. Half the women in the world want me very much. The other half want me more than that. And that leaves all the men who want you even more. But I want you more than all of them combined. My dreams are relentless. I wake up in the morning and my cock is aching and I drag it around like that for sixteen, eighteen hours so I can go to bed again and wake up with it hurting more. I want you more than I ever wanted any woman, more than I thought it was possible to want a woman, and I thought today, when I'd come back, after I'd spent three hellish weeks away from the woman I adore, arranging everything so we could be together, that today we might actually be alone, in our own space, with no danger of being disturbed, at last. And instead I get this...child."

Ida hung her head. She took one halting step toward him, but Max was already walking away.

"Go home," he said over his shoulder. "Go home to your mommy and daddy."

Ida moved stiffly, stone-dry and silent, out the door. She pulled it firmly shut behind her, propelled herself along the walkway and down the stairwell to her parents' car. She knew that Max wouldn't follow her and he didn't. She unlocked the car door, adjusted the rearview mirror, and carefully maneuvered out of the apartment complex and onto the street. She sat through a red light. It was only after the light changed to green and Ida had driven through that she began to bawl in high, screaming sobs.

At some point she realized she couldn't see where she was going, so she lifted her foot off the gas and coasted into a vacant parking lot. The car came to a gentle stop, she leaned over and dug around in the glove compartment for a Kleenex, blew her nose four times, then looked around. The road was unfamiliar. But then it would be, she thought. She had just come from her fiancé's new apartment, where she'd never been before—and might never be again.

She wiped around her eyes with the back of her hand and pulled out into traffic. When she glanced at the little clock on the dashboard, she realized she had been in his apartment for under an hour.

Ida drove until she reached the next major intersection, turned right, and in half a minute knew just where she was. The city was not impossible, she thought. If somebody blindfolded her and dumped her on a streetcorner, she might survive after all.

She drove north. What she felt, even more than sadness, was surprise. She had always known that someday her true love would come. In the meantime, waiting on that future happiness, the life she lived before Max was the only kind of life she'd ever wanted, because it had allowed her to stay intact. She had never felt the need to be anything that she wasn't, to do things she didn't want to do. She had assumed—was it foolish?—that when her true love came, he, too, would want her exactly as she was. He wouldn't ask her to change because he wouldn't want her to. She had thought that was what love was—to come as you were.

Now Max, for reasons she couldn't fathom, was asking for something different.

So she was faced with a choice. Either option was awful: She could change for Max, or not change and go on without him.

Ida had dedicated her life to staying the same. She was intractable, and anyone who mattered understood this. Her parents, of course, and Shoe, who people called intractable but who was really flexible to a fault. Johnny understood. No one had tried to bend her for years.

Maybe Max knows something I don't, she thought. Maybe I'm more resilient than I think. Still, it seemed to her that if she were going to bend, perhaps she should've bent earlier on, that in waiting so very long she might have doomed herself. Maybe, she thought with sore, stunned wonder, my life had its price after all.

She slowed on the final stretch into town. Up ahead was the blue-gray of Henry's house. She saw his car out front and thought about stopping for a visit. Henry knew her. He could tell if she was in need of reform. But the car behind Ida honked and instead she hit the gas and kept going.

At twenty-two, she had defied her parents for the last time when she refused to move out of the house. They knew what this meant—that she would live at home until she married, and if she didn't marry (and this seemed increasingly likely as she grew ever more completely into who she was), that she would live with them forever.

They let her stay. That was what she wanted, and

besides, Ida was easy to have around. It was only when faced with the world outside that she collapsed into something unseemly. The difficult daughter lay just beyond those trees. As the car raced down into the hollow, Ida turned to face the cemetery entrance.

Shoe lived the life Ida would have abhorred, and Ida was grateful to her for doing it, for enduring all that for both of them and letting her off the hook. Shoe lived, somehow, to spare Ida the indignities that accompanied life. Ida had listened to all of her sister's stories with interest but without real curiosity, never wanting to experience the things firsthand, never feeling as if she were missing anything. If all that Shoe had done and seen was living, Ida did not care for life.

She blew a kiss toward her sister's grave, the car sailed up the far side of the valley and a minute later, she spied Moses ahead, walking home in his brown corduroy coat, his hands shoved in his pockets, the hood hanging halfway off his head. Ida came up beside him and pulled over. When Moses turned to the car, she raised a hand from the steering wheel in greeting, then leaned over and opened the passenger door.

"Hop in," she said.

Moses climbed in and shut the door. She helped him fasten his seatbelt, then continued down the street.

"Where were you?"

"Granddad was showing slides," he said. "He met me after school, then I walked back with him to his class."

"Slides of what?"

"Girls and boys working in factories. They liked to

use children because they had small hands."

"Was it interesting?"

Moses nodded. A moment later she turned onto their street.

"Did you see Max?" he asked.

"I did."

"When is he coming again?"

"I don't know," Ida said, because she didn't. "Do you miss him?"

Moses nodded again.

I had years and years, she thought as she pulled into the driveway. Those years would have to suffice. If something was wrong with her, it would have to be set to rights now by a mighty act of will. She decided this necessity, this mandate to somehow change, must be adulthood. The time had come at last to find out this thing she had protected herself from for years on end.

She was not curious, not in the least. But despite herself, Ida felt a growing curiosity about something else. So that night she called Emily.

CHAPTER FIFTEEN

Ida had always had an odd grudge against Emily. For starters, Johnny had once said she was like Ida and Shoe fused together. She was not. She wasn't like either one and the very suggestion made Ida angry.

Worse, Emily herself had always seemed to operate on the assumption that she and Ida were old friends, which they were not—nor could they ever be. Emily was some kind of journalist. Every day she went out and talked to strangers. Ida could not be true friends with someone like that.

To top it off, Emily had once written to Ida that one of her paintings had saved Emily's life. It seemed a preposterous thing to say. Ida didn't know why a person would need to save her life in the first place, and if she did need saving, she should paint her own paintings in order to do so. Ida's paintings were personal. This woman could not understand them very well, whatever she might think.

But Ida called her anyway, ready to hear Emily out, to glean what wisdom she might from her. She couldn't ask

Max why her sister had left him: He might take offense at the question. And Ida didn't know any of his friends. She'd never met his family. Shoe was dead and could not be reached for comment. This Emily would have to do.

When Ida identified herself, Emily sounded surprised but friendly.

"How are you?" she asked. "How's Moses?"

"Fine," Ida said. "Everybody's fine."

"Is he okay?"

"He's fine," Ida said, more firmly. "That's why I'm calling, actually. Not about Moses, but about something connected with him."

"Oh," Emily said. "Okay."

"I wondered why my sister left him. The father, I mean."

Emily didn't answer right away.

"What he was like?" Ida asked.

"You know, I never met him. I didn't know Shoe when she was with him. I only met her when she was four months pregnant."

"I know. But Johnny thought you might know something."

"Oh," Emily said. "He did, did he."

"Yes."

"How is Johnny?"

"He's fine," Ida said, then realized she hadn't talked to him since Christmas, and even then, she hadn't asked him how he was.

"I haven't talked to him since the funeral."

"Oh," Ida said.

"Some parts of the will worked out better than others," Emily said.

It took a moment before Ida recalled Emily's part in her sister's will. But that had been a joke—Emily must know that.

"Well, I'm sure you'll find somebody better suited to you," Ida said.

She meant no cruelty. She meant, in fact, to be encouraging—but also, it was true, as a warning to this woman that, if she entertained any romantic notions about Johnny, the match would never come to pass. It simply wasn't meant to be.

"We'll see," said Emily. "So. You want to know about Shoe and Helmut."

"Helmut?"

Emily laughed.

"Are you sure that's his name?"

"I'm sure," Emily said. "Though come to think of it, she only called him that to annoy him. He went by something else."

"What?"

"I don't remember. Why?"

Ida ignored her question. "What did he look like?"

"I never saw a photo," Emily said. "But I remember one thing she told me. He liked to tan. She said he'd go to a tanning booth every week."

Ida closed her eyes, then opened them again. "And do you know why my sister left him?"

Emily sighed a short sigh. "You know that once a decision was made, Shoe seldom talked about it."

"I know," Ida said. "She didn't like to be reminded there were other options."

"Huh," Emily said. "I guess I wouldn't put it quite that way. But no matter." She sighed again. "Can I ask why you're asking? Why now, I mean."

"Well, I'm curious."

"He hasn't contacted you?"

"How could he?" Ida said. "Shoe made sure he couldn't find her."

"Oh, he could always have found her," Emily said. "She just made sure he didn't have a reason to."

"I don't get it," Ida said. "If he loved her, why didn't he follow her?"

"He didn't love her," Emily said.

People—rude people—used to ask Ida if she was jealous of her sister. Though Ida could tell they didn't believe her, she always told them no. Yet now, in the midst of her panic, she felt a weak wave of relief.

"I used to worry," Emily said. "I wrote that piece, you know, about her murder. I used her real name. I mentioned Moses. Sometimes I'm sorry I wrote it, or published it, at any rate. Of course I wanted it published, at the time. I wanted everyone to read it. But I don't know why, now. It's not like it brought her back. And if he'd seen the thing, it might've done more harm than good. If it did any good at all."

Ida didn't care about this woman's professional qualms. "So what if he did see your story?" she said. "If he bothered to track down Moses, he'd only be doing it because he loves him."

"I don't believe that," Emily said. "He'd do it because Moses is his."

"Same thing."

"It's not the same thing," Emily said. "Shoe said he had an ego a mile wide. She said if he had a child—especially a son—the kid's whole life would be about him. She said it wouldn't matter what the kid wanted, what the kid liked or what the kid was like. He'd want to make the kid over in his image. And in order to do that, he'd try to take Moses away from her."

"I seriously doubt that. He wouldn't tear Moses away from the only family he's ever known."

"People do it all the time."

"Well, I'm sure if he showed up here, we could work something out."

"I don't think so."

"How would you know?"

"I wouldn't know. But Shoe knew."

"That's exactly what Johnny said. But that doesn't tell me anything."

"She defied him," Emily said. "She said it was the smallest act of defiance she'd ever performed but for how he reacted, it might as well have been huge."

"Why did she defy him?" Ida wondered if it had something to do with sex.

"He didn't like her feet."

Ida tried out a scornful laugh, but she was too worked up, and instead it sounded like wheezing.

"You know Shoe, the metaphorical weight she attributed to everything. According to her, he did the same.

They both thought that way, small to large. I think that's probably why she fell in love with him. She said they understood one another absolutely. In that respect, at least."

Ida fought off another wave of jealousy. "But what about her feet?"

"Promise me first that he hasn't been in touch with you."

Ida sat in the hall closet, her knees pulled up to her chest, her head pressed against one wall. A dozen coats hung beside her in the dark, mixing their musty smells. She breathed them in and said nothing.

"Has he contacted you?"

"As a matter of fact, he has."

"Oh God," Emily said. "This is all my fault."

"Nothing's your fault. For your information, we're going to be married. And I guess we have you to thank. Would you like an invitation?"

"Ida," Emily said. "Does Johnny know?"

"Not exactly."

"When will you tell him?"

"When we announce the engagement. Very soon."

"And you want to marry him?"

"I've never wanted anyone else."

"Does he let you have your head?"

Ida snorted. "I'm not a horse. And I'm not like Shoe. Shoe always took these stands at the sake of her own happiness."

"Not that one," Emily said.

"We're in love," Ida said. "You wouldn't understand."

"I would," Emily said. "But there are certain things I wouldn't give up for love."

"I would."

"I wouldn't give up myself. And I wouldn't give up my child."

"But this isn't about giving up a child," Ida protested.

"It is if his values are fundamentally opposed to yours. Because the risk is very real that Moses would be pulled into a world that doesn't have a thing to do with you. Shoe knew a man like Helmut would never let his children make their own way in life. He terrified her."

Ida had never known Shoe to be terrified of anyone. But then she recalled what had really happened: Shoe had met her match.

"Love manifests itself in lots of ways," Emily said.

"I'm sure you're right," Ida said politely.

"When it isn't good love, they say it isn't love at all, but it is."

"Maybe so," Ida said.

"They say it isn't love when it feels bad, but sometimes it is. Sometimes that's how you know it's love."

Ida said nothing. How dare this woman lecture her on love.

"I used to think it couldn't be love if it felt bad," Emily continued. "Or if the person didn't understand you. If it wasn't working, if anything went wrong, then it wasn't love."

"I left something on the stove," Ida lied.

"I was wrong. So then I thought, if it's love it doesn't matter if he doesn't understand me, if we can't talk to each other, if we make each other miserable. The important thing is that it's love, because love is real and love runs deeper than happiness and I wanted to live a real life."

"Something is burning," Ida said.

"It is love," Emily said. "But it doesn't matter."

"I really have to go," Ida said.

"That kind of love won't change anything," Emily said.

"It will," Ida said. "It'll change me."

Love was real. Ida had always known this. What her sister had felt for Max had obviously been something less than what Ida felt, or else Shoe had just been too scared to let go of the world she knew. Ida wasn't. What was falling in love but entering another world, the world of the beloved? And if things got a little scary once in a while, you just pushed on through. And if it felt a little strange sometimes, if it even felt like a dark tunnel, Ida believed that when she came out on the far side, whoever she'd become by then, she would be a good person in a good place, better than the person she'd left behind. Already I'm blossoming, she thought. Already my world has expanded. I'm not losing myself at all.

Her past was infantile, criminal with waste. She recalled the weeks he was away—not those first weeks, which were, she thought, what it must be like coming down off some drug, but what followed, those peaceful days—and decided peace was just another word for backsliding. Living was not about peace. She could feel peace when she was dead. Living was not about comfort, she understood that now. She had been too comfortable all along, had lived her whole life to avoid feeling uncomfortable, and that was no way to live. If she wanted to grow, it might be that a little discomfort was in order.

CHAPTER SIXTEEN

The last time Emily or Johnny saw Shoe alive was on a trip through Dinosaur National Monument, two months before she died. They camped and hiked and floated through the red Gates of Lodore on a raft. But first they gathered in a supermarket parking lot in Utah, so Shoe could buy the groceries.

Whenever they met up for trips, Shoe insisted on buying nearly everything with her food stamps. It made her feel generous, expansive. It made her feel like a provider. And the excitement of free food had never worn off for her. She'd stand in line, flipping through her coupons, hand them over with a flourish and then, exiting through the whoosh of the automatic doors, turn to Moses.

"What do we say?"

As soon as he was old enough, Moses came in on cue: "Thank you, Uncle Sam."

Shoe took particular pleasure in flashing her stamps around high-end grocery stores in high-end towns peopled with the outdoor adventure types and yuppies she disdained. Usually the clerks had never seen them before.

It was late afternoon when they drove out of Vernal and evening before they reached their campsite on the Green River. They roasted turkey dogs and baked beans for dinner, washed them down with Colorado-bought beer, and waited for the sun to set. It took its sweet time, a week shy of the summer solstice. The moon crept up in the east. Then it was time for dessert.

"And these little babies come to you," Shoe announced, as she'd announced the main course earlier, "courtesy of the U.S. Government."

She held out a bag of marshmallows, first to Moses, then to Emily, then to Johnny.

"These have coconut on them," observed Johnny, who didn't like coconut.

"Toasted coconut," Shoe said. "You can always pick it off. I'm surprised food stamps even cover marshmallows. They can't have any nutritional value."

"Marshmallows contain gelatin," Emily said. "That's good for your nails."

Johnny wandered away with his marshmallow in search of the river. Moses jumped up and ran after him. As soon as they were out of earshot, Shoe leaned forward.

"Johnny's got a new girlfriend," she announced. "I met her."

"And?"

"Goddamn yippie. Dull as dishwater."

"Maybe she's just shy."

"She isn't shy," Shoe scoffed, then shook her head. "Why must you always give these women the benefit of the doubt? Aren't you jealous at all?"

"Should I be?"

"I know you like him."

"I could never be with Johnny."

"Why not?"

"He's too beautiful for me. Women would always be trying to steal him away."

"Fuck that."

Emily did not reply.

Shoe looked across the campfire at her friend. "Listen to me. He's had girls throwing themselves at him since the fifth grade. He's like pudding now, he's so passive. So you can't leave it up to him. And if you do, you're not doing him any favors, believe me. I asked this girl why she likes Johnny. She said he meets almost every point on her list."

"What list?"

"Exactly. What list. She's one of those girls who makes lists of what they're looking for in a mate. I mean, you need to write it down? If you need to write it down, how important can it be?"

Moses returned to the campfire, with his uncle close behind him. Johnny had been in the backcountry the past six weeks, surveying owls. He'd grown a beard, shaggy hair and muscles.

"Where's your marshmallow?" Emily asked.

"It dissolved in the river," Johnny said. He looked discouraged.

"Hold on," she said. "I have an idea."

Emily reached for the bag of marshmallows and skewered a fresh one. Shoe picked up the point she had been making and ran with it.

"Look," she said to Emily. "You've got this grocery list. You've got a dozen things on it. But you head out the door because you need milk. When you get to the store, you realize you forgot your list. You end up forgetting a couple things on the list. You still get the milk, though. The bread, the eggs. You make it home with the important stuff."

"I don't," said Johnny. "I'll buy a bunch of stuff and never get the thing I set out for."

Shoe shot Emily a glance. Emily smiled and slowly waved her marshmallow over the campfire.

"Then you didn't really need it," Shoe said.

"I didn't need the other stuff either," Johnny said. "But I forgot my list. So I bought it."

"I'll bet you didn't make a list in the first place," Shoe said.

"That's true," Johnny admitted.

"People with real goals don't need to write them down. They don't wake up after twenty years and say, 'Gee, I meant to do this with my life, not that. Why didn't I write down what I wanted?' People who write stuff down are lame. In fact," Shoe continued, "I'll go so far as to say there are two kinds of people in the world. List-makers and non-list-makers."

"I make a list every day," Emily said. "Otherwise I forget what I need to get done."

"I'm talking about life lists," said Shoe. "I'm talking

about girls who won't date guys unless they're six feet tall. Men who won't date women unless they're under thirty. Women who won't date men unless they're earning more than $50,000. I'm talking about people living statistic-riddled, criteria-ridden, categorizable lives."

Emily lifted her stick away from the flames. She tested the marshmallow with her index finger, then turned to Moses.

"Like coconut?"

He nodded.

"Okay. Here's what we're gonna do. You're gonna suck the crusty outside off this thing. The inside part stays on the stick for Uncle Johnny. So you have to make your lips real gentle. Got it?"

Moses nodded again. He opened his mouth wide and settled his lips loosely around the marshmallow. When Emily pulled back on the stick, the white insides still clung to it, coconut-free. She lowered this back over the flames while Moses smacked his lips.

Twenty seconds later, Emily handed the rest of the marshmallow to Johnny. He swallowed it whole, then searched across the flames until his eyes met hers.

"Thank you, Uncle Sam," he said.

"Welcome," she said.

Johnny and Emily rose early the next morning. This had become their habit on camping trips, to rise early, to walk together and watch the sun rise. But from the canyon, they wouldn't see the sun for hours. So they borrowed Shoe's truck and drove to Harpers Corner, one of the high points of the park. The air grew cooler as they climbed, but the sun was climbing too. It was well past the horizon when they reached the top. They parked the truck, then followed a trail into a stand of juniper and piñon trees, with Johnny leading the way.

"How's your job?" Emily called up to him.

"Good," Johnny said. "I get to spend a lot of time outside. And I hike around a lot, so I'm always stumbling onto weird, amazing stuff. Then it's like I'm a kid again. Like life is for Moses now."

"Are you alone a lot?"

"Sometimes," Johnny said. "Sometimes I'll go a week without seeing another human."

"How's that?"

Johnny turned and studied her from under his baseball cap. "Honestly?"

Emily nodded.

"I love it," he said.

They burst out laughing, then hiked in silence until they reached the overlook. They walked out on the cliff as far as they could and leaned over the chain-link fence. Four thousand feet below them, the Green and Yampa Rivers met. Just beyond the confluence, a yellow raft floated by. In three more days, they would float there too.

"They'd be surprised if we spit on them," Johnny said.

"We're too high," Emily said. "Our spit would never make it."

"Sure it would."

"It's too far. It'd break up and evaporate before it ever reached them."

"I doubt it," Johnny said. "My spit is pretty viscous."

Side by side they leaned out across the metal rail and watched the sun creep higher over the canyon cliffs. Neither wanted to break the silence, though both had things they could've said. They liked silence, when it felt right. It seemed more eloquent. And this was the closest thing to perfect happiness either of them had felt in some time.

Finally, Emily made an announcement.

"I can't spit."

"You don't say," Johnny said.

"Not to speak of. It just dribbles out. I can't get any projection."

"I can help you with that," Johnny said.

"Can you really?"

He nodded. "I think I can."

The four of them left their campsite late that morning to reach the Gates of Lodore, where their raft trip would begin. They climbed out of the canyon, Shoe and Emily up front, Johnny and Moses in the back. Shoe waited until they'd reached pavement to make her confession.

"I'm going back to school."

Emily looked at her. "When?"

"This fall," Shoe said. "I registered last week."

"Good," said Emily.

Shoe nodded.

"What convinced you?"

"The idiots." Shoe lifted the long braid off her back and flung it over her right shoulder. "Always the idiots."

"Whatever it takes," Emily said.

"Idiots with college degrees making three times more than me while I get varicose veins, not to mention all my grease burns. Have I ever shown you those?"

Emily nodded.

"Anyway, I've got some things I want to find out more about."

"Like what?"

"Theology."

"What else?"

"Doesn't matter to me," Shoe said. "I'm gonna be a minister."

They rolled along through the high country, miles of sagebrush, lush now, with purple lupine blooming in the green grass. The land was vast. The road was deserted. They could see three states and a hundred miles in every direction, with no other humans in sight.

It was a warm June day. With the windows rolled down, Moses and Johnny could hear the AM radio up front. But they couldn't see what Shoe and Emily saw up ahead—first dots, then black bands that moved across the pavement.

Shoe slowed down. Then they heard her speak. "What in God's name?"

Thirty seconds more and the truck was rolling over the bands, crickets that flooded the road, migrating some-where. They could hear some hopping, others crunching under the tires. They could smell the carnage too.

Shoe rolled the truck to a stop. They climbed out, carefully. When their feet touched the pavement, the nearest crickets turned and hopped away. The crickets were three inches long, some black, some deep red, all moving east.

The four of them wandered up and down the road, turning in circles to take it all in. The sun beat on the backs of their necks, where they'd forgotten to put sunscreen. Moses walked up to clusters where the crickets had stopped to eat their flattened friends. He stamped his foot to scare them away, so they wouldn't be run over too. Johnny fetched his camera from the truck and sprinted up the road. Emily raced past Johnny in the opposite direction, both of them dodging crickets.

He lay down on the center line to shoot the crickets at eye level. Emily grabbed her notebook out of the truck and started scribbling.

Moses approached her, stepping gingerly. "What's that for?" he asked.

"Oh, somebody's going to want to read about this," she said.

After fifteen or twenty minutes, Johnny and Moses climbed back in the truckbed. Emily sat up front with Shoe again, who drove on, cringing as the tires leveled wave upon wave of crickets, until they left the last straggling band of them behind.

Shoe sighed. Emily scratched her head with her pen and wrote some more. She never did sell that story.

CHAPTER SEVENTEEN

Max kept saying that he wanted everything to be perfect. The next time they were together, Ida made sure it was.

She took care to smile, once they were naked. "I need your help," she said.

"Oh, darling," Max said. "I need yours too."

She managed to get through the next part without gagging. Each time she started to, she choked it down, suspecting he might not forgive her for something like that. Afterwards they traded places. His tongue hurt, which surprised her. When that was over they lay side by side on his big white bed. From the corner of her eye she saw him watching her and waiting, but Ida felt so empty she couldn't move. He took a hand and ran it in front of her face. Ida blinked.

"Say something," he said.

"I feel strange," she said.

Max eyed her.

"I had no idea," she said, which was true. In fact, she still had no idea. She was not entirely sure what had just happened between them, but her limbs were shaking. She thought it might be fury.

"I won't take you until we're married," Max said.

Virginity was no burden in her eyes, and no prize either. She felt neither pride nor shame regarding hers, a simple biological fact that at this point was largely accidental. She hadn't been saving herself for marriage. She wasn't even sure she'd been saving herself for him.

Max rolled toward her. He took one of her hands and wrapped it around him. "What do you think?" he said. "Is this or is this not the most gorgeous cock you have ever seen?"

"It is," she said, but without looking. She gazed into his eyes instead and wondered if he knew she'd lied. She had never seen one before his, not a live one, and Max must know that.

Maybe that's the point, she thought, that I am willing to lie for him, even to him. Maybe that's love.

It was a careful line she walked, this dissembling. She had to stroke his ego, a thing done by means of superlatives that only took on genuine meaning when held against some previous and inferior model; at the same time, it seemed to Ida that he took great pleasure in her virginity. So she was a virgin, but Max had to be the best she'd ever had.

He was a man of paradox and a man of extremes. Ida had loved these things in the beginning and she still did, but she understood now that they were tricky, especially when they bore on her. And it was bad timing—was it not?—that for the first time ever, Ida felt dissatisfied with herself. Dissatisfaction with her life was a familiar thing, particularly when she was still in school and had to face her unsympathetic peers every day. But however unhappy those encounters had been, as soon as she could steal away from them, the dark muddle of their unwelcome world fell away and she was fine again. And she had always known that when she graduated, or quit, as it turned out, she would not be going back out into their world, and all would be well. There had never been anything wrong with her.

Now her life was incomparable: She was in love. But this love, or lover, held up a mirror to her, and Ida saw that the woman reflected there was scarcely a woman at all. Lying on her back, feeling her eyes stare into space and the twitching all through her torso, Ida asked him when they could do that again. Tomorrow, he said. I want you to do that to me every day for the next fifty years.

Fine, she said. No problem. She turned her head and smiled straight at him as she promised to check off every item on his wish list: yes, yes, yes. Delicious, Ida said when he prompted, the most delicious thing I've ever tasted, though the truth was that she'd had to brace herself to keep it down. I had no idea, she said again, and shook her head slowly from side to side.

You were perfect, whispered Max. Your mouth is perfect.

Ida smiled and wiped small tears from the corners of her eyes.

Left to her own devices, Ida decided she could pull off true love. She was learning the ropes—what to tell Max, how to tell him, what never to tell him. But there were other people involved in the mix. There was Moses, who told Max things about Ida that only caused problems.

One day, just as she was lifting cinnamon cookies from the tray, Moses and Max came bursting in the kitchen door, laughing and shouting. Ida laughed too, as Moses barreled into her, but Max stayed in the door. He only ducked his head inside and fixed her with a look.

Ida was learning this look, the one that meant she had done something wrong. She smiled, but something coiled up inside her. When Max failed to smile back it coiled tighter. He turned, shut the side door, and moved across the room. Placing himself just behind her, he leaned down and murmured in her ear.

"What's this about you and the Magician of Horses?"

Ida recalled the foggy field, the horses emerging from the mist, and Moses with the final apple. She could smell the damp night air. Moses had put his hand into hers— that had been the first time—and they had moved through those shifting, stomping walls.

"No." Moses climbed up onto a stool behind the kitchen counter and watched while Ida poured him a tall glass of apple juice. "She's the magician. Henry just painted her."

We fed the apples to the horses, Ida thought, and kept the people free from sin.

"Oh." Max flicked at a crumb on the counter and

moved away from her. "Right."

Later, walking Max out to his car, Ida suggested they take a quick drive to the lake. Max shook his head.

"This man's in love with you," he said.

Ida clasped her hands behind her back. "He'll be okay," she said.

"No, he won't," said Max. "How the hell could he? And I don't want him hanging around you, panting like a dog and hoping some scraps drop off your table."

"No scraps," Ida said.

"It's puzzling," Max said, "but I get the distinct impression that you don't even see what's wrong with this situation."

"What situation?" Ida asked.

Max looked at her just long enough for her to see she'd disappointed him. Then he sighed and looked away. "How often do you see this guy?"

"I used to see him a lot," she said. "Now, hardly at all."

"And you know that he's in love with you?"

Ida didn't know whether to nod or shake her head—she didn't know whether she knew that or not—and so, by degrees, her head fell to one side. "I guess," she said.

"No guess about it," Max said. "None whatsoever." Still he studied her with that same narrow look. "And he knows about me?"

Ida nodded regretfully. "He does," she said.

"What's the matter? You seem sad."

"I am sad," she said. "It was very sad, when he found out."

"Sad for him or sad for you?"

"Sad for both of us. He was my best friend."

Max fixed her with a solemn look. "Ida. Has this best friend of yours ever made a pass at you?"

Ida blushed. She clasped her hands once more.

"That's what I thought." Max unlocked his car door, reached in, and brought out a small bright bag. He handed it to her.

"You think he's such a good friend," Max said. "You put this on the next time you go over there and you see if your fine fuck can keep his eyes on any of your paintings for more than two seconds. I know about these sensitive guys who walk around pretending like they've got more honor than the rest of us. The only reason they've got more is because no woman in her right mind will let them near her."

Ida peeked inside the bag. Some kind of shirt.

"Why are you loyal to this guy?" Max asked her. "You can't be loyal to everyone."

"I don't see why not," Ida said.

"Then you've never been loyal to anyone."

This wounded Ida; it also shocked her. Of course you could be loyal to everyone—everyone worth being loyal to. "I am loyal," she insisted.

Max nodded slowly. "I don't want you to see him anymore. Obviously, I can't tell you what to do, but you won't see him if you care about me at all."

"I hardly see him as it is."

This time, Max's sigh was almost a groan. He looked at her as if she'd deeply grieved him.

"That's not what I wanted to hear." He made a move

toward his car.

Ida grabbed his arm.

"There's nothing more to discuss," Max said. "I asked of you something simple. I asked you to make your terms clear. I wanted him to know that you were unavailable. And the words had to come from your mouth. He had to see them falling from the lips he wants to kiss."

"You're using past tense," Ida said.

Max cocked his head. Sometimes it made her think of a parrot, when he did that, the way his eyes were calculating but strangely flat. "Was I?" he said.

"It's a false choice," Ida said.

Max made another move toward his car door, but she held on to him.

"There's no conflict of interest," she said. "I love you in such different ways."

"So now you love him," Max said.

"But I don't want to marry him."

"Well, if you can't find a little more loyalty in your heart, you may find he's the only man who'll marry you."

Ida stopped short. Max had told her on more than one occasion that she could have any man her heart desired. Of course she hadn't believed him, but she hadn't expected him to reverse his position so easily, either.

"You still don't get it, do you," Max said. "You should want to choose, to make clear your allegiance. If the roles were reversed—and believe me, they could be ten times a day—I would avoid any situation or circumstance that an interested party might construe as false, or real, encouragement."

"So would I!" Ida cried. "Not for your sake, but for his."

Max tapped his chest. "For my sake. I don't give a damn about him."

"Henry is no threat."

"Every man is a threat," Max said. "And this one knows how to play you. He feeds you an idea of yourself, one he knows you like. And that idea you like is what you think he likes too, what he wants. But I can tell you what he really wants. So could any man. You watch the next time you see him. See if his hand doesn't move toward his pants."

Ida stepped backwards. She folded the arms of her overcoat across herself as Max fit himself into his car. He hunched forward as he started up the engine. But then Max rolled down his window and motioned her over.

"Moses tells me you take him with you when you go to the cemetery."

Ida nodded. "Or he takes me. Whichever."

"But isn't that morbid?"

"Morbid." She thought a moment. "Sure."

She knew better than to argue about that word. In high school, after reading Ida's paper on Wuthering Heights, her literature teacher had taken her aside to explain that when Heathcliff dug up Katherine's grave to hold her to his breast, Brontë had not intended that to be romantic but morbid. Morbid, she'd said again, and shuddered—theatrically, Ida had thought at the time—as if to illustrate the problem, and the correct response.

At one level, Ida had understood. She understood, as

she always did in such encounters, that there was something wrong with her own response, but what it was she could not say. Heathcliff's impulse was pure and passionate. It had always seemed to her an impulse born of love.

After Max drove away she hurried inside and looked up the word in the dictionary. "Suggesting an unhealthy mental state; unwholesomely gloomy, sensitive, etc. A morbid interest in death."

The antonym, she noticed just before she shut the book, was "cheerful." But what if one showed a cheerful interest in death? What was the word for that?

When she removed the T-shirt from its shiny bag, slipped off her coat and changed into it, the fabric squeezed her breasts and cut into her armpits. At first she thought Max had gotten her a child's size, but then she read the label and remembered that she'd seen women wearing tight-fitting T-shirts like this in the movies and on TV. Baby tees, they called them.

She spent the rest of the afternoon in front of her bedroom mirror. The shirt made her breasts look huge, her stomach flat. She'd never worn anything like this in front of Henry. He had propositioned her anyway, it was true—Ida blushed again at the recollection—but she had turned him down and they had gone on, much like before. Hadn't they? Henry was not manipulating her. Henry liked her. Henry loved her.

Ida stood before the mirror and turned from side to side. She thought of Henry seeing her in this shirt and was struck with shame, even with a kind of horror. She took off the T-shirt and put her smock back on.

What did it mean to love a man and not want him for a lover? It was a half-hearted sort of love, she thought, almost a slap in the face. Now that Ida had a lover, someone who had already taken a dozen liberties with her that Henry never would, she wondered what possible kindness she could extend to Henry, what possible happiness could honestly pass between them.

And Max knew her. Sometimes she found his criticisms confusing, her instincts didn't seem to bear them out, but then again, she had ignored criticism all her life. Why should it ring true now? These things he touched on—about Henry, about her siblings, about her—were probably right. Max had gone out into the world and he saw it very clearly. Ida had dedicated her life to remaining blind.

Something was wrong with her. It had been wrong for years and years. The girls she'd gone to high school with were all married now, all having babies. Ida had never liked them, no, but then again, her friend was not a proper friend, Henry, a bachelor for life, and making passes at her. And before Max came into her life, that one strange friend was all she had.

It seemed to Ida that she'd made a bad job of her life, indeed. She had enjoyed herself, that was true, but here she was, already past thirty with nothing to show for it, no life wisdom, not even any scars. She had indulged herself to an absurd degree, and her family had let her get away with it. They'd let her live like Peter Pan, which meant she hadn't lived at all.

Still, it was exhausting, trying to get these things right. She'd never had an instinct for how to behave like other people, and she could see she still didn't. She memorized the proper attitudes, but there was no internal capacity, no built-in compass. It was like math in school. What was the use in working problem after problem if one never mastered the general principles underlying them? Only then would things fall into place.

And the problem now was her life. Understanding had never been so important. It was not a comfortable feeling, this dissatisfaction with her own status quo— trying to change, on the one hand, and then on the other, still trying to understand precisely why she needed to. The effort took its toll.

She lost her appetite. Ida still came to the table, eager to be with her family, but the food became irrelevant. Sometimes she placed a forkful of something in her mouth and then realized she didn't want it, that under no circumstances could she make herself swallow it. Other times, she just forgot the food was there. Her stomach grew lean, almost hollow, but she wasn't hungry. Her jeans sagged at the waist. She couldn't sleep. And once again, she couldn't paint.

These symptoms were unfamiliar, all very strange. At times she felt as if she'd been invaded by some hostile organism, but the organism was hard to isolate, hard to name. It might be this dissatisfaction taking its toll on her. Then again, the affliction might be love.

In thinking so hard about life, Ida left behind the terrain of her heart and entered into a different terrain, the one her sister had occupied for so many years. Ida came to see, as Shoe had before her, that progress was a simple exercise of will, of mind over matter. In the end it was Shoe, not Max, who completed the circuit back to her heart. For it seemed to Ida that she had begun to know Shoe from the inside now. And to love her sister more than she had when she was still alive.

CHAPTER EIGHTEEN

Johnny flew home for the Easter weekend and his parents' wedding anniversary, which fell that Saturday. These were his official reasons for coming, anyway, though his family was not religious and he'd never even sent his parents an anniversary card before. When Ida met him at the airport gate, Johnny set down his bag and looked around.

"Who drove?" he asked.

"I did." Ida grabbed the bag and slung it across her shoulder.

"Who drove down with you?"

"Nobody," Ida said, and started away.

Johnny trailed her all the way out to the parking lot. He stood by as she laid his bag in the trunk. Only then did she turn and really look at him.

"You wanna get a drink?"

"Now?" Johnny glanced at his watch, then glanced again to make sure he'd moved it ahead to Eastern Standard Time. "Sure. I guess I know a place or two."

"That's okay," she said. "I know a place."

Johnny offered to drive them into the city, but Ida shook her head. So Johnny sat back and talked, about the government, about his government job, about the new woman he wasn't exactly seeing.

"Uh-huh!" she said in response, and that was all, nodding distractedly, eyeing the lunch-hour traffic. "Wow."

She drove them to a strip mall on the outskirts of Cincinnati, parked, and led the way into the bar.

"You should eat something," Ida said, once they had got their drinks.

"I had breakfast on the plane. Twice. Why don't you eat?" he asked.

"I can't," she said. But when the waitress stopped by, she ordered herself a second beer.

Ida had gotten skinny. The missing weight honed the bones of her face and made her eyes seem even larger. She looked a little wild and a little lost, Johnny thought, like a cat who can't find its way home.

"How's Mom?"

"Oh." Ida sighed. "She's living for Moses now. Wants him to grow up to be another adventure-monger."

"Is that so bad?"

Ida shook her head. "Adventure is good. But motive is everything. As you know." She smiled at the table. "That's why you must not hold me back."

Johnny studied his beer, confused. What adventure did she have in mind? And what motive? Ida had always acted according to the dictates of her heart. Until recently, those dictates had been disarmingly simple.

"Oh, yeah," she said. "Mom's got a new doctor. He just prescribed something for her."

"What?"

"Some antidepressant. Acts like a sedative, though. She's back in bed all the time."

"Great," Johnny said. "That seems like the last thing she needs."

Ida stared at her bottle. She tapped an index finger against the brown glass. "That's what I said."

"So whose idea was it? It couldn't have been Dad's."

"It wasn't." Ida pushed away her bottle. "Let's call Max," she said. "He's right around the corner. He's dying to meet you."

"He's at work?" Johnny said.

"I doubt it." Ida sprang up. "I'll be right back."

Johnny watched his sister maneuver through the lunch crowd toward the phone, already buzzed. Maybe she hadn't eaten breakfast either. What struck him next was the thing she did when she reached the phone, the thing no one else would give a second thought: She dialed the number, then turned back to face the room. Odd, thought Johnny. Ida had always put her back to strangers when given the choice.

She passed the bar on her return, and a man at the counter shot out his arm and caught her by the wrist. Johnny put down his beer and started from the booth, then stopped as Ida rotated her arm. They both looked at her watch, then the man looked at her and let her go.

Johnny sank back down. That was another sister, he

thought. Another situation. He sighed and drank his beer.

Ida's face was flushed when she returned, from drink or shame, he wasn't sure. She slapped a hand around her bottle and took a long pull.

"You're not yourself," he said.

"You mean I've changed."

Johnny laughed a dry breath of laugh. "All right," he said.

An irritable silence fell between them.

"So I've changed," she said suddenly. "Change is essential."

Johnny laughed again. She sounded like an evolutionary biologist.

Ida lifted her beer, brought it to her mouth, swallowed. Johnny could see by the way her mouth bunched around the liquid that she still didn't enjoy it. She drained the bottle anyway. "Laugh," she said. "We'll see who has the last laugh."

Her eyes drifted out into the room. She began to talk about Max, more in the style of a speech than a conversation, almost as if she were reciting something from memory. She spoke of Max's way with people. Of his uncanny ability to assess a person's motives, of his shrewd judgment in all things human. Then Johnny realized she was reciting. He had heard her describe Max in just this way when they talked at Christmas.

"He's going to manage my career," she announced.

"You want that?" Johnny asked. "To be managed, I mean."

Ida laid her palms flat on the table and leaned toward

him. She smiled a conspiratorial smile. For a moment, Johnny thought she was going to tell him the truth about Max, whatever that was.

"Johnny," she whispered. "Do you inventory yourself?"

Before he could respond, he felt somebody loom over their table. Johnny looked up. The man was so tall it was startling. His handshake was firm and probably rehearsed. He had a long, closely shaved face, and a huge white smile that stood out against his tan. He slid in next to Ida, spread his hands on the table, and waited.

The waitress reappeared. Max ordered for himself and for Ida, though she swore she couldn't eat and wanted nothing more to drink.

"Darling," Max said, and Johnny watched one of his hands slip underneath the table. Max lowered his voice, but not enough. "You have to keep up your strength. If not for your sake, then for mine."

Max turned his light brown eyes from her to Johnny and grinned. There was something conspiratorial about his smile too, but Johnny didn't think he and Ida shared the same conspiracy. His grin seemed slightly wicked.

"You live way the hell out West," said Max. "Good for you. I was out there once or twice."

"Good for you," said Johnny. "Whereabouts?"

Max waved his hand. "I guess it's beautiful, but it's not the kind of beauty that makes you feel at home."

"That depends," Johnny said.

"Of course." Max nodded, large, emphatic nods. "Absolutely depends. I misspoke just now. What I meant to say was that it isn't a warm beauty. Not like your sister's here."

Max had plans for that beauty, he said. Any month now, they were going to move to a big city.

"Where the action is," Ida put in, and laughed. Johnny was not sure how to read the laughter.

"She's going to waste here," Max said. "A woman like her belongs in a place where she'll be appreciated."

"You mean her art," Johnny said.

"I mean her gorgeous self." Max waved his hand again. "I'll find a market for her art anywhere we go. She's too talented and I'm too connected not to."

Max likened her to a flower blooming in the wilderness. What was the use if no one could see it? But in a big city, Max said, Philadelphia or New York, people on street corners would stop and stare. In the great museums, people would turn away from famous paintings of other women, long-dead women, to watch her walk by. New York would fall at her feet, he said. She was what everybody wanted.

"Maybe you could try out Cincinnati first," Johnny suggested. "As a trial run."

"What for?" Max shouted. "Cinci is old hat."

Ida smiled and said nothing. It was her silence that impressed Johnny more than her smiles, though it was clear Max inspired in her a steady stream of mirth. She listened to his rumbling voice spin out their thrilling future with her head tipped to one side, her gaze thoughtful, and laughed softly into her beer.

Johnny listened too. Yes, he thought. I've heard that

voice before.

"Ida tells me you're going to manage her career."

Max nodded.

"How does that work?"

"First we get a portfolio together and find the right niche. Then we get her in shows and galleries. Introduce her to some of my clients. Help her plan her next direction."

"What does that entail?"

"Which part?"

"The next direction. How do you plan out something like that?"

"You don't," Ida said, and laughed.

Max smiled tightly, but Ida was looking out the window and didn't notice. When a moving van parked on the street pulled away, she brought the fingers of one hand to rest lightly on Max's sleeve. With her other hand, she pointed beyond the bar's plate-glass window, to where the van had been.

"What?" Max searched the street almost frantically. "What is it, sweetheart?"

Ida didn't answer him, just continued to point, serene and faithful, her arm and finger forming one intrepid line.

"It's the dogwood," Johnny said.

Max frowned and shook his head.

"There was a van," Johnny explained. "You couldn't see the tree until it pulled away."

"I didn't know they were in bloom," Ida said.

Johnny caught his sister's eye.

"I haven't gotten out much this spring," she said.

Johnny tried to pick up the tab when it arrived, but Max wouldn't hear of it. On their way out he slapped Johnny on the back, then disappeared around a corner with Ida. Five minutes later, when she returned alone, Johnny took the wheel.

Driving north, they passed through tiny towns that stretched their lengths along the highway. No sooner had they shot past one than they were passing through another. Johnny had forgotten how the empty spaces here didn't last. And even those spaces weren't really empty. They were divided into fields and pastures touched by human hands. There were furrows and fences and, everywhere, signs of habitation.

At one point he tried to tease his sister about being a flower in the wilderness.

Ida smiled. "You know it was always my favorite thing to be," she said. "But I was playing games up there in my imagination." She tapped her head, with its dark heavy hair twisted on top. "I always knew that when he came for me I'd leave all that behind and embark on my real life."

Johnny suspected her games of the imagination were alive and well. For starters, she'd convinced herself this new life was somehow more real than the old one. And Max was not an outstanding representative for real life, not in Johnny's book.

"So in your real life you want to walk around and decorate some city?" he asked.

Ida smiled again. "With my paintings. Not with me."

"But he's serious."

"Not so serious. That's the key to Max. Once you get

it, you'll adore him."

"Shoe said the key to Max is that you're forced to convince yourself he isn't serious, when in fact he is."

Ida was silent. They passed a young tree with bright plastic eggs, purple and pink and yellow, hanging from its slight branches. They passed long rows of crops already growing green. Coming into town, they passed the slate blue house of Ida's friend, Henry.

"So," she said finally. "I guess you talked to Emily."

"I didn't need to talk to Emily to know it was the same guy," Johnny said. "Anyway, I didn't talk to her. She left a message on my machine."

A message he had not erased, though it had been three weeks. Yesterday, before he drove north to Salt Lake City, he'd listened to it four times in a row.

He cleared his throat. "How is she?"

"Oh, I don't know. She mentioned the will. That provision about you guys getting married. She said it wasn't working out like Shoe had planned."

"All Emily or I ever asked of Shoe was to stay alive." Johnny had to clear his throat a second time. "We owe her nothing now. Our debts to her are canceled."

"What makes you think marriage was Shoe's idea?"

"Who else's would it be?"

"Emily's. She's not getting any younger."

"She's the same age as you!"

"Well." Ida considered. "I rest my case."

When Johnny didn't respond, she yawned and continued.

"Anyway, she's not your type."

"What do you mean?"

"She isn't beautiful enough."

"Yes, she is."

"No," Ida said. "You're five times better-looking than she is. You need to be with someone really gorgeous. Beautiful people have a special bond."

"Is that right."

"It's a different kind of love than normal people's. In a certain way, it's more profound."

"What a load of crap." Johnny rolled down his window and spat. "Did Max say that?"

"Uh-huh. And so I work much harder now, on my appearance. It's important to age gracefully and the devil's in the details, you know. I pay attention to my nails, my skin. I try to preserve that youthful glow. Funny, how when you're young you take all that for granted. Now that I'm losing it, though, I notice it so much! Do you know what I'm talking about?"

"No."

"It's a kind of sheen that high school girls have, a glint across their cheekbones. Older women just don't have it. And they hollow out around the eyes. Their skin starts to loosen. It's really awful. At the funeral, I saw it happening already to your friend."

"Emily will always be beautiful," Johnny said.

"Well, of course, in a certain spiritual way she might."

"No, not just in a spiritual way!"

"I thought you didn't like her."

"Of course I like her. You'd have to be crazy not to like her."

"But you never talk to her."

"I can't."

"Why not?"

"After Shoe's will? If Emily and I ever got together now, that'd be like saying, 'Good job, Shoe, getting yourself killed!'"

"I'm missing the connection. But it's just as well. I wanted to surprise you with Max's identity. Emily knew that, and she betrayed my confidence by telling you first. I can't abide a tattle-tale."

"You shouldn't have told her if you were worried about that," Johnny said. "You should have known her first loyalty would be to Shoe."

"She made me tell her," Ida said. "And Shoe is dead."

"Lucky for you," Johnny said.

"What do you mean?"

"If Shoe was alive, you and Max never would've met."

"That's a nasty thing to say."

Johnny supposed it was, in a certain way, but he didn't apologize. They sailed down the long hill past the cemetery. Both of them kept their eyes fixed straight ahead. Then they sailed up again and past the college campus with its stone bridges, red brick buildings and tall oak trees.

He hadn't been back for an Ohio spring in years, and now his head felt loose on his shoulders. He felt like he might drown in all the soft shades of green. Off to the right, white swans floated on the campus pond, beside a bed of red and yellow tulips. Johnny put up a hand to shield his eyes.

"Does he know you know?" Johnny asked.

Ida nodded. "I brought it up last month."

Johnny pulled into the driveway and shut off the engine, but neither one got out.

"When was he planning to bring it up?"

"I didn't ask him."

"Why not?"

Ida stared out the window and didn't answer.

"Are you saying we're all a lot safer if we act like everything's okay?"

"Safer." Ida thought a moment. "Probably."

"Mom and Dad still don't know?"

"Nope. Moses neither. We wanted it to be a surprise."

"Some surprise," Johnny said.

"Yes."

"And you trust him."

"Yes."

"Don't think he's using you to get to Moses?"

"You asked me that before." This time, though, she smiled. "If anything, he uses Moses to get to me."

"Well," Johnny said. "I guess it's working."

They got out of the car. Johnny went to the trunk and lifted out his suitcase just as the bells of the Catholic church in the center of town began to toll. They looked at one another.

"Henry believes," she said, and gazed off toward the church. "Jesus rising from the dead and all."

Johnny nodded to himself.

"Max says it's because he's got nothing better to believe in."

Johnny found that a mite presumptuous, and perhaps faulty in its logic as well. He himself had nothing better to believe in, and still did not believe.

"How is Henry?" Johnny asked.

"I don't see him much these days." Ida frowned. "I guess he's probably at mass."

"Now?"

"Good Friday services. Didn't Christ die at three in the afternoon?"

Johnny didn't know. The Tumarkins were not a religious family, though he and his sisters regarded their father's style of nonbelief as rather innocent. He had never known anything else.

Their mother's style was something sadder: failed belief. If their father had no need of God, their mother's universe was just too dark to admit God's light. When they met, their father might have thought he was getting a freethinking compatriot, but it seemed to Johnny and his sisters that their mother might have benefited from the prospect of an afterlife more than most.

Johnny and Ida stood in place until the tones of the last bell died away. Then they headed up the driveway to the house they'd both grown up in.

"How's the painting?" he asked.

"Oh, not so good," she said.

That night, when the rest of the family had turned in, Johnny stayed up and listened while his mother rhapsodized about the future. It was very bright, she said. Max was just what the doctor ordered: Ida was coming out of her shell after all these years and Moses would have a father.

Johnny listened and watched while his mother sewed a button on one of Moses' shirts. He recognized the shirt as one of his from twenty years before.

She'd always done her mending late at night, by the yellowish light of a table lamp. He watched her pull up on the needle, watched the thread go taut, and watched her face. Impossible, twenty years ago, to imagine her face today. Now every line made sense. They'd been easy to get used to. You always forgot, Johnny thought, what someone looked like without them.

"Your father and I won't be here forever," Mrs. Tumarkin said, and Johnny knew she spoke the truth. "It's better for Ida to move on before we do."

She tied off the knot behind the button, cut the thread, and folded up the old plaid shirt.

"Now Ida has a chance. A once-in-a-lifetime chance to live."

No one in the family was a worse romantic than their mother, Johnny thought, because no one was more unhappy. Mrs. Tumarkin couldn't comprehend Ida's style of living any better than she could comprehend Shoe's. Shoe had lived the life her mother believed she wanted to live herself, but Shoe's life had only been romantic in its exploits; Shoe herself had never been a romantic. She'd always been an idealist. There was a difference.

"I heard you're seeing a new doctor," Johnny said.

"He's wonderful," Mrs. Tumarkin said. "Max put me in touch with him."

"Does everyone do everything Max tells them to do?"

Mrs. Tumarkin widened her eyes in surprise. "Max has never told me to do anything."

"Did he tell you his plans for Ida?"

"Why, yes," she said. "He's going to help her see the world."

"And did he tell you he's Moses' father?"

Mrs. Tumarkin smiled slyly. "Not in so many words," she said. "But I suspected."

"Does Dad suspect?"

"Oh, your father. I told him. He said I was just being romantic."

"There's nothing romantic about it," Johnny said. "This whole situation should give you the creeps."

"Why?" cried Mrs. Tumarkin. "I think it's lovely. It's like a wonderful play, by Shakespeare or Oscar Wilde."

"Look," Johnny said. "Ida thinks she's in love with him. There's nothing to do about that now. But would you do me a favor? Would you keep an eye on her? And would you check in with Dr. Gibson? He never prescribed you any drugs, did he? Dr. Gibson just told you to get out of the house once in a while. See the world, you know."

Mrs. Tumarkin put down her sewing. "Johnny," she said.

He lifted the plaid shirt to his face long enough to feel the soft cotton against his skin and inhale any lingering odor of the past. His mother lost her stern expression and smiled at him in the half-dark.

"And what do you think of Ida's young man?" she asked shyly.

Johnny laid the shirt back on the table. "I don't trust

him," he said.

"I think you don't like him."

"I don't like him either."

"Well, I declare!" she cried, and laughed gaily.

Johnny rose to his feet. "What's so funny?"

"You've become so...decisive!"

Johnny turned and left. But the sound of her laughter followed him up the dark stairs to his old room, Moses' bedroom now. Tonight they shared, his nephew laid out in his familiar sleeping bag on the floor. Johnny stepped over him, glad for the company, and climbed into the bed, where he eventually fell asleep.

CHAPTER NINETEEN

Saturday afternoon Max showed up with two boxes balanced in his hands, wrapped in glossy blue paper. One box was for Professor and Mrs. Tumarkin; the other Max handed to Moses.

"Open it now," he said.

Moses tore away the paper, then lifted the lid off the box so his aunt and uncle could see.

"Cool," Moses said. "Thanks, Max." He left the shoes in their box, nestled in white tissue.

Max's smile wilted slightly. "Do you know what those are?" he asked.

"Tennis shoes," said Moses.

"Basketball shoes," said Ida.

"Air Jordans," said Johnny.

When no more information was forthcoming, Moses smiled. For a six-year-old, the smile was polite.

Max's mouth fell slowly open. "Don't you know about Air Jordans?"

Moses nodded. "They're basketball shoes," he said.

Max gazed at the boy for one long moment. Then his still-open mouth curved upward. "Do you have a basketball?" he asked.

Moses turned and looked at his aunt and uncle. Johnny nodded.

"Let's shoot some hoops," Max said.

Ida had been trying to nibble at a plate of crackers since Max arrived. Now she pushed away the plate and leapt to her feet. "Oh, I know just the place," she cried.

Johnny toyed with the idea of not going. He didn't really want to. Then he looked at Moses and changed his mind. He'd come to investigate the situation—for Ida's sake, and for his nephew's—and by God, he would investigate it.

The court Ida led them to had already been visited by spring. The cracks that snaked across the concrete surface were crowded with young dandelions in bright bloom. The chain link that fenced in the court was obscured in spots by heavy vines. Much of the growth was dead and brown, but new vines were starting, the leaves small and tender. A cluster of trees suspended their limbs over one end of the court. Beneath the limbs, a luxuriant clump of violets had sprung up in the rubble.

Some of the vines held old pods, left over from the previous autumn. Ida detached one of these from the fence, coaxed opened the pod with her finger, loosed a few seeds from inside and blew them up, into the air. Moses leapt after the white fluff, jumping and spinning, trying to catch the floating seeds in his hands.

Max took one look at the court, turned to Johnny

and rolled his eyes. "Your sister adores decay," he said. "It's a wonder her teeth are so perfect."

It was not a full court. There was only one hoop, with a washed-out backboard and a snarled chain net. Two old metal posts on either side of the court had probably held up a tennis net, once upon a time. In fact, in one of the corners, Max found a tennis ball.

He crouched down beside it, but didn't touch it. "White!" he cried. "White! Do you know how long it's been since I've seen a white tennis ball?"

Johnny did not know. And he couldn't decide, from Max's reaction, whether he was horrified or delighted. Max straightened again and walked over to Ida, who was still releasing the white parachute seeds, one by one, into the air.

"Ida," he said. "Moses can't play basketball here."

"But he can shoot here," Ida said. "No one ever comes here."

"That's the trouble," Max said. "He'll never get a game."

Max led Moses to the hoop, while Johnny and Ida backed up against a section in the chain-link fence that looked like it might support some of their weight. They backed up without thinking, quiet and deferential, watching as Max bent over, hands on his knees, and he and Moses looked eye to eye.

"He does that with kids," whispered Ida, full of admiration. "Because he's so tall. He's very conscious of these things."

Max talked to Moses for several minutes. Moses

nodded now and then. Max palmed the ball in one of his long hands, then handed it across. Moses pivoted from him toward the hoop. Max talked some more.

Ida twined her fingers through the links in the metal fence and let her torso fall forward in a clean line. "He could practice hoops here," she repeated, almost to herself. "In privacy."

"Sure he could," Johnny said. "Moses will decide for himself."

From where she hung, Ida turned and smiled over her shoulder at him. "You like the weeds?" she asked.

"I love the weeds," Johnny said. "Why do you think I came back to Ohio?"

Ida stood up again. When she let go of the fence, Johnny noticed her palms were crisscrossed in dark red lines. She rubbed at these with her thumb. "Of course, these aren't really weeds," she said cheerfully. "Weeds are unwanted."

She paced away and plucked three long-stemmed dandelions from the pavement. Two of the yellow flowers she tucked into her dark hair, then walked back to Johnny, reached over and placed the third one behind his ear.

"Pretty," she said. "Shoe always said you were the prettiest."

Ida was happy now. She was her old self. Johnny looked at her and smiled.

"I like blond with bright yellow," she added, admiring the flower in his hair. "I think I always have."

Moses was trying to throw overhand, but he couldn't get the ball up high enough. After each attempt he rushed forward to grab the ball again, then moved back to a space just in front of Max. Max kept on talking in a low, soothing voice, very different from the one he'd used yesterday in the bar.

This was a good voice. This was a kind voice. This was the sort of voice that would inspire allegiance. Occasionally Max would rest both hands on the boy's shoulders. This seemed to be Max at his best.

Moses might fare all right in this deal, Johnny thought. Maybe that was the bright side—not Ida gaining a husband, but Moses gaining a father.

"I should go frost the cake," Ida said suddenly.

She left him and approached the others. Halfway there, Max turned and looked at her. "When you walk down the aisle, we'll get a real wreath of flowers for your beautiful hair," he said. He left Moses and came to her.

She whispered something, and Max nodded. Johnny watched as she reached up a hand to Max's face, moved her thumb along the underside of his jaw. One kiss, a long look, another kiss.

Max was still gazing at her when he called out to Moses. "Say goodbye to Mommy."

But Moses was concentrating on his shooting and did not respond.

Max opened his mouth to call out a second time, but Ida reached up and put her fingers to his lips.

"What?" said Max.

Ida didn't answer, only shook her head. She lifted away her fingers, waved them at Johnny, and headed home. Max shrugged and joined Johnny up against the fence.

"Basketball changed my life," he said.

Johnny didn't know what to say to that, so he waited.

"None of the girls would go out with me before I joined the team. A year later, the same girls who'd turned me down were asking me out."

"Did you go out with them?"

"A couple."

"Why?"

"Why not?" asked Max.

Moses was getting tired. He trailed his basketball to the shady corner where it had rolled and come to rest amid the violets. When he reached the ball, instead of retrieving it one more time, he sat down on top of it. With his elbows on his knees, his chin in his hands, he surveyed his surroundings.

"You want Moses to get all the girls?"

"Just the good ones." Max raised an arm and motioned for Moses to join them. Moses rose to his feet, turned and picked up his basketball. He carried it in both arms, across his stomach.

Leaving the court, Max asked Johnny if he'd played sports in high school.

Johnny had played soccer, and loved it. But he shook his head.

"At my school, it was the only way to be popular," Max said. "I started out a lot like Ida. Inside, we're the same. I worked to transform myself on the outside. Ida never did."

"Ida didn't care about being popular," Johnny said.

Moses tried dribbling on the sidewalk and soon lost

control of the ball. It bounced out into the street and hit the far curb. He dashed after it, as it rolled toward a sewer grate.

"Watch for cars," called Max, then turned and looked at Johnny. "Everybody cares. That's part of being human. Before the year is out," he said, "she'll have more friends than she knows what to do with."

Johnny recalled Ida's words the day before concerning Max, how he was only half-serious, how this was his greatest charm. It would have been charming, Johnny thought, if it were true.

Moses retrieved his basketball from the gutter across the street, waited until a car drove past, then shouted to them that he wanted to visit his mom's grave.

"Today?" cried Max.

Moses nodded.

Until that moment, Johnny had been resolved not to go to the cemetery. He'd formed his resolve yesterday, shortly after his plane had left the ground, about the time they turned off the seatbelt sign, somewhere over Colorado. But Max seemed more put off at the prospect than he was. This didn't make Johnny braver, but it made him curious.

"Come on," Johnny said. "I know a shortcut."

He thought he'd lead the way, but it turned out Moses knew the same shortcut. Johnny watched the boy's limbs swing in front of him, already emerging from the soft round flesh of early childhood into something lean and full of bones. They marched south, descended into the park, and kept walking until they came to the weedy bushes that fringed the cemetery.

When their daughter had died so precipitously at thirty-four, Johnny's parents had decided to go ahead and purchase a family plot. Shoe was buried there now, at the top of the hill. But when Johnny reached Shoe's grave, he discovered that the undertaker or the caretaker, whoever handled those things, had already gotten to work. To one side of his sister, someone had placed the stones for his parents as well. Their names were inscribed, with a date of birth for each and the anticipatory dash.

Johnny hadn't expected this. He was already backing away when Moses turned to him. "We catch the mice at Henry's house and here is where we let them go," he said. "Mom liked mice."

Max shuddered. Moses turned back to his mother's stone. Some daffodils bloomed beside the pink granite, but they were past their prime, the edges beginning to brown.

"You can't catch as many mice now," Moses said, no longer addressing Johnny, but the tombstone. "They only come in when it's cold."

They left Moses alone at his mother's grave and wandered a short way down the hill. Below was a small brick square of a house, built for the caretaker once upon a time, Johnny imagined. He was surprised to see a car parked beside it now. Maybe somebody lived there still.

It was an old cemetery, with obelisks of rough white marble, and some of the oldest markers, thin gray slabs of stone, cracked down the middle. Steep hills. No wide open spaces, no vistas, and no one looking in. It was a lush cemetery, too. Forest encroached on every side, with dogwood, redbud and forsythia all in bloom. Shoe had told Johnny, more than once, that she wanted to be buried here. When I'm dead, she had said, I want to be smothered in spring and fall. But she was drunk when she said it.

"So your sister was murdered," Max said. "Shot with her own gun."

"That's what they're afraid of," Johnny said.

"Drugs involved?"

"No one knows."

"But the other victim was a drug dealer."

"Yeah." Johnny opened his mouth to elaborate, then stopped himself. The last person he wanted to discuss Shoe's murder with was this guy. But Max was watching him, waiting for something more.

"Yeah, he was," Johnny repeated.

He stepped into the undergrowth, where a Civil War-era tombstone was being claimed by the surrounding woods. That kind of disappearance happened here. Johnny thought of tearing at the encroaching trees and weeds and vines, but it was spring. Those things had just made it back from the dead themselves.

Max cleared his throat and Johnny spun around.

"She was pretty," Max said.

"Did you see a photo?" Johnny asked, though he knew Max had seen more than that.

"I saw her," Max said. "She was a pretty girl."

Johnny nodded. He stepped out of the woods and glanced back up the hill.

"But do you appreciate—" Max shouted—"that your sister Ida is a goddamn knockout?"

"Probably not," said Johnny. "Not a goddamn knockout, no. I guess not."

Max looked at him strangely.

"She's talented and smart," Johnny volunteered. "Not street smart, though."

"God, no," said Max. "But she doesn't need to be. She's got me now."

"But you're the one who's going to put her on the street," Johnny pointed out.

Now Max looked hard at Johnny, his face fiercely attentive.

"On the street, but not out on the street. We won't be living hand-to-mouth, I can assure you. My whole life has been building toward this. Besides, between your sisters, Moses has seen enough of rural America to last him a lifetime."

"Not for Shoe's taste."

Johnny was sorry the minute he said it. He opened his mouth to take it back, just as Max reached out and put a hand on his shoulder. Once again, Johnny was struck by the disparity in their heights—and by the conviction Max would put that disparity to his advantage, if he could.

"Pardon me for what I'm about to say," Max began, "but isn't your sister buried up there?" He stared at Johnny with his light eyes until Johnny looked away. "Besides, what makes you think it was the setting Susan was concerned with? Ida's the key."

"Change the setting and you change Ida," Johnny

said, almost against his will.

"Ida has a right to change," Max said. "More than that, she has a need."

Johnny stared at the space between his tennis shoes.

"Correct me if I'm wrong, but it seems to me that you and Ida are forever thinking how your dead sister would've wanted Moses raised. Always trying to raise him according to her design." Max pointed up the hill. "But as I said: Susan's not in charge anymore. The queen bee has departed the hive, God rest her soul, and the rest of your family can stop acting like drones, trying to do her bidding."

Johnny raised his face to Max in disbelief. "I don't know what Ida's told you—"

"Nothing." Max shook his head gravely. "Nothing."

Johnny turned and marched back up the narrow asphalt drive to fetch his nephew. Somehow Max had read his mind. Read it, and then put it to work for himself somehow. Because Shoe had run the show. She wrote her will so she could keep right on running the show once she was gone. Max was right.

Except Max was wrong. Johnny was twelve when Shoe left home. He seldom saw her after that until he headed west for college, and once he did, the rest of the family saw her even less. She'd always taught him to think for himself, as a little kid and later on as an adult. So how was Shoe to blame for his choices, for anybody's choices but her own? If Johnny worried about Ida now, or Moses, it wasn't because of Shoe. Just like it wasn't Shoe's fault if he missed Emily.

Johnny topped the hill but slowed when he saw his nephew. Moses was kneeling in the new grass over his mother's coffin. Moses was sinking his face into the sweet spring grass.

"—but you're way out of line," Johnny mumbled, to no one but himself.

When Ida found out they'd gone to the cemetery, her eyes grew wide and strange. Johnny watched her turn those eyes on Max, dark with accusation. Betrayal, he thought, although he didn't understand the nature of the betrayal. Max seemed to take her look for something else and tried to kiss her forehead. She ducked away.

Laughing, Max tried again.

Ida pushed past him and marched from the room. Max began to follow, then stopped himself in the doorway by shoving both hands up hard against the frame. He stayed there a moment, shrugged his broad shoulders, and turned back to the room.

"Let's get some beer," he said to Johnny.

The beer was in the wine cellar, off the main basement, a tiny, dank room under the front porch. Max held the cellar door open while Johnny scanned the shelves with a flashlight.

"Support me," Max said. "If you don't support me, you don't support her."

"That's debatable," Johnny said, and reached for a six-pack on the lowest shelf. The cellar door creaked on its hinges, Max stepped into the small space beside Johnny and the door fell shut behind them.

"Support me," he said, "or I'll make sure your sister never has anything to do with you again."

Johnny laughed, set the beer back on its shelf, and straightened. "Ida told me you really know how to assess people."

Max waited.

"Assess this." Johnny raised the flashlight, then his middle finger in front of it.

Max opened the cellar door. He moved out into the basement and Johnny followed him.

"You've got a lot to lose," Max said quietly.

"Good," Johnny said. "I wouldn't have it any other way."

But as they climbed the basement stairs, Johnny began to wonder what, exactly, Max meant. Did he mean losing Ida to marriage, and Moses as well? Or did he mean something more—losing this sister the same way he'd lost the other one?

He recalled their visit to the cemetery, Max's near-assertion that everyone was better off with Shoe dead. Shot with her own gun, he had said. Maybe that was Max's style, to somehow use the victim's effects against her. Some kind of poetic justice. But Max seemed too self-serving for vengeance, too self-absorbed. Maybe he just needed Shoe out of the way in order to get to his son.

Either way, Ida was another matter. She was going along with Max's plan. She was not in the way as her big sister had been. Johnny was.

Dinner went late, thanks to Max, a far better conversationalist than any Tumarkin could ever hope to be. Several times Max posed a question to one of Johnny's parents, waited until they'd started talking, then reached under the table for Ida, sitting next to him. Each time, Johnny watched her twitch.

At nine, Ida and Max put Moses to bed at nine, then she walked Max out to his car. When she returned, Johnny pretended not to notice she was still buttoning up her blouse. She came over to the couch and tapped him on the shoulder, and together they crept out to the backyard with two dozen plastic eggs, already filled with candy.

They had always loved the hunt. The Easter egg hunt in particular had been no-holds-barred competition for years and years, until Johnny was twelve, Ida sixteen, and their parents announced there would be no more hunts. They said they'd gotten too violent—Johnny had tackled Ida at least twice the year before and she'd jumped on his back—and besides, weren't they a bit embarrassed to still be hunting Easter eggs at their age?

Johnny and Ida had looked at one another blankly. No, they realized, they weren't embarrassed. Until then, they hadn't given it a moment's thought. And Shoe had never let on anything was wrong, though now that they thought of it, she had held back for the last few years and mostly shouted incitements to them.

"Never mind," Ida had said to him then. "Someday we'll have kids and the fun can start all over again."

Fifteen years later, they hadn't had kids, but Johnny still recalled the hiding places, both the places he had looked first as a child, and the places he hadn't thought to look. Now, hiding his dozen eggs, he chuckled to himself, little congratulatory chuckles, hoping Ida might turn around and admire some of his spots. But Ida was lost in thought.

"I've been mulling over something you asked me yesterday," Johnny said, to draw her out. "You asked me if I inventory myself."

Ida nodded. She stood in the center of the lawn, an old woven Easter basket in the crook of one arm. Her hair had been up at dinner, but now it was down, he noticed, falling around her shoulders. She was, maybe, a little gorgeous after all.

"I have no idea what you're talking about," Johnny said. "Do you inventory yourself?"

Ida shook her head, but drifted toward him. "Here," she said, and one by one, transferred her remaining eggs into his basket. "I'm feeling uninspired. But I like to watch you."

She followed at his elbow as he crossed back and forth, surveying various locations. "I was talking about sex," she said.

"You mean performance?"

"No," she said. "I mean body parts."

Johnny turned to look at her.

"What I mean is," Ida clarified, "do you take stock of your penis?"

Johnny shook his head. "It takes stock of me," he said.

"You don't think of it in relation to other men's."

Johnny shook his head again.

"You don't take pride in it."

"Well." Johnny smiled.

"You have all those opportunities to compare," she said. "In lavatories."

"You mean the size?"

"That, and whether it's good-looking."

Johnny burst out laughing. Ida tried laughing too.

"Because you see, I've got no innate sense about that kind of thing. I might recognize a really ugly penis if I saw one, but I don't think I'd know if one was beautiful. And I wondered what the criteria might be."

"I don't think there are any," Johnny said. "Beauty's in the eye of the beholder. Besides, you're the artist. Maybe the beautiful penis is the one you want to paint."

Ida was silent for a moment. Johnny was fairly sure she had never painted a penis in her life.

"If I were a man," she said slowly, "I don't think I'd talk about my penis. I don't think I'd admire it. I don't think I'd have a personal relationship with it."

"Does Max?"

"Oh," she said. "Who knows." She lifted a blue egg from Johnny's basket, opened the lid on the gas grill and laid it inside. "He accused me of ruining Mom and Dad's anniversary."

"How? I thought they had a fine time."

"I didn't ruin it for them," she said. "I ruined it for Max."

They stood in the spring darkness, eyeing one another.

"He wanted it to be perfect," she explained, and a weird smile played at the edges of her mouth. "He says I could be perfect too, if I just took my pills."

"What pills?"

"This new drug for people with social anxiety disorder." Ida smiled weirdly again. "It's easily treatable."

"Have you got social anxiety disorder?"

"Apparently."

Johnny lifted the last egg, bright orange, from the basket. He set it between two large rocks in the garden wall, then sank onto one of them. Ida sank onto the other.

"I guess that's bad."

"Apparently. I mean, it's a disorder and all."

"Shyness is a disorder?"

"I'm not just shy. I'm debilitated." Ida looked at him. "That's what the doctor said."

"Which doctor?"

"Dr. Milton. Same one as Mom's."

"So he wrote you a prescription too?"

"He did," she said. "I just haven't filled it."

"Why not?"

Ida looked worried. "Do you think I should?"

"No. I just wondered why you haven't."

"I'm not sure why," she said slowly, "but I suspect because Max asked me to."

"Ha!" Johnny slapped her on the knee, but Ida shook her head.

"I'm not being contrary. I don't care about taking a stand, like Shoe, or being independent. I just want Max to love me the way I am."

Johnny considered this distinction, and whether it mattered. Motive is everything, Shoe used to say, but if some kinds of independence were unintentional, were they less real for that? Ida could say she had no interest in taking a stand, but in her own way, she took one every day. Maybe her insistence on remaining herself was her so-called disorder.

He thought back to something else Max had said to him that afternoon in the cemetery: Ida has a right to change.

Sure she does, thought Johnny. A right, not an obligation. He was about to say this when Ida broke the silence.

"I know I'm different from other people." Her voice was low, her face pleading. She took a deep breath and went on. "The trouble is, I've never known why it matters. I have never understood, with all the things that go on in this world, why I am such a crime. Have you?"

What Johnny wanted was to pull her close and, if she felt like it, let her rest her head on his shoulder. But they were not a physical family. Only Shoe had broken free of that with her fierce bear hugs and unpredictable kisses. She had willed herself not to worry about overstepping her bounds, but Johnny still worried. So instead of slipping an arm around his sister, he just shook his head.

CHAPTER TWENTY

Easter morning, Johnny woke to a small hand gripping his shoulder. He opened his eyes and saw Moses standing there.

"Come on," Moses said.

Johnny thought he must be ready for his hunt. "Don't you want to wait for Grandma and Granddad?" Johnny asked. "They'll want to watch too."

"There isn't time," Moses said.

Johnny stumbled to the bathroom and, standing over the toilet, regarded his penis in dawn's early light. It was the proper shape. When called upon, it performed its functions. Johnny had no complaints. But should he take more pride in it? Would that lead to more pride in his manliness? If it did, would the world which never made entire sense to him fall into place, the way it had for Max? Did he want it to and should it?

Johnny made his way downstairs, where Ida was stooped over the kitchen table, dashing off a note to their parents. She looked up at him from under a straw hat—

Emily's hat—and smiled.

"So you're coming after all," she said. "I thought maybe you'd sleep in, since you went yesterday."

"Went where?" Johnny said.

"To the cemetery."

Johnny had not known they were going to the cemetery.

"What about the Easter egg hunt?" he said.

"When we get back," she said.

On the walk, Johnny and Ida tried to stroll, to watch the dew sparkle, to smell the April morning air, but Moses was impatient. He tugged on both their arms.

"Come on," he said. "We're gonna miss it."

"Miss what?" said Ida.

"The resurrection," he said, and shot ahead of them.

Ida, who had been sauntering toward the cemetery with an insouciant smile, distracted by her tight new dress, almost bored, lost that smile and stopped in her tracks. "Moses," she called. "That was two thousand years ago."

"Not Jesus," shouted Moses, dancing side to side now and almost frantic. "Mom!"

There is little to do when awaiting a resurrection. Johnny had no previous experience in such matters, and scant faith in this one occurring, so he looked to his nephew for clues on how to behave. Moses stretched out on his side in the grass that covered his mother's grave, the same way he used to stretch out on her bed in the middle of the day. Johnny sat beside the grave, his knees up, his back propped against the side of his father's stone. Ida sank down slowly, careful to keep her knees together so her underwear wouldn't show.

There seemed to be nothing particularly sacred in the vigil. They talked about fishing and plucked at blades of grass and wondered how it was that Moses knew so much about Christ's passion, and people rising from the dead.

"That's not all," said Moses, chock-full of stories. "The first Moses, when he was born, it was a dangerous time because the king was killing little Jewish boys. So his mother, she was scared and made a basket and coated it with pitch and then she put him in it and put it on the river and he floated away until a princess found him in the reeds. He was raised to be a prince of Egypt. But in the end, he came back to his people. He led them to the promised land."

"Where did you learn this stuff?" Johnny asked him. "I know they didn't teach you this at school."

"No," Moses said proudly. "Henry taught me." And it came out that in the last few weeks, while Ida had been slipping down to Cincinnati, Moses had been slipping off to visit his friend on the south edge of town.

"He's lonely," Moses said, and stole a look at his aunt.

Ida glanced up the hill toward where Henry lived, just a dash along the brick road and through the woods. Then she glanced down at her tight dress and away.

Johnny got to his feet and gestured for his sister to follow him. They left Moses at the grave and headed downhill, past a row of children's graves with little stone lambs on top, then across the unmown grass, long and fine and glossy, still damp with dew. They stopped when they were out of earshot.

"Do you think we should tell him?" Johnny asked.

"He won't believe us. Better if he finds out for himself."

"This'll take all day," Johnny said.

"I've got no plans," Ida said.

They laughed.

"It's very sweet," she said.

Johnny nodded.

"But I suppose it can't end well," she added.

Johnny shook his head.

"There's nothing for it," she said. "Far as I can see."

They heard a car's engine at the cemetery gate, turned and saw their parents. Professor Tumarkin rolled down his window as the car approached them.

"We thought we'd pay a visit too," he called.

So began the family's Easter vigil. Ida's coffeecake was transported to the cemetery and everyone sat down beside the family headstones and ate it. Later in the morning there were games of Go Fish and SlapJack in the grass. A few people walked by in their Easter best, offering fresh flowers to their departed and strange looks to the Tumarkins, but no one in the family appeared to mind except Mrs. Tumarkin, who smoothed her skirt each time and turned away her face.

When Ida and Johnny went back to the house for lunch, Ida changed out of her new dress. She returned to the kitchen in bermuda shorts and a sleeveless blouse older than she was, patterned with large pink and gold flowers. She had wrapped her hair in a pale pink chiffon scarf and carried a large straw bag that said MEXICO on the side. She packed a sack lunch for Moses and put it in the bag, along with some Easter candy and a Monopoly game that poked out the top, between the handle loops. When they left the house she put on her rhinestone-studded cat's-eye sunglasses, then slipped her arm through Johnny's as they walked.

At the cemetery, they spent the next three hours playing Monopoly. Moses was the pistol, in honor of his mother, who had always chosen that piece when she was alive.

When the adults needed to use the restroom, they walked over to the park nearby. But Moses was unwilling to let the grave out of his sight for a single minute. When he needed to go, and he only went twice, he walked backward from the grave, keeping his eyes fixed on his mother's stone, and slipped among the nearest weedy trees that fringed the cemetery property. At the last possible moment, he turned his back on the grave, swung his eyes over his shoulder, and peed.

The second time, he was spied out by a passerby. The woman turned and looked at Ida and Johnny, lounging beside the Monopoly board.

"Don't you have any respect for the dead?" she demanded.

Johnny changed five of his yellow tens for a fifty in powder blue before he looked at the woman. "I think the better question," he said, "is whether the dead have any respect for us."

She stood a moment longer, while Moses rearranged his pants and rezipped his fly, then hurried on. "Some parents," she threw back at them.

The sun sank behind the trees on the cemetery's west end, and kept on sinking. The grandparents began to discuss dinner. Johnny thought they could set up a hibachi and barbecue there, but Professor Tumarkin said that was going too far. Besides, said Mrs. Tumarkin, she and Ida had an Easter dinner all ready to go.

Let's wait a little longer, Ida said.

They waited until the sun had dropped from view. Finally Moses rose to his feet. "We can go now," he told them. He marched slowly down the hill, into the deeper shadows, and climbed into the backseat of the car. Johnny and Ida trailed silently behind, then piled in on either side of him, not touching, but close enough that he might feel some warmth from their bodies. Professor Tumarkin got behind the wheel and turned the car back toward the gate.

It had been a clean and sparkling day. Throughout, Johnny had seen the lines between and around things clearly. Once the light had left the tops of the cemetery trees, though, dusk seemed to settle on the little valley quickly. Everything smudged and lost color. The fine young leaves went indistinct.

"Mom isn't God," Moses announced.

Professor Tumarkin had stopped before exiting the cemetery. He dug around in his pants pocket, extracted a large white handkerchief, and loudly blew his nose. Then he turned slowly onto the highway and accelerated up the hill.

Ida slipped a sunburned arm around Moses, but though the sun was gone she still wore her cat's-eye sunglasses and kept her face turned firmly to her window. Mrs. Tumarkin pulled a tissue from her purse and dabbed once, neatly, at each eye.

Moses looked around the car at everyone. "Even when Jesus resurrected, he didn't stick around for long," he said.

Nobody met his eyes but Johnny. They gazed at one another and then, like men on horseback, beyond.

CHAPTER TWENTY-ONE

Monday afternoon, Ida and Moses dropped Johnny at the airport, then drove to the Cincinnati zoo. It was a long drive, and Ida spent most of it wondering if she ought to call Max to join them, but she wasn't ready to face him yet. Yesterday's mood hadn't worn away. Her head was not right. He wouldn't want her like this.

Moses had never been to a zoo before. Everything amazed him, and his amazement was infectious. They left the front gates at a run to see the elephants, but stopped once for an ostrich, then a giraffe, and soon were stopping for everything. When Ida and Moses came upon the massive walrus, they both stared in disbelief. It spouted water through its air holes, and they laughed so hard that people turned away from the animal to study them instead.

Ida spoke in a fake European accent, one she was too shy to use on Max. They ate stale cotton candy. They lay on the grass, raising their limbs in the air and wriggling them like spiders, then holding their stomachs when they laughed too long. When a peacock strolled by, Moses jumped to his feet and began to stalk it. Without meaning to, he took on the movements of the bird. His head swept back and forth and he strutted with small, flat steps. Lying in the April sun watching him, Ida realized those things she had expected love to bring her—helpless laughter, unbridled, galloping joy—love had brought. But it was Moses who brought them, not Max.

It was love, with Max; it just wasn't love as she'd imagined it.

Life was large with Max, but the scale of that life seemed to dwarf her. Ida knew now she was not large. She could try to stretch herself to fit, she had and she would, but she wondered if she ever could be large enough. Could any woman? Could Shoe?

Ida rose to her feet and trailed after Moses, content just to watch him. They came upon another telephone, and Ida realized she had to call. Max would find out about the zoo one way or another, from Moses if not from her. If Moses told him first, there would be no explaining her way out. What could she say?

I didn't want to see you. I wasn't right in the head.

Why not, darling, he would ask her. What was the matter?

I missed my brother.

I missed my sister.

I realized I was in love with your son.

Or worse still: I felt too much like myself.

She took up the receiver and punched in his number, keeping one eye on Moses. When he turned back to look at her, she motioned him over. The answering machine came on. Ida smiled.

"It's me," she said sweetly. "We're in town, at the zoo. Wish you could be here with us. I would've called you sooner, but we did this on the spur of the moment..."

That was almost true. She prattled on, trying for lightness, brightness, not even knowing what she said as the words spilled forth, then stopped and held out the phone to Moses. He put the receiver to his ear, listened hard, then brought the rest of the piece to rest against his chin.

"Yesterday was Easter," he began. "We spent the whole day—"

Moses looked up at her. "I got the beep," he said, and handed her back the phone.

"Aha," Ida said. Good, she thought.

But driving home, she realized it didn't matter, what came over the machine. The problem wasn't how Max found out yesterday's sin, which he would find out soon enough anyway, but in the sin itself—not just going to the cemetery this time, but waiting there for the resurrection.

Max still drove up at least once a week to visit. He said he liked their little town. He said it was sweet. And he was teaching Moses all about basketball.

Ida would send the two of them down to the court alone, then join them later, or have some special treat waiting when they got home. It seemed only right for Max to have a chance to get to know his own son, one-on-one. Moses liked Max, and when the time came to tell him Max was his father, she imagined they'd become a family quite naturally. But when Max called that evening to tell her he was coming up the next day, Ida felt almost as much dread as she did anticipation. She wondered if she ought to tell Max about the Easter vigil herself. She thought about somehow lying to Moses, or telling Moses to lie to Max, but knowing all the while that was one line she would not cross.

Max drove up on Wednesday. It was nearly five when he and Moses returned from their hour on the court, shouting and happy. Max said nothing about the weekend, but Ida couldn't relax, and when he suggested they drive out to the lake, she almost refused. There would be a confrontation, and then the place would be colored by that. They'd never want to return.

Still she went, taking his hand as she led him along the top of the earthen dam to the far end, where the water crashed over the concrete spill and the stream resumed its course far below. Ida climbed onto the metal rail that separated them from the lake, and looked out over the water. All the ice had melted. The sun was bright. She rolled up her sleeves, then swung her legs over the top rail and perched on it.

"You're sunburned," Max cried.

"That's from Sunday," Ida said. "First burn of the season."

She smiled hopefully at Max and gestured out onto the lake. "In the winter, sometimes it freezes up enough to ice-skate. I used to dream that someday I'd have a pond almost this big in my backyard. Then on Christmas Eve we'd go out with a long pushbroom and sweep away the snow and everyone would ice-skate until midnight."

"Everyone" wasn't anyone Ida knew in real life—not yet—but she felt she would. The dream was too real not to come true. And there was more, of course. There was a moon, and stars, and gentle white flakes falling from the black night sky. There was music spilling across the ice, and a few people dancing. They drank hot chocolate and peppermint schnapps from a thermos and the steam rose up before their faces and disappeared. There were hills beyond the pond, evergreens and wild animals and, from the house, bright points of colored Christmas lights.

There was merriment, joy and laughter. There was a way of life, where people wore long underwear all winter and wrapped their heads in hand-knitted mufflers and somebody out on the lake, somebody Ida loved well—or would one day—wore a big old hat with earflaps, and hummed off-key. It was one of the lives she'd dreamed for herself. She had seen it clearly and painted what she saw, as she had painted many of the lives she'd dreamed of one day living.

Maybe that's what Emily meant, she thought suddenly. Maybe the painting she found in that thrift store was one of those lives, and I didn't save hers; I let her borrow one of my lives after she'd run out of her own.

Max stepped behind Ida and wrapped his arms around her stomach. He rested his chin on her shoulder, so that their heads were side by side. She leaned against him.

"When we live in New York," he murmured, "I'll take

you to Rockefeller Plaza every weekend. They've got an ice-skating rink right there in the middle of the city. You see it on TV all the time. Your parents can see you skating on national television. We'll buy you a skating outfit with one of those short, ruffled skirts. At Christmastime, when the place is all decorated, it's fucking fantastic."

"That sounds nice," Ida said. On the far side of the spill, two dogwoods had come into bloom. Ida started to point them out, then thought better of it. She rested her ears on the sound of the creek below, her eyes on the trees. As long as these things continued, even without her, everything would be okay.

Max brushed his mouth against her ear. "I've been thinking," he whispered, "about your mother."

"What about her?" Ida said.

"Is she getting out more?"

"I don't think so. No." The truth was that with the new medication, she was getting out less, but Ida was afraid to say this. She didn't want Max to think she was criticizing his choice in doctors.

"What does she do all day?"

"I don't know," Ida said. "Not much, I don't think."

"There's nothing for her to do," Max said. "You do it all."

Ida waited. She didn't know yet if this was going to be a criticism or a compliment. She didn't know if he was championing her or her mother.

"Is that all right?" she asked finally.

Max shrugged.

"Are you saying I usurped my mother's job?"

Max shrugged again. "Not usurped," he said. "But maybe that's why she's depressed."

"I thought you thought I did the right thing, staying at home."

"Right for you," Max said. "But consider this, sweetheart. A home is like an organism. If one part isn't healthy, it affects the rest. So if it wasn't right for her, it couldn't really be right for you either."

"But I'm not what depressed her," Ida said, trying not to become upset. "It was Shoe's death that did it."

"If that's true," Max said, "it's only because your mother lived vicariously through your sister. There was a problem there before Susan died. Your mother is in perfect physical health, but she's carrying on like an invalid. She atrophied years ago. Now she can't run her own household. She can't watch her own grandson. She doesn't even know when he slips out of the house for one-, two-hour-long stretches."

Ida had not expected this. She groped for something to say.

"You knew," Max said.

She nodded.

"You didn't tell me."

Ida shook her head. "I only found out Sunday."

"When were you planning to tell me?"

Ida hesitated. She couldn't see her way to a good answer. So she shrugged.

"It slipped your mind?"

Shrugging had been the wrong choice. Sometimes there was more than one wrong choice. Sometimes there was no right one. But Max let it go.

"This is the last time we're leaving him alone with her," he announced. "And another thing. I asked him how many times he snuck out on your mother's watch. Only twice, he told me, but I think he's lying, already, to protect people. Now the disturbed organism that is your home is infecting him too. Already."

Ida swallowed. She could feel her face burning.

"It's not your fault," Max said. "But it isn't healthy. How could it be, when your own mother resents you?"

Ida spun around to face him and lost her balance on the rail. She fell backwards, but Max caught her and lowered her down to the grass. She lay on her back, staring up at the cloudless spring sky, until Max's face loomed over her.

"Are you all right?" he asked.

Ida shook her head.

"That's why I think the sooner we get you out of there, the better for everyone involved."

Ida cradled her stomach and curled onto her side.

"Darling," Max said. "I thought you knew all this already."

Ida said nothing. But when Max studied her, she felt his scrutiny and sat up. When he continued his study, she rose to her feet and made a show of brushing herself off.

"I'm not making this up," he said, laughing slightly. "Your mother told me she felt that way—toward her own daughter. And she's telling me! I thought it was irresponsible at the time, but after this incident with Moses, I see just how irresponsible she is."

Ida tapped his arm. "Let's go," she said.

"What for?" said Max. "We just got here."

Ida started away without him. She walked the length of the dam, and then on to the parking lot before she turned and looked back. Max was moving toward her, though far behind. When he reached the car, he unlocked her door without a word and walked around to his side. Ida got in.

"You can't expect me to be happy to hear this," she said.

Max was angry. "I don't want you to be happy. I didn't tell you this to make you happy. I told you this because it concerns our son. And I told you for your own good. But you just killed the messenger."

He started up the engine, but before he could put the car into reverse, Ida leaned over and placed her hand on his.

"I'm sorry," she said.

Max would not look at her. He moved the gear shift and they rolled out of the lot. Neither spoke again until they were halfway to town.

"I forgive you," he said then, "because your family is so strange. I think you failed to learn certain kinds of etiquette. Maybe that's not your fault."

Ida felt as if someone had stuck her with an IV. Drip by drip, her veins flooded with indignation. It forced her eyes open wide, and then her mouth. She had to clench her jaw to keep from speaking, while she fumbled in her bag for her old sunglasses to hide her eyes. She didn't want Max to see this expression and ask why she had the wrong look on her face.

"Anyway," Max continued, "your mother was only

half the problem with this particular incident. That cocksucking Catholic 'friend' of yours needs to keep the fuck away from my son. If it weren't for him, Sunday never would have happened."

Ida had already decided not to argue with him about Sunday, not to suggest Sunday was perhaps a good thing or that she, for one, would probably hold that particular Easter dear for years to come.

"I doubt Henry ever said that come Easter Shoe would rise from the dead."

"Well, Ida," Max shouted, "we'll never know what he said, will we? It's bad enough his name is Moses, but now I have to hear him recount the entire Old Testament while we're out shooting hoops. And what the hell is 'pitch'?"

"I think it's like tar."

For a moment, Max's expression went blank. Then he scowled again.

"God only knows how many years before all this Judeo-Christian crap gets purged from his head."

"You know, Max," Ida said, "you can't really blame Henry for this. Most of the country is Christian. Resurrection is an appealing notion to anyone."

"Anyone who fucked up this life."

"Religion's here to stay," Ida said.

"You're still protecting that fuck!"

"I'm not protecting anybody."

"Take off those sunglasses. I can't see your eyes."

Ida took them off.

"Thank you," Max said. "Those things make you look about fifty years old."

"Someday I'll be fifty years old."

"But you won't look fifty," he said.

"Not till I'm fifty-five."

Max smiled. They'd come upon a long white fence with horses running on the other side when he pulled over suddenly. Beyond rolling hills, she could see the steeple on one of the town's churches.

"Why did you take Moses?"

"When?"

"That time with the horses, after dark. You took Moses with you."

Ida groped for his meaning. "It wasn't a date," she said finally.

Max made a face. "I hope to God you never dated that guy. I meant, why did you take Moses inside the fence with you?"

"So he could feel them," Ida said.

Max laughed. "Couldn't you just take him to a petting zoo?"

It was Ida's turn to laugh.

"Understand me," Max said. "You were magnificent. But you endangered yourself and Moses. Darling, they could've trampled you both to death."

"They could have," Ida said. "But they never would have. That was the point."

He popped the car back into gear and pulled back onto the county road.

"I don't get it," he said.

Ida had always expected to unfold before her lover as

effortlessly as the petals of a poppy before the morning sun. But though Max loved her, he didn't really approve of her. Since the zoo, Ida had begun to wonder if whatever it was she fell in love with in Max was whatever he'd handed on to Moses, if the best part of the father was just shades of the son. But thinking this did her no good at all.

I love Max, she told herself. And Moses is a little boy.

Lately it seemed to Ida as if she'd become almost as scared as Shoe—in her case, loving a little boy because she was scared of grown men. She wasn't scared of Johnny or her father, true, but they were blood relations and did not count. Henry didn't really count, either. She had never thought of him as a hot-blooded man the way that Max was. To have a real man would take some getting used to, she saw that now, but it was the only way that she would ever become a real woman. Each time she doubted Max, she reproved herself: Max had to be the one.

"God only sends the lifeboat around once," she wrote down on a scrap of paper. She had heard that somewhere. She taped those words above her desk.

"Whosoever loses his life shall find it," she scribbled on another scrap. She had heard that one, or something like it, in church once with Henry. These words she didn't tape above her desk, though, for fear Max might see them and think she was becoming religious.

It's now or never, Ida thought. I've made my resolution. I can do this. And so I shall.

In the bedroom, her determination served her well. She watched his videos and viewed his magazines with an impassive, knowing face. Some of it was interesting, some of it was silly. Some of it disgusted her and some of it she liked. But no matter what she thought or felt, she paid attention. She studied smut with the kind of absorption she had once given to her painting. She knew, now, that there would be a test.

Smut embarrassed her. Not the sexual acts themselves, but the show that seemed to surround them. Max wanted her to talk about these acts, so at first Ida tried to describe them in strictly physical terms. But there wasn't much to that, so she abandoned the facts and instead spun out a little Max-style story, with a setting and a plot line for the two of them. The plot line wasn't overly involved. She tried to keep the events relevant to the activity at hand. If something curious happened back there behind her mind's eye, if she came across distracting details, she left them out.

One day after they had finished, he ran them a warm bath. When he climbed in to join her, Ida moved to the opposite end of the tub, and fit herself in next to the faucet. They lay in the water, immobile, seemingly stricken and admiring one another. She wondered if he might finally take her.

"Do you want me?" she said.

"Always." Max bit his upper lip and stared at her. "Always, Ida."

"Once we're married, Moses might get suspicious if we lock ourselves up in the bathroom like this."

"He's suspicious now," Max said.

They laughed.

"Take down your hair," Max said.

Ida took down her hair. The ends dragged gently through the water.

"You like my feet?" she asked.

"I love your feet," Max said.

Ida lifted her left foot and placed it between his legs.

"You don't think they're rough?" she said. "Unsightly?"

Max shook his head. She waggled her toes against him. They watched together for a little while, then Max's eyes closed and Ida watched alone.

"Good," she said.

CHAPTER TWENTY-TWO

Ten days after his visit home, Johnny called from Utah.

"Good God," Ida said. "You again."

"Still want to spend your life with him?"

"Ten years."

Johnny snorted. "And then you're going to kill yourself?"

"No," Ida said slowly. "And then he's going to die."

"Then all hope isn't lost."

Ida was silent.

"When you talked to Emily, did she tell you why Shoe left him?"

"She started to. I didn't let her finish."

"What did she say?"

"She said he didn't like Shoe's feet. But I don't have that problem."

"What are you saying?"

"I'm saying he likes my feet. He thinks I have attractive feet. And as long as he thinks that, we'll be fine."

"Ida." Johnny made a half-formed noise and she

could tell that he was groping for the right words. "Listen."

"I'm listening."

"Thanks. Ida. I'm not convinced you love this guy."

"Don't be foolish."

"Do you love him?"

"Of course I love him. I told you before, Johnny. Max is the most amazing man in the world. If I can't love him, I'll never love anybody."

"Now you're talking crazy."

"He's top of the heap. Cream of the crop. King of the hill."

Johnny laughed softly.

"Besides," she said. "I already made up my mind."

"That's what an engagement is for," Johnny said, "to give you an opportunity to change it."

"I'm bound and determined," Ida said. "I can take it."

"This is a marriage we're talking about. What you're talking about sounds more like a military mission. Which you don't have to choose to accept, by the way. You can decline any time."

"I'm committed," Ida said.

"You're talking funny. Are you taking that drug?"

"No. I'm just funnier than I used to be."

"I noticed that," Johnny said. "But I'll tell you what I've been thinking. I've been thinking you might want to come out here for a little while. Do a little tour of the West."

"I've always wanted to tour the West," Ida said wistfully. "I've always admired that huckleberry. That fine mountain fruit."

"That's what I thought," Johnny said. "You know I'm not too far from those mountains."

"I know it well. I've perused the maps many times."

"A couple more weeks and Moses will be out of school. Then you could both come. I could show him how to use that fishing pole."

"We'll all come," she said. "Moses, me, and Max. We're like the holy trinity. Only, not holy. Not me and Max, at any rate."

"Well," Johnny said. "I was thinking this might be more like a retreat for you. A chance to think. Clear your head."

"Oh, no. Thinking will just get me into trouble. Much like this conversation."

"You're doing it again," Johnny said.

Ida sighed.

"Ignoring a problem doesn't make it go away."

"Oh, you should talk."

"I should?"

"Don't make me say her name. At least in my case, there isn't any other option. Plus there's Moses to consider."

"That's what I mean," Johnny said.

"What do you mean?"

"I mean I think you might be doing this to hold on to Moses."

"Oh, no," she said. "Moses isn't going anywhere."

"Has it ever occurred to you he might be courting you just to get close to Moses?"

"Gee, thanks. You asked me that already. Ad nauseum, in fact."

"I'm serious, Ida."

"I know," she said. "It must be hard for you to fathom why a man would want me."

Johnny ignored this. "Has it ever crossed your mind—" his voice shook, and he took a moment to steady it "—the possibility that Max had Shoe killed just to get to his son?"

Ida laughed. "I miss you," she said. "Even though you don't respect me."

"This is serious," Johnny said.

"Dead serious," said Ida. "Just like Max."

"Ida," Johnny said. "You're scaring me."

"Don't be scared," she said. "I'm not."

CHAPTER TWENTY-THREE

The call came from the Boulder County Sheriff's Department the very next day: They had picked up a man wanted in connection with Shoe's murder, living in Las Vegas under an assumed identity. His fingerprints had been lifted from Shoe's truck, and there was more evidence connecting him to the drug dealer, possibly killed with her gun. They would know more soon, the detective told Professor Tumarkin. Shoe might have just been an innocent bystander, in the wrong place at the wrong time. This was what Johnny had believed all along—until he met Max.

The same day Johnny's father phoned him with this news, Johnny phoned Emily. That Friday, she drove north and he drove south to reach Flagstaff, where the snow was still heavy on the mountains outside town, the spring flowers just coming into bloom. They met at a run-down bar near the railroad tracks, where freight trains rushed past in the dark to drown out their conversation, and the special was orange Kool-Aid spiked with vodka. Johnny arrived first, ordered two, and carried the drinks in their plastic football cups to a booth near the front, where he could wait and watch for her.

The drink was vile but oddly tasty, and Johnny enjoyed his for several minutes before it occurred to him that all the ice in Emily's drink would melt and dilute the Kool-Aid before she could enjoy it. He was in the process of transferring the ice cubes from her cup to his when she arrived.

"Ice thief," she said.

Johnny had meant to leap to his feet and embrace her, but it was too late. Emily had already slipped into the booth across from him. She unbuttoned her jacket, laid her right hand on the table, then covered it with her left. Her hair was much shorter than it had been at the funeral. It swung away from her head in a lively, fetching fashion.

"Long time no see," said Emily.

Johnny nodded.

"How's tricks?" she asked.

"Tricks." Johnny nodded again. "Pretty tricky."

"Is that mine?"

He pushed the drink across the table toward her. Emily tasted it. She made a face, licked her lips, then tasted it again.

"I love it," she said. "All it needs is some ice."

Johnny lifted his spoon just as a waitress appeared with chips and salsa. He waited until she set them down and went away again, then began a slow transfer of ice cubes from his own cup back to Emily's.

"So," she said, supervising. "You wanted to see me."

"Yes," Johnny said. "Thanks for coming."

He stole a look at her face, but her eyes were carefully fixed on the movement of ice. Suddenly she raised a hand.

"That's enough," she said. "Thanks."

Of course, Emily had already heard the news—Johnny had told her about the apprehended suspect earlier that week when he phoned. But he had wanted to talk it over in person.

"I wanted Max to be the killer," he confessed. "It seemed like a handy way to solve the problem."

"Which problem?"

"The Max problem."

"He's already got a girlfriend," Emily said. "Maybe that'll help."

A train screamed past. Johnny waited while Emily picked a tortilla chip from the paper-lined basket between them. She dunked it in salsa, shook it carefully, and devoured it before the noise faded and she could go on.

"I made some phone calls. Just in case. Didn't turn up much of interest, except a former girlfriend he lived with in college. Asked her if Max was capable of murder. She had this laugh like Santa Claus—ho, ho, ho—and said he was an egomaniacal prick, not a felon. But then she told me something really intriguing."

Emily paused to reach for another chip.

"Looks like the girl he left her for—this would be at least ten years ago, mind you—looks like they're still together. She said she saw them at a party last Christmas, holding hands."

"No," said Johnny.

"That's what I said. 'Ho, ho, ho,' she said. 'Yes.' After she spotted the two of them she left the party and didn't come back until they were gone. Said it might've been ten years, but that still didn't mean she had to talk to him."

"Has he been with this woman the whole time?"

"Dunno," said Emily. "But if he has been…"

If he had been, the math was easy enough. Not only was Max two-timing with Ida; he'd been two-timing with Shoe.

"It's good news, really," Emily said. "Between that and the police getting their man, we should be celebrating."

But instead, they sat across from one another in their booth and did not speak. Johnny looked out into the room. Emily studied a tiny scar along her index finger.

"I wanted Max to be the killer," he repeated. "I would've liked it better."

"I know," said Emily. "But you should be glad he's not. It would've been terrible for Moses."

"It's terrible anyway. His mother's still dead. His father's just a prick who'll never be convicted. At least if Max was the killer, he could do time. And we'd know she couldn't have helped it, that she was just a victim."

Emily raised her gaze from the scar to him. "Don't piss me off," she said.

"You know what I'm saying. You knew my sister as well as anyone did."

"We've had this conversation," Emily said. "I'm not

having it again. Just because Max didn't murder Shoe does not make it her fault. She was in the wrong place at the wrong time. It could've happened to anyone."

"Not to anyone."

"If you need to forgive her, then forgive her. As far as I'm concerned, there's nothing to forgive." She slid out of the booth. "Let's shoot some pool or get out of here."

He rose and followed her into the narrow back room. They shot and drank, shot and drank, long swallows of Kool-Aid in steady succession. When they had finished off the first round, they ordered refills through an opening in the cement-block wall. The bartender poured more liquid from a pitcher on the counter and handed back the football cups, then as an afterthought, the pitcher. They proceeded to get drunk.

Several times they wandered over to the love meter against one wall, where Johnny fed in a quarter and gripped the outstretched plastic hand. The machine measured his prowess as a lover, and registered something different each time.

"You are inconstant," Emily finally concluded. "But getting hotter, on the whole."

When other people showed up, they moved to the front room for a slovenly game of checkers, followed by Battleship and Indian poker. At midnight, they drifted into the back room once more and sat down at the piano, their backs to the pool players, side by side. Emily bent her head over the keyboard and began to pick out a tune, something pretty and a little sad—like her, Johnny thought.

They weren't really alone anymore, but they could pretend. When they were together they were able to shut out everyone and everything else. It seemed to him they became their own island, corporation, kingdom, and this was the way it had always been with Emily. He wanted to tell her this.

"We were the only ones who could have saved her," he said instead.

"That kind of thing doesn't always work."

"What kind of thing?"

"Saving. Saviors. Being saved."

"It does," said Johnny. "You'd know it does if you'd ever been saved."

Emily stopped playing. Her head fell back and she gazed into the shadows on the ceiling. "I was saved."

"Who saved you?"

"Shoe," she said, and resumed her song on the piano. "Ida, and then Shoe."

Johnny was jealous. He turned his face away and looked around the room. It was narrow and small, with just space enough for two pool tables, one old piano, a broken pinball machine and the love meter. The bartender's square face appeared through the hole in the wall, scanned the crowd, then disappeared again. Somebody at the table behind them racked up, and Emily and Johnny had to lean in opposite directions to let him break. Afterwards, they drew back together again, closer than before.

"The problem," Emily resumed, "is we're not talking about one big save, not with Shoe. She needed lots of little rescues, over and over."

"That's right," Johnny said.

"You couldn't be there every time."

Johnny had saved his sister more than once, but few people knew that because he never wrestled an assailant to the ground. Shoe didn't need an action hero, just someone to keep her distracted so she didn't run toward danger with open arms. He believed that keeping her from the killer's reach would've entailed very little, probably just sitting in the cab of the truck with her and pointing in the opposite direction when the guy showed up around the bend. By making conversation, by occupying her brain sufficiently, Johnny was sure he could've saved her yet again.

"And you know what?" Emily added. "You didn't need to be. She was figuring things out. Did you know she wanted to be a minister?"

"A what?"

"A minister. She was going back to school. I'm telling you, Johnny, she was making plans to live. Not to die."

It was late. They leaned into one another. But soon Emily got to her feet and yawned.

"I'm exhausted," she announced.

Johnny was exhausted too. They left the bar and walked the three blocks to their cheap motel, this time with separate beds. When Johnny went to use the toilet, he was careful not to break the seal. He slid it off with care to give to Emily, but when he emerged from the bathroom, she was already in her bed, a small shape under the ugly quilted bedspread.

Instead of curtains, their hotel window was hung with a venetian blind, so plenty of cold white fluorescent light from the street could seep into the room. Johnny looked over to where she lay in the half-light and felt more than lonely. He felt forlorn. He wanted to talk to Emily about Emily, but he did not know how. They were like two supporting actors without their lead. They'd have to relearn everything without Shoe.

Maybe in the morning they could take a drive up into the snow, or to the Painted Desert, or even back to the Grand Canyon, he thought, reprising a trip they'd done years before. Maybe they wouldn't speak for hours—that would be all right. The whole weekend stretched before them. He lay against the puffy motel pillow, very still, and tried to detect the rhythm of Emily's breathing, but the sounds of night traffic on the highway running beneath their window were too loud, and she was too far away, besides.

When he woke in the morning, Emily was gone. At the bathroom sink, under a half-filled cup of water, she had left a note.

"See you at the trial," she wrote. "Whenever that is."

Johnny folded the note and put it in his pocket.

He doubted there would be a trial. Even if there were, he doubted the man on trial for his sister's murder would know what Johnny wanted to know: Had she been glad to go? And which was worse—wanting to die when you should go on living, or wanting to live and then being killed? He recalled the last conversation he'd had with

Shoe, about a month before she died.

"I've been lonely most my life," she had said, "always looking for someone who understood. Lately, I've begun to suspect God might understand."

"Really?" Johnny had forgotten that his sister was not an atheist, like him, that she'd never disdained faith, exactly; she had disdained people who relied on God for anything, including the companionship she craved so badly. The only way to have a true faith, she used to say, was to believe without needing to believe. Otherwise, faith was self-serving and suspect.

"I need someone to know my thoughts," she had said. "Someone I can trust. God's very convenient for this purpose, I realize. But I'm no longer convinced that my need for God proves God isn't out there."

Johnny wondered if she'd gone to her death believing in such a God. For her sake, he hoped so. But it was meager comfort to a man who did not believe in such a God himself.

CHAPTER TWENTY-FOUR

The weekend Shoe turned thirty-four, she decided to go up on the mountain and think things through. She had high hopes for thirty-four. She thought it might mark a significant turning point in her life, and it did.

She left on Saturday morning with sufficient munitions for two nights on the mountain, three days. Jasper, the head chef, and his New Age-manager-girlfriend Isis took Moses for the weekend. In exchange, Shoe took their Australian shepherd, Exene. They said Exene needed the exercise, but Shoe knew they sent her along for protection. Recalling the dog was prone to flatulence, Shoe made her ride in the truckbed.

Saturday she and the dog hiked up in rain, then lightning, passing timberline in mid-afternoon, just as the storm blew over. They pitched camp about six.

With no wood to burn, she sat on a rock and cooked a packet of freeze-dried shrimp Creole over her camp stove. Exene wandered off and then returned with the skeleton of some small animal clamped between her jaws.

A pink tinge remained where the head once joined on.

Shoe listened to Exene gnaw the bones. When the dog grew bored with that, she began circling in on Shoe, tight and then tighter, the white bones of the deceased animal jutting out on all sides of her mouth, looking stupid and creepy at the same time.

Finally Shoe set down her fork. "Get away from me," she said flatly.

Instead, Exene got right in her face. Shoe jumped to her feet. They chased each other around the fire until Shoe started laughing, and Exene finally dropped her prize. They watched the sun go down, then crawled into the tent, Shoe in her sleeping bag and Exene on top of Shoe's feet.

Here in close quarters, Shoe heard her panting and smelled it too, the stench of death. She turned her face into the bag, then into her own armpit to escape it. She lay like this, nearly warm as night settled in, and thought about space. Not outer space, with its floating astronauts, its asteroids, galaxies, and those black places where nothing resides. Inner space. Which, like its relative, felt to her like it was still expanding.

She'd told her bosses that she was hiking up here to get in touch with herself, but that wasn't really accurate. It wasn't herself she wanted to touch; it was all that space inside that wasn't her. Shoe suspected it might be what some people meant by God.

She happened to be of a religious inclination, though she had never received much training along those lines and maybe for this reason took some time to recognize the inclination for what it was. Professor Tumarkin had always maintained that religion weakened the walls of children's souls, however he defined those. He said if you never had God to begin with, you'd never feel the need later on, that you couldn't miss a thing you've never had. Shoe found his argument less than convincing, having missed things she'd never had all her life. In youth, she called this boredom, and thought that's all it was.

For a while, she tended to her own homegrown religion: the exquisite conversion of fear into fearlessness. She never fully understood why tempting fate made her euphoric, but that mystery was part of what made it irresistible. It had little to do with faith or anything she'd call God. It felt more like an addiction, and an unhealthy one at that. After Moses she gave it up, or tried to. Besides, plenty of fears attached themselves to Moses, fears that couldn't be confronted or converted into some transcendent feeling, fears that would take a lifetime to overcome, and not her lifetime, but his.

But though she loved the world more once her son was in it, sometimes this everyday world wasn't enough. She came to know the dimensions of the hole in her spirit, the leak in her soul, and began to ponder not simply how to fill it, but its very nature. Was her desire to confront fear a mere addiction or something more, something almost religious? What, really, was the difference between the two?

One day it finally came to her, how God and her addiction intertwined. Simply put, she was afraid of God.

This revelation took her by storm. It had never occurred to her that she could be afraid of God. She thought only God-fearing people were afraid of God. She thought she wasn't the God-fearing type, seeing as how she didn't believe in God. Yet the more she thought about it, the more it seemed to her that what she really was, God-wise, was afraid.

Her fear of God was a fear of believing in God and being wrong. This was why she'd never bothered trying—not because God didn't matter but because God mattered too much. Taking that leap of faith was just too risky. What if she took a running jump out there and then discovered it was all a big mistake? She'd fall—maybe forever.

A big old fear like that must have been there all along, Shoe thought, but she'd put off thinking about it for years. She hadn't recognized her resistance to belief for what it was. Once she did, she began to suspect her old way of life might have been leading up to this one challenge. Maybe every delicious wave that had ever washed over her when she chose to face a fear was just a precursor to what might come. Because it would have to be sweet beyond the bounds of sanity, overcoming a fear like that. Assuming one even survived.

Afterwards, of course, fear would lose any lingering charm. Fear couldn't mean much when there was nothing left to fear. And with a true belief in God, she thought, there wouldn't be. For Shoe, that prospect was like flushing the last cigarettes in the world down the toilet. Once the temptation was destroyed, she would be free.

With these things in mind, she went up on the

mountain like the original Moses to find God. All that space inside her where she was not might prove to be God's space, but secretly she was hoping for something more—nothing fancy, no burning bushes, but some kind of a sign.

Such hope was embarrassing. She understood that it was a glaring contradiction, since a real sign, any physical manifestation of God, would undermine the whole challenge of faith, and Shoe had never believed you could have your cake and eat it too. But it had taken her thirty-four years to get this far. She hoped God, if there was such a being, might take pity and meet her halfway.

She slept well through the night. Sunday morning was overcast and cold and Shoe and Exene spent most of it above timberline, hiking from one alpine lake to the next. In the early afternoon the lightning returned. In the event of a storm above timberline, guidebooks used to say to take shelter by crawling under a rock. Then the books said not to do this. They said the lightning traveled through the rock, or around it. So Shoe and Exene just kept walking.

Around three, the sky began to clear. Shoe removed her poncho and put it inside her pack. Then Exene shook out her fur and Shoe got wet anyway.

They crossed another pass in late afternoon. Below them lay an otherwordly lake with long, white fingers of rock stretching below its surface and glowing ghostly through the strange blue water. Beside the lake stood a small army of spruces. When they reached the trees, Shoe spotted the remains of a campsite. There she laid down her pack and began collecting firewood.

It took a while to smoke out the wood, but she got a good fire going before sundown, put some water on to boil, and sat down to wait for some kind of sign. Exene ate her food, then disappeared again. It was dusk and Shoe was just beginning preparations for a s'more when the dog came running back into camp with a deer head in her mouth.

The skin had been stripped from its face. All that was left was bloody meat and muscle and gaping, lidless eyes. It filled Shoe with a strange panic.

"All right, Exene," she said. "You've made your point."

Shoe chased her out of camp, and kept chasing the dog until Exene dropped the head somewhere in the woods. As they made their way back, the trunks of the trees grew indistinct. Shoe watched the darkness advance on the day and grew depressed.

She'd gone out into nature to find the God who fashioned her soul. She had climbed all those mountaintops and built that fire. She had tried to maintain internal stillness and quiet. It seemed like enough to attract God's attention, but God had never showed. Now what?

The next morning they headed back down. It was closing in on three when they passed the wooden outhouse beside the trailhead and, a second later, a guy on his way to use it. He and Shoe looked each other over. Shady, she thought, but no shadier than some of the guys she'd slept with.

"Backpacking?" he asked her.

She stopped, nodded.

"By yourself?"

Exene strained forward with a low growl. "Not really," Shoe said, and walked on.

There was a truck parked beside hers and leaning up against it, a skinny, long-haired guy about her age. She figured the two were together. She would've figured it even if there weren't only two vehicles in sight. They had the same look—played out and wound up—common to certain addicts. She gave him a slight wave, then turned her back to unlock her door. A moment later, he tapped her lightly on the shoulder.

"Can I hitch a ride with you?" He was sweating, although it was a cool day for August, and his eyes skittered around her toward something else.

Shoe turned, but all she could see was the outhouse. Then she realized that was it—he was watching the outhouse, watching for his companion to come out. This man was hoping to skip out on that one. But why?

Shoe opened the door of her truck and Exene jumped up and in. This time she let her. "Where you headed?" she asked.

"Into Nederland," he said. "My friend was supposed to pick me up out here, but I don't think he's coming."

This, she was certain, was a lie.

"Sure," she said, tossing her pack in the bed of the truck. "Hop in."

Once he was in, her passenger laid his daypack on the

floor of the truck, leaned over, and started fiddling with it. They were rolling out of the parking lot before the first guy reappeared. When he did, Shoe only saw him in her rearview mirror. He walked slowly, looked around a couple times, then came to a standstill. His eyes drifted toward her truck just before it disappeared around a bend in the dirt, but her passenger was still down there, doubled over and out of view.

Shoe counted to twenty in her head. "You can sit up now," she said.

From where he crouched, the skinny man swiveled his head to look at her. He was still sweating, though he was out of the sun.

When he did sit up again, she noticed the needle marks in the crook of his arm. Heroin, maybe, but he didn't have that look. He popped his head over his shoulder a couple times at the road behind them. Crank, she thought. Not Shoe's addict of choice, but Exene curled up on the seat between them and closed her eyes. No growls for this guy.

"Did you make your connection?" Shoe asked.

His hands were shaking. He put them to his head.

When he continued to say nothing—and what, she thought, is he going to say to me—she turned on the radio. The reception wasn't good yet, but a few more twists and turns heading east and it would be better. She didn't want to talk anyway. It had been a disappointing pilgrimage.

She let her head fall back against the headrest, suddenly tired now that she was off her feet. The sun shone warmly for the first time in days. Shoe just drove and watched the cloud of dirt that rose from the road that would lead them back home, or wherever they were headed.

That time of day, that and the light in August, always put her in mind of school, though it was more than a dozen years since she'd attended one. In just a few more weeks, at just that time, doors all over America would again swing open and children of all colors and creeds would spill out onto city sidewalks and suburban streets. For now, the children were still in the local pool or laid out in front of televisions. But the shadows were lengthening. Summer would retire soon. Shoe's own son would start first grade. He said he was looking forward to it. She made a mental note to ask him why.

Shoe was still watching the dust through the rearview mirror when she saw the other truck from the parking lot appear in it. Her traveling companion turned his head for the twentieth time and saw the truck too.

"Fuck," he said, and slunk down in his seat.

The truck, a bigger, newer one than hers, gained on them with alarming speed. Just when it was close enough that she could recognize the guy behind the wheel, he flashed his headlights.

"He wants me to stop," Shoe said.

"Don't." Her passenger was cowering beside her. "He's got a gun."

"You don't?"

He shook his head.

Shoe felt the old chill begin behind her forehead, the

first pulse so delicious her mouth dropped open. She pressed on the accelerator, but by now the guy was on her tail. With one surge, he rammed into them. It took her three or four seconds to comprehend that this was what had happened. Once she did, she turned and looked at her companion. He looked back, terrified.

But she was exquisitely happy. She had gone without the thrill of immediate danger for so long that to be visited with it now, so unexpectedly, brought tears to her eyes.

"Can you shoot?" she asked.

When he nodded, she gestured to the glove compartment.

"Roll down your window, lean out fast, and shoot out his tire."

His eyes went wide. Shoe felt the pulsing in her temple, the pulse she still could not distinguish from joy. She might not understand this feeling, but she knew it as intimately as that space inside her. This feeling belonged in that space. They remained the perfect fit.

The gun came out and with it, candy. Hershey's miniatures spilled across the floor. From the corner of her eye she spied the yellow wrapper of a Mr. Goodbar.

"Can you grab me one of those?" she asked.

Her companion turned and stared at her. He looked appalled.

"After you shoot," she added.

He rolled down the window and the truck rammed them again. Just as the two trucks parted bumpers, her companion flung his torso around the open window and fired her gun. Two shots. There were, she was fairly certain, two bullets left.

With the sound of gunfire, Exene began to bark. Shoe felt something stretching out inside of her, then realized she was laughing. She watched in her rearview mirror as the other truck swerved right and then, in what seemed like slow motion, collapsed against a tree. Shoe pulled her foot off the gas pedal and scanned the rearview mirror to see which tire he took out. Instead, on that other windshield, she saw the blood.

Exene wouldn't stop barking now, growling and barking. Shoe sank a hand into her fur and noticed the hand was shaking. She made herself speak.

"You shot him," she said.

"It was an accident."

"You weren't supposed to shoot him."

"He was a bad man."

From the corner of her eye she watched him, still handling her gun, and nodded while his head inched back toward his hands.

"I know," she said. "I know that."

Her left arm rested on the windowsill, her own open window, and she noticed now the way the breeze felt moving through the little hairs, how kind and soft the air was. It was the softest air she could remember. It seemed to bless her skin.

With one small motion, he turned the gun on her.

"Aha," she said. "How quickly we forget."

"I need the truck," he said.

"I guess so," she said.

Exene's barking continued. He was jumpy and she

thought the dog's noise probably wasn't helping.

"Shut up," he said. "I need to think."

Shoe didn't like the way he kept jerking his head at Exene. She turned up the radio to try and block out the dog's racket. Nirvana came in clean, so she knew they were closing in on civilization. Only a couple miles now until they hit pavement. Then houses would pop up, maybe even people. But there on that dirt road, they were neither in nature nor civilization. For now, she and Exene had to travel through this no-man's-land with a gun, her gun, trained on them by a killer.

"Listen," Shoe said. "You go to the police. You tell them it was self-defense."

"They won't believe it."

"They'll believe it. You've got my testimony to back you up."

Exene wouldn't stop barking.

"Can't you shut her up?"

"Let me put her in the back." Shoe lifted her foot off the gas and let the truck roll to a stop. She climbed out on shaking legs and motioned Exene to follow. Once both were standing in the road without him, Shoe knew what to do. She'd give him the truck and send him on his way.

She drew a deep breath, raised a hand and waved goodbye. "Vaya con dios," she said.

He slid into the driver's seat, and rested one hand on the wheel. This is it, she thought, already calculating how many miles until they hit the highway. It might be they could hitch even before then. They had been walking all day, but she could walk into the evening and into tomorrow if that's what it took. Exene could too. She stood beside Shoe in the road, barking frantically.

"Shut up your dog," he said.

This confounded Shoe, maybe more than anything so far, because Exene's barking was no longer his concern. All he had to do now was drive away. And though there were a hundred things she could have said at that moment, because she did not understand this man, because she had miscalculated and this had shaken her confidence badly, Shoe reverted to the little girl she'd begun life as, the one afraid of getting in trouble.

"She's not my dog," Shoe said.

Only when he slid from the truck and fired the gun did she understand her betrayal.

Exene had been sent to the mountains for her health. A breeze, carrying more of that beautiful soft air, swept up the road and lifted her thick fur. Shoe knelt beside her in the dirt. She reached to scratch a spot just above the dog's eyes.

The instant she touched the dog, she knew Exene was dead. Shoe almost sobbed. And then an astounding thought struck—God had not ignored her. No. God had tried to tell her something after all. The skeleton without a head and then the head without a body, the stench of death, all that was a warning. And now this man had killed the messenger. One shouldn't kill the messenger, she thought, however bad the news. Shoe rose to her feet again.

"Put her out of her misery," she said, though Exene was past suffering. Shoe wanted him to blow that final bullet. By her calculations, there could only be one more.

One at most. She could not absolutely recall.

"Put your hands over your head," he said.

She put her hands over her head.

"Walk." He gestured toward the woods. "Go on."

But she saw no use in walking now. She wouldn't save her life by walking into those woods. A line came to her from a story she couldn't remember. "I know," she said, "that you are a good man."

He blinked several times. Then he stepped behind her, planted the gun between her shoulder blades, and she began to move.

They walked into the woods, not far, fifteen or twenty feet. The woods were nicer than the road, Shoe thought, but she preferred the view back there. She liked the before and after of a road, the past and future together in one place. Now, she'd traded in that perspective for cool gray shade and the smell of ponderosa pine. Too much pine, thought Shoe. This forest needs a fire to sweep through and cull some trees. Humans can't do anything right.

"Stop," he said. She stopped, and looked over her shoulder, though she hadn't meant to do this either. At some point she'd quit doing what she wanted to do. She couldn't decide whether this had just happened, or had been happening most of her life.

"Just tie me to a tree and leave me," she begged.

"I haven't got any rope."

In her laugh, she heard the lilt of hysteria.

He set a hand on top of her head and pushed her down until her knees buckled and she landed on them with a muffled thud in a bed of old pine needles. The smell of resin rose around her. She took it into her lungs as he slid the revolver up her spine to the nape of her neck.

They say your life flashes before your eyes at such a moment, but all Shoe could see was the forest floor, so lifeless. She didn't want to die there. Let me die in sunlight, she silently prayed, or in rain. It didn't seem too much to ask.

"I'm sorry," he said.

"Not sorry enough," she said.

If God bothered to send me that warning, she thought, then God must bother to exist. If God exists, there is something beyond this life. She wanted to convince herself, and the two fears jockeyed against each other, the fear of becoming nothing versus the fear of becoming a fool.

Then, as if he'd read her mind, the man issued the single most sinister suggestion ever made to Shoe— perhaps to anyone, she thought.

"Say your prayers," he said.

But there was one who mattered more to her than God.

"I have a son," Shoe said.

Silence.

"He hasn't got a father."

The man hesitated. She stole another look at him and he looked outright puzzled. He seemed to think it over. Then the cloud passed. His eyes cleared. He shook his head.

"Everyone's got a father," he said.

CHAPTER TWENTY-FIVE

The sun still hung in the sky when they stepped into the bar, so it felt like afternoon. Inside, there weren't any windows, so it felt much later.

Now when Max came to town he ate dinner with the whole family, but he and Ida still liked their after-dinner drink. They usually took it at the bar where they had met for their first date, and got their favorite booth, which Ida liked because it was close to the fish tank, and Max liked because it was close to the bar.

It wasn't hard to get the booth tonight. Finals were over and the college students had headed home or at least headed somewhere else for the summer. Most of the tables were empty. They settled in, a waiter came to fetch them drinks, and Max slipped one of his hands under the table.

"Hi," Ida said.

"Hi," said Max. "Let's just sit here for the rest of the night with my hand on your thigh and you tell me everything that's happened since the last time I saw you."

His hand crept between her legs.

"I would," Ida said. "But I can't think right now."

"Neither can I," said Max. He took the hand away just as the waiter returned, set it against his glass, lifted the glass and clinked it against Ida's.

"I thought of something," she said.

"I'm dying to hear it," Max said.

"Johnny wants us to visit."

Max made a face.

"You don't like Johnny."

"It's not your brother I dislike," Max said. "It's his attitude. Has he always been like this?"

"Like what?"

Max laughed and shook his head. "I'll bet your brother told you not to marry me."

"What makes you say that?"

"I've seen his type before," Max said. "Stuck in a rut, doesn't know what to do with his life, and here comes his gorgeous sister, moving on, getting married, starting up a family. It's okay for him to be down as long as you're down too. But now he's freaking out."

Max had been wrong to pit her against her mother, that day at the lake, but at least there had been some truth in that. Johnny was different. Max should know better than to try to come between Ida and her brother.

"He might be a little depressed," Ida admitted.

"More than a little," Max said. "What's the matter with him, anyway? Doesn't he have a girlfriend? He's not a bad-looking guy."

"He's beautiful," Ida said.

Max eyed her sharply. "More beautiful than me?"

Ida grinned.

"I'm serious," said Max.

Of course he was.

Max had dropped comments about her brother before, but it had never occurred to Ida to defend him. She hadn't wanted to. Honestly, she hadn't realized she could. But since Johnny's visit, she had discovered a deeper loyalty to him than she'd known in those early months with Max, back when she thought she was getting at something, standing up to her siblings, emerging triumphant from the shadow of their opinion of her. Now she understood that she'd never been in their shadows to begin with.

"He's invited us to come out West for a visit."

"How long?" Max said.

"Two, three weeks. Let's go."

"I've been," said Max. "There's nothing out there but space and rocks."

"Sounds like the moon," Ida said.

"It's not. If it were the moon, I'd be the last man on earth to try and stop you. I'd be right behind you in line for my ticket. I'd have been there and back half a dozen times."

"I know you would," she said. "Still, I'd like to see this space and rocks for myself."

"Listen." Max lifted his long hands and settled them on her shoulders. "What about all those other years when you didn't go West? Those other thirty-three years? Why does it have to be now?"

"Actually, we went to Yellowstone when I was five. I

got stuck in some quicksand. I saw a bear."

"Your brother is trying to break us up."

Ida shook her head. "He couldn't if he wanted to."

"The guy doesn't have a life of his own, so he's gotta mess around with ours."

"Johnny's not like that."

"He's going to get you out there and try to keep you out there. He's going to try and brainwash you, now, before we're engaged."

"You mean before we're married," Ida said.

"Before we're engaged. He's afraid of what might happen once I ask you to marry me."

She had believed them engaged for some time, since February, in fact, when he had gone away and she had kissed no one. Those had been the terms of their agreement. She had upheld her end. Max knew that. Now she was so taken aback she could not think what to say.

"What is it?" he said. "When you frown like that, you bring out those little lines between your eyebrows."

Ida set her index finger above the bridge of her nose and rubbed it back and forth. "I think we'll go," she said slowly. "Moses and me. Even if you don't."

"Good. Go." Max left the booth and headed for the bar.

Ida didn't know what to do, so she finished her drink, tipping back the glass until the ice cubes fell against her nose. Then she stood, pulled her dress into place, and walked blindly through the bar, past the large illuminated fish, until her shoulder met the swinging door and she pushed through and found the bathroom. She ducked inside, and was about to turn the lock when Max came in and caught her in his arms.

"Don't leave me," he said. When he let her go, Ida turned to the toilet paper dispenser, unrolled a long stretch, bunched it and blew her nose.

"Promise me," Max said.

Ida dropped the toilet paper into the trash. She had promised him this several times before, but she had never realized he meant it so literally. Before she could think how to answer him, Max locked the bathroom door and tossed her over his shoulder. Ida glimpsed herself in the mirror, her dress riding up in back, and then he set her on the counter beside the sink. For a few consoling seconds, she forgot they were fighting and felt like a child, perched somewhere surprising in a short dress. Life seemed straightforward and fun. She started swinging her legs off the edge, but stopped when he addressed her.

"Look at you," he whispered.

Ida's thighs had gotten tight and sleek from losing weight and fooling around, but Max would not take her. The fact had puzzled her almost from the start, and it puzzled her still. The virginity was hers: Why did he prize it more than she did? She wrapped her legs around his hips and pulled him toward her. He tugged aside her underwear with one finger.

"I'm of half a mind to take you right here."

"Good," she said.

"I won't," he said. "Not until all the obstacles are out of our way."

"I thought they were out of the way. I thought that's

what your trip this winter was about."

"My obstacles are out of the way," Max said. "Yours aren't."

"What obstacles?"

Max let go of her underpants with a snap, slipped off her right shoe and let it clatter to the floor. He cupped the heel of her foot in his palm and stooped over it.

"Obstacles to your loyalty."

"Such as?"

"Such as your brother." His lips enveloped her big toe. "Such as Henry."

Ida was about to argue when Max bit down hard. She had to clap a hand over her mouth to keep from crying out. In the mirror behind her, Max watched himself.

"I told you what I wanted." He released her foot, and his hands settled lightly onto her thighs. "I've waited all these months for a sign from you. No sign. If I believed in God, I would have prayed to him a thousand times a day to make you love me half as much as I love you. I trusted you and you betrayed my trust. I gave you everything I had to give. You said big deal."

His hands ranged over her as he spoke. When a knock came on the bathroom door, both of them were panting as if they'd just run a long race. Ida cleared her throat.

"Yes?" she called.

"We've got two women waiting," came a female voice. "And I really need to go."

They looked at one another and started to laugh. Ida slipped from the counter and looked wildly around for a place to hide, but there was no stall, not even a cabinet. So she stomped her foot back in her shoe and tugged down the hem of her dress. Max placed his hand in the small of her back, released the lock, and they marched past the women, back out to the bar and to their table, where his fresh drink was waiting.

He tested it before he spoke.

"Your brother is a problem," he said. "But just a peripheral problem."

Ida's head fell to one side. She couldn't believe he was resuming their earlier conversation.

"He's not the one killing the love between us," Max said.

Her drink was gone, so she reached for his.

"Your sister," Max said.

Ida looked him over. "My sister is dead," she said.

Max nodded patiently. "I want to know what she told you about me."

"Nothing," Ida said. Her right toe still throbbed. She wondered if his teeth had left a mark.

"She badmouthed people. I know she badmouthed me. I was the only person who wasn't afraid to stand up to her. She badmouthed you, for Chrissakes, her sweet little obedient sister."

Ida pressed her hands over her ears.

"Darling," he said. "This is for your own good."

She rose, but only halfway, because of the angle of the table to the booth.

"If you walk out on me," he said, "don't come back."

Ida raised a hand to slap him, but halfway to his face, she swung her hand up and away instead, to motion over the waiter. She ordered another drink then sat back down, ashamed because she'd nearly lost her temper or because she hadn't, quite. She played with her coaster instead of looking at him.

"Why are you doing this to me," she muttered.

"That's the wrong question," Max said. "The question is, why are you letting her do this to us."

Ida neatly folded the scalloped edges of her coaster while some grief deeper than she'd ever known yawned open inside her. She had to force herself to speak. "Whatever she said about me—if, in fact, she said anything at all—"

"Hold it right there." Max set the fingers of one hand against her lips. "Are you calling me a liar?"

Ida shook her head. Max removed his fingers and continued.

"Because it sounded suspiciously close to that. If we surveyed ten people in this bar, I'll bet nine would say you were calling me a liar. And the tenth vote, the dissenting opinion, would probably be mine, because I'm trying to give you the benefit of the doubt."

"All I'm saying is that whatever she said didn't mean much in the end. She willed the care of Moses to me."

Max rolled his eyes.

"What?" Ida said.

"What else was she going to do? What other choice did she have?"

Ida's eyes slid away. She might have chosen you, Ida thought.

Max took hold of her face and slowly tipped back her

chin. "What did she say?"

"Nothing."

"Look at me." Max searched her face. "There's something," he said.

"I know why she left you."

Max laughed. "Tell me. I'm dying to hear this."

"You didn't like her feet."

Max laughed again. He dropped his hand and let her go. "Is that what she told you?"

"She didn't tell me," Ida said. "Her friend did."

"What friend?"

"Emily. The one who wrote the story after Shoe was killed. The story that brought you here."

"Oh, that interfering bitch."

"I thought you'd never met."

"We haven't. Yet you're taking her word over mine."

Ida didn't have the courage to inform him that she'd been the one to call Emily, and not the other way around.

"Did you tell her who I was?"

"Not exactly," Ida said. "Why?"

"'Not exactly,'" Max repeated, his voice thick with scorn. "Well, thanks to whatever great impression you and your sister gave of me, she's been digging around. She contacted an old professor of mine, and a business associate. Who knows who else."

Ida sat bewildered. It was puzzling, to be sure, that Emily would do this. But what really confused her was that he appeared to somehow be holding her, Ida, to blame. In some vague way, she came to Emily's defense for the first time.

"She's been through the wringer," Ida said, though she hadn't understood what Shoe meant by those words until this moment. "Something happened to her once."

And now, she thought, it's happening to me.

"Something happened to all of us, Ida, with the possible exception of you. That's no excuse for sniffing around in the affairs of a man she's never even met. Of course she didn't find anything!" he shouted. "What's she going to find, except that I graduated with honors? That my fraternity started a special award in my honor after I left? That I have occasional poor taste in women!"

Ida waited, sitting on her hands now so she didn't use them for something strange.

"I'd like to blame your sister, Ida, but I can't, because your sister was crazy. I know that sounds like a harsh appraisal, but frankly, I don't know what else to call her."

"Don't call her anything." Ida had pondered the mystery of her sister's feet for weeks now. She still didn't understand why this particular criticism would drive Shoe away. Yet somehow, Shoe's choices were making more sense to Ida all the time.

"Your sister did a number on you. Why do you think your life has turned out as it has? Because she took everything for herself. You—beautiful, talented, brilliant—and yet here you are, where you've always been, when you could have done anything you wanted with your life. Anything. It wasn't until I showed up that you even began to understand what life could be."

"That isn't true," Ida objected.

Max raised his hand. "Hear me out," he said. "We

have to make this work. It's the only way to a happy ending."

"I knew what life could be," Ida said, then revised. "I knew what I wanted it to be."

Max nodded emphatically. "When I found you," he said, "that was your strength. But you're ten times stronger now. You just have to choose."

She had chosen between Max and Henry, believing it was for the best. Chosen between Max's world and the different futures she'd dreamed for herself, but those dreams might never have materialized anyway. Sometimes she thought she'd chosen between Max and her painting, though he'd never asked her to. Now he wanted her to give up her family—her very idea of family. And maybe he was right. But Ida had learned she did not like to choose.

"I told you before," Max said. "Loyalty has its price. You're no good to anyone until you get that right."

"I won't choose. And remember, Max, you once said I'd never done a thing I didn't want to do."

Max blinked as if she'd stumped him.

"I remember it well," she said. "It was in this very restaurant. And you seemed to admire that fact."

"You misremember," Max said. "If you had never done anything you didn't want to do, all that would signify is that you were a very lucky girl."

Ida took a deep breath. "Oh," she said. "That's too bad," she said. Because that's when I fell in love with you.

The waiter brought her drink. Ida drank it.

"Before you break up with me," she said, "I have three

things to say to you."

"I'm only breaking up with you because you won't let us stay together. You've made that quite impossible."

"Three things," Ida said.

"I'm listening," Max said.

"I love you," Ida said. "I hadn't realized it would matter so little."

"If you loved me as I loved you, nothing would have mattered more."

She hadn't realized, either, that you could go on loving someone with so little cause.

Ida fixed her eyes on the fish tank, but this didn't help. She saw the blue fish swimming there as it always had, but where had the orange fish gone? How could the blue fish be expected to carry on like that, alone? Or, being such an uncommon color, had it always been alone?

"My second point," she finally managed, "is Shoe. I didn't understand about the feet because I never got the whole story, but even so, I feel like I understand it now. She was always quick. I think she was a kind of genius, the way she apprehended things."

Max snorted.

"And thirdly," Ida continued. "You shouldn't have told me."

"Told you what?"

"Told me that Shoe talked about me behind my back. You shouldn't have."

"Look," Max said. "I'm sorry. But that's what you need to know about your sister. I guarantee you, if there's anyone in your family who doesn't deserve your loyalty, it's her. I only told you to save us."

"It was unnecessary. It had no earthly bearing on us. It was unkind."

"It only hurts because you're afraid to choose."

"If you loved me as I love you, you would not have told me. And you would not have needed to tell me. If you loved me as I love you, nothing could ever come between us."

"You're wrong. Something can always come between people. God knows I've learned that with you."

Ida spoke carefully. "Whatever it is you think is wrong with me, it isn't about Shoe. It isn't about anybody but you and me. And all that's wrong with you and me is that it isn't me you want."

"I wanted you, Ida. I never wanted a woman more."

"I think it isn't a woman you want at all. And I don't believe you'll ever find what you're looking for."

"Oh, I'll find her all right. Just not in your family." He rose to his full height, walked to the bar, and paid the bill. Together, in silence, they moved outside.

It was the first of June, and the day was long. Though the sun had set, there was still light and color in the sky. Ida stopped on the sidewalk and looked around her.

In town, summer was her favorite season, when the students cleared out, professors and families left on vacation, and just enough people remained to keep the town in working order. Of course it was humid. Sometimes the air was so thick that a ghostly haze hung above the river and sifted through the trees. But there was sweet shade everywhere in daytime, and for now the green leaves, in all their shades and incarnations, still held a touch of tenderness.

Ida remembered all the summer evenings she'd wandered up the bricks of Main Street with her parents to get an ice cream cone, or alone, to sit under the water tower. There was the movie theater, the library, the bank, all in plain view. Just across the street were the wide wooden doors of Henry's Catholic church. This town was the only place she had ever really known, for Max lived on the outskirts of Cincinnati, and you couldn't know strip malls the same way, not in a car, not darting into different spots each time.

She turned and looked at him. "Let's take a walk," she said.

Max stood by his car door, resting his arms on the roof. "I'm really tired," he said.

Ida moved across the pavement. She stepped off the curb and into the street. "I love to walk," she said. "I had a hundred walks we could have taken."

Max waved a hand as if he were swatting at a mosquito. Ida didn't know if this was the case, or if the gesture was meant for her. She stood before him for a moment, uncertain, then raised a flat hand in farewell. He fit himself into his car while she stood by, biting the crook of one finger and faintly smiling. When his headlights came on, she drifted across Main Street, and was headed home when the car swung around and rolled past. She turned her head away as his taillights receded and then her whole body, veering onto campus so she wouldn't have to look down the long stretch of road before her and watch those two red circles disappear from view.

Halfway across campus, it occurred to her that she could keep going. The light diminished as she walked, and under cover of evening, with no one around, Ida raised her head and swung her arms. She recalled an incident the afternoon of Shoe's funeral, in the downstairs bathroom, when Ida had decided to take a bath and all those mourners had milled about just outside the door, so impatient it made them unruly, like a pack of wild animals. She had begun to panic, worked herself into a corner, and Johnny had come in to spring her from the trap. He'd helped her mimic tears, because she couldn't muster the tears when she needed them, not when they would have made her explicable to all those other human beings.

She had always struggled to explain herself without ever knowing how. She had believed an explanation was required, but there were other ways. One could simply refuse to explain, if one had the courage. She didn't, but someone like Max, the master explainer, just locked himself into the women's room and marched out without a word.

And Shoe, in turn, fled him with scarcely a word of explanation to anyone. If only she had explained that once, Ida thought, just a little warning, just a tip. But Shoe would not have seen the use in that. Like Ida, Shoe thought an explanation was tantamout to a defense—and unlike Ida, would not have thought any of her actions required one.

By the time Ida reached the cemetery it was dark, but there were fireflies to guide her up the hill, and the sound of frogs singing in the ditch to keep her company. She reached Shoe's grave and knelt down before the stone, palms flat and fingers splayed so the bluegrass that had taken hold in ten months' time pushed up between them.

"So thick," she whispered. Then she rolled onto her back and stretched out on the grave, her eyes on the deepening dark of the sky. "He didn't want me either," she said.

But oh, he had seemed to. He had seemed to understand, in the beginning, so that for once she didn't have to explain.

It was surely an irony, Ida thought, that the sister who had protected her all their lives had, in the end, brought this disaster down upon her, had set in motion events that would destroy the very thing in Ida they had both sought to protect. Until now, Ida had thought her way of life had spared her from suffering, rejection, the dreary compromises of a normal human life. In fact, she'd been spared something more. She only recognized that now because, like any innocent, Ida couldn't know what she was protected from until she'd lost that protection.

It was not only the aches and pains of worldly experience that she'd been spared, but the uncertainty that she had lived her life properly. For the most extraordinary fact of Ida's life was not that she had lived it out in the safety of her parents' protection or even with her childhood identity intact and suspended in time, but that she'd lived her whole life in serene confidence that everything was as it should be, that everything was going according to plan.

And now that confidence was gone.

At thirty-three, Ida realized her true love would never find her in this small Ohio town, that her paintings would go undiscovered, and that there was a chance she'd made a horrible mistake, more than ten years back, when she'd decided never to leave home. In this moment, Ida felt her sister's death more deeply than she had when it happened, felt as if a floor had given way and she had fallen through. Lying on her back, she saw her own life in a clear and cold and utterly alien light.

She jumped up, spooked, and hurried into the bushes, blindly pushing her way through until she had escaped the cemetery and staggered out onto the old abandoned brick road that led up the hill. When she reached the farmhouse, the recently mown lawn, the fireflies lighting up here and then there, she stood for some time, still and silent, before she looked up at the second floor.

There was a light on in the back bedroom, the one Henry used as his studio. Ida continued up the hill, stopping again at the bottom of his rickety wooden stairs to recall the cold night late last fall when they'd returned from their walk out on the tracks. There had been a gibbous moon that night—luna linda—and clean black shadows. They had gone out into no place and come back again.

She climbed the steps carefully, quietly, and rapped on Henry's kitchen door. When he didn't come, she almost turned and left, but then she raised her fist and tried again. A moment later she heard footsteps in the middle room, a light came on in the kitchen, and her friend appeared, squinting behind his glasses. When he could make her out, he dropped his eyes and opened the door.

"I'll bet you're out of beer beans," Ida said.

"No, I'm not," Henry said. He sounded as belligerent as ever.

"One helping, please."

"They're in the refrigerator. I'll have to heat them up."

Ida stepped into the kitchen after him, leaned against one of the cupboards, and slid down until she was sitting on the floor with its patchwork of missing tiles. Her dress rode up her thighs, but Ida didn't care.

"I guess the mice have all moved out for summer," she said.

"Pretty much." Henry stood at the kitchen sink with his sleeves rolled up, scrubbing out a pan.

She pressed her palms to the cool floor and watched as he lifted the towel from the handle of the refrigerator door. He dried the pan, pulled a jar of beans from the refrigerator, and dumped in half of them, then set the pan on the stove and fiddled with the blue flame underneath. Ida grew calm.

"I didn't think you liked my beans," he said.

"I don't," Ida said.

Henry remained at the stove, his back to her, stirring the contents of the pan. Ida got to her feet and wandered from the kitchen, but she listened to the spoon's metal scrape as she drifted back through the dark middle room. The screaming man was missing from its wall, and she wondered if Moses had said something to him. In its place hung the Magician of Horses. Ida stopped in the semidarkness to study it.

"That's going in a show," Henry called. "Next month."

Ida moved on, through the sitting room and into his studio, where she had seen the light from below. His easel was empty, but off to the side she saw a painting of a face she knew well. The face belonged to Moses.

She was still looking at her nephew's portrait when Henry came in behind her. He handed her a bowl full of beans but wouldn't meet her eyes. She took the bowl in both her palms and stood with it, surveying the room. When the phone rang, Henry left her standing there. A moment later she heard his Texas twang flare in anger.

"Hell, no," he said. "I'm not gonna let her talk to you."

Ida moved into the doorway. "I'll take it," she said. She set her bowl of beans down on the phone table, took a seat in her favorite armchair, and put the receiver to her ear.

"Max," she said.

"You don't waste time, do you."

Ida reached for her beans, settled them into her lap, lifted a forkful, and blew across them. "Life's too short," she said. "You taught me that."

"You fucking bitch. It's over."

Ida looked at her watch. "Really," she said. "I thought it was over an hour ago." She put the forkful of beans in her mouth. They were just shy of scalding, and delicious.

Max raged on. Ida brought up another forkful and blew across it. "Where are you?" she said. "How did you know I was here?"

Max roared, setting off aches in a dozen parts of her body. Ida picked up the bowl and carried it with her to the window, but this only offered a limited view of the street. When he took a break from shouting, the sound of her own voice was pleasantly sane. "Are you on your cell phone?"

"I'm coming over," Max said. "I'll be there in two minutes. We'll settle this once and for all."

He hung up. Ida took up another forkful of beans, put them in her mouth, and sucked on them a while. Then she walked back toward the kitchen, enjoying the clip-clop of her shoes on the bare wood floors. Max's place had wall-to-wall carpeting.

When she found him, Henry was cleaning out his pan a second time.

"Thank you for the beans," she said.

He turned to look at her. Ida leaned forward and kissed him lightly on the mouth. His mustache smelled like cigarettes and paint.

"He's coming over," she said. "I'm sorry about that, but you don't want to meet him. Take your car and drive somewhere. Just for an hour or so."

"I'll be damned," Henry swore.

Ida kissed him again, on the cheek this time. "Not you," she said. "Please go."

Henry dug into his pocket, fished out his keys, and studied them. "You've changed," he said.

"Not so much," Ida said.

He turned at the door and looked back at her. "Ida," he said. "You were the only woman I ever cried over losing." Then Henry walked out the door and down the steps.

Ida picked up her bowl and carried it with her onto

his tiny landing. She sat down in time to see the final remnants of the Ohio sun disappear into Indiana. She was still watching the sky and forking down beans when she heard Max's car turn onto the street. And then she realized something really surprising: She'd gotten back her appetite.

She sighed, if not with contentment, then with resignation. Well, she told herself, this nightmare's coming to an end. But it was just beginning.

CHAPTER TWENTY-SIX

Ida made it home somehow, the night Max—or she—called it quits. She left the slate-blue farmhouse, walked out onto the highway's center line and followed it back into town, kicking stones down its middle when she found them, half-hoping someone would come along a little too fast in his truck and put her out of her misery. But every truck slowed down. Every car swerved. She made it safely back to the bedroom she'd slept in all her life, with the princess curtains and childhood desk she had never thought to question until Max. He had said so many things to her that night, accused her of so many things, that by the time she crept into bed she'd already lost track of most of them.

In the morning it took seven or eight seconds to remember she'd lost him and then desolation set in again. Since it was summer vacation Moses didn't leave for school, and spending those hours with him was a comfort. But there were also moments when it hurt to look at him because he reminded her of Max. For three days she staggered around, then Max called.

"I wanted to tell you." His voice was husky, and he kept clearing his throat. "In the bathroom, the little girl's room."

"Yes."

"I wanted to tell you. You were so fucking perfect. That gasp."

Ida waited for the real reason he had called. Maybe, she thought, he'd called to apologize. Finally she said, "I was in pain."

"I know you were. I know that. You know I never adored anyone more. And no one ever crushed me the way you did. You know that, don't you? You and your beautiful mouth. Your hands. Your sweet, tight little—"

"Stop."

He stopped.

"You can't do this anymore. You lost the right."

She heard a fumbling on the other end. "I'm sorry," came his voice. Then the receiver clicked and he was gone.

When the registered letter came in the mail a week later, the letter from his lawyer, announcing his intent to sue for custody of Moses, she read it through twice, then went to the telephone and dialed his number in Cincinnati. A woman answered. When Ida asked for Max, the woman asked who was calling.

"Ida," she said. "Ida Tumarkin."

There was a pause. "He doesn't want to talk to you," the woman said.

Ida froze. She could not think what to say. Finally, in a voice she didn't recognize, Ida said, "Put him on."

And then he was there, so suddenly, where he had not been for days. "What," he said.

"I wanted to ask you something."

"So ask me. I've got a meeting with my lawyer in twenty minutes."

"I just wanted to ask you—" Ida broke into a spastic, short-lived laugh. "When you said you'd protect me, what were you planning to protect me from?"

"I can't protect you from yourself," he said, "if that's what you mean. That's the one thing in the world even I can't protect you from."

Countless meetings and interviews led up to the hearing. A custody analyst interviewed Ida and her parents, Moses, and then Max and his parents. Moses told the analyst, told everyone, he wanted to stay with his aunt.

For this reason, Ida wanted Moses to testify in court. It seemed to her simple enough: The boy should live where he wanted. He knew where that was. Enough said. But the Tumarkins' lawyer said differently. He said it might look bad if their side wanted Moses on the stand and Max's side did not—it might allow Max to gain the moral high ground. By sparing him the trauma of the courtroom, Max could claim he was more interested in the boy's welfare.

"Besides," Frank Hurley told her, "at Moses' age, what the child wants isn't a legal consideration."

Ida was enraged. But Max and his lawyer knew what Moses had said. They'd seen the tape, and Ida clung to that. She told herself that if Max loved Moses—and he must, for a thousand reasons—he would have to let Moses decide this one. If he loved Moses at all.

It has to be about love. That's what Ida whispered to herself first thing each morning, and last thing after she turned out her bedside light at night. She was talking about Max and Moses. But she was also talking about Max and herself.

Through that long summer when Max refused to speak to her, Ida held out hope. In fact, she took his refusal as possible proof that he still loved her. He knows if he talks to me, he'll lose his resolve, she reasoned.

That September, when her family's lawyer informed her that Max was engaged, Ida shrugged. She knew that where Max was concerned, engagement was one thing and marriage another. Perhaps this engagement was for show. For show and for security—to keep him from running back to her, since that was probably what he wanted to do.

In October, when she learned that Max was charging her as mentally incompetent, Ida merely nodded. Frank said it was not an unheard-of or even particularly uncommon procedure; Ida suspected the real reason for the charge was spite. It was the spite, somehow, that saved her from despair.

In building their own case, Johnny wanted to fight fire with fire. He knew Max would hire the best, most aggressive lawyer money could find—someone who specialized in custody battles, which the Tumarkins' lawyer did not, and someone who'd leave no stone unturned in order to discredit them. Indeed, someone willing to humiliate them. Johnny called and told Frank about Mrs. Tumarkin and the new doctor Max had sent her to, the one who set her up with an antidepressant so effective her family hardly saw her anymore. He told him Max had seduced Ida. And he told him that Max had not only been seeing his fiancée while he was with Ida, but while he was with Shoe. Johnny insisted they could nail Max to the wall with that fact alone, because it revealed his true character, and revealing Max's character was the key to keeping Moses.

Unfortunately, these facts only seemed to distress the Tumarkins' lawyer. He wanted to steer clear of Max almost entirely.

"Even if he's a philanderer," Frank argued, "that's not to say he couldn't be a loving father."

"We're not accusing him of philandering," Johnny said. "We're accusing him of deception. Lies, manipulation. This is a character assassination. And believe me, his is one character that needs to be assassinated."

"In a court of law, he's blameless."

"So is the devil," Johnny said.

The day before the hearing, Johnny flew east. In Denver, he caught the same connecting flight as Emily, who'd called to tell him she'd be in town for the hearing. Johnny supposed that made sense—she loved Moses too. And it put an idea in his head, a proposition.

It was late afternoon when they landed in Cincinnati, already dark by the time they picked up the rental car. But though the dark lent him courage, Johnny waited until they were almost to town before he finally summoned enough to lay out his proposal. He cleared his throat.

"I had an idea."

"Did you?"

"It involves us both."

When Emily didn't respond, he asked, "Do you want to hear it?"

"Sure."

He laughed nervously. "We adopt Moses."

Emily said nothing. Johny hurried on. "Ida's at a disadvantage as a single woman. But as a married couple, we wouldn't be."

"A sort of business arrangement, you're saying."

"A family arrangement," Johnny said.

Emily shook her head. "Seems too desperate."

"Why? That's what Max did and no one seems to think he's desperate."

"But Max got engaged months before the hearing, not during it. He'd been dating his fiancée for years before that."

"Before he dated Ida, you mean. And Shoe."

"That's right," said Emily. "Anyway, no matter how you slice it, we're at a disadvantage. We'll always be at a disadvantage to Max because he's the father."

They drove past the campus in silence. Emily was right, of course. His idea wouldn't have worked. Johnny was just relieved she hadn't taken offense.

"Why don't you stay with us?" he asked.

"I'll come by and visit," she said. "I don't think you'll want me in your house this week."

"At least stay for dinner."

Emily looked uncomfortable. "We'll see," she said.

She slowed for the turn onto the cul-de-sac, pulled into his family's driveway and shut off the engine.

"I'll just pop in to say hello." She pulled the keys from the ignition and opened her car door.

Johnny followed her up the driveway.

"Anyway," she called over her shoulder, "it's not like we'd be any improvement on his current home environment. Right?"

When Johnny caught up to her at the front door, Emily rang the doorbell, turned and faced him.

"I'll never forgive you for asking me that," she said.

Emily stayed for dinner, but it was a strained affair. Mrs. Tumarkin was absent as usual, and Ida was silent. They ate take-out Chinese, but at the end of the meal, when Johnny proposed that everyone read off the fortune from their cookie, Ida just shook her head and left the table. A few minutes later, Johnny left too to take some food upstairs to his mom.

The door of his parents' bedroom was slightly open. He pushed it over the thick carpet and crossed to the pillow. Only then did he look down.

His mother's hair was black. That was the first shock. She had been dyeing it for years, but always nut brown, the shade it had been when they were little. Against the pale pillow, around her paler face, the black did more than age her. It made her look garish.

He put down the tray of food, reached out, and took

hold of her shoulder, afraid to shake her, afraid to wake her at all. But her eyes opened, slowly, and fixed on him more slowly still. He saw her eyes catch, then focus, and thought of fog, the way an object will seem to materialize out of nothing. He was the object. The nothingness seemed to be everything else.

"Hi, Mom," he said.

"Well, Johnny." She lay a moment, gazing up at him, then propped herself up slightly. Johnny sat down on the edge of the bed.

"Are you okay?" he said.

"Yes..." They seemed to wait together through a long pause. "It's this medicine the doctor has me on."

"Maybe you shouldn't take it."

A crease of worry came and went between her eyes. She sighed and looked around the room. "Well," she said finally. "It's winter again. Isn't it."

"Yes," Johnny said. "The custody hearing starts in the morning. I flew back for it and so did Emily. Why don't you put on a sweater and come downstairs and join us? Ida baked some Christmas cookies. We'll put some coffee on. You look like you could use a cup."

Mrs. Tumarkin muttered something under her breath.

"What?" asked Johnny.

"Christmas cookies!" she exploded. "What's the use?"

Johnny had no response to this. Since Shoe's death, it had seemed to him there wasn't much use in anything. He knew his mother suffered from the same malady. But he looked at her now and realized his own mistake. He wanted to rejoin the living.

Neither of them spoke for several minutes. He looked around the room and thought maybe his mother was drifting back to sleep. I'll let her, he thought. He heard his nephew's laughter float up from the kitchen and itched to return downstairs, but when he glanced back at her she was watching him, her eyes strangely bright.

"Moses needs a father," she said. When Johnny said nothing, she added sagely, "A boy that age always does."

"He never had a father when Shoe was alive. I didn't hear you complaining then."

"Well, what was I going to say? We didn't know he had a father then. Max didn't know he was a father. And besides, Shoe was strong."

Johnny didn't understand what she was driving at. But he got up, went to the door and closed it. Then he stood at the foot of the bed.

"You don't want us getting custody?"

"It isn't us getting custody," she said. "It's Ida."

Johnny let this sink in. Then he shook his head. When she saw he was still confused, his mother waved her hands impatiently. They knocked against each other in midair.

"What kind of mother can she make him? Both of his parents are so strong. Adventurers. Rebels. He needs to be with somebody who can handle him. Someone who understands him."

"What for?" Johnny said. "You raised Ida, and you don't understand her at all."

"Maybe if I had, she would have turned out better."

Johnny walked back around the bed. He leaned over his mother, tried to look deep into her eyes, but could not. There was something in the way he couldn't get past. He gripped her shoulders.

"You listen to me, now. I don't know why you've got it in for Ida, and it doesn't matter now because this isn't about you and her. It's about your grandson."

"But I know that," she said. "That's what I've been saying all along."

Johnny shook her gently. When her head snapped back on her neck he let go, dismayed.

"Mom, you've got to listen to me now. Do you know what sort of man Max is?"

"Do you?"

"I know what he did to Ida."

She waved her hands again.

"What does that mean?" Johnny demanded.

"He did nothing to Ida, far as I can tell. According to him, they never had a relationship."

"But you know they did."

She smiled at him slyly.

Johnny swallowed. "Are you calling her a liar?"

"Of course not." Mrs. Tumarkin reached up and patted him on the shoulder. Her speech, like her gestures, was strangely languid. "Ida's honest to a fault. She's also naive. Very susceptible. This tall, handsome man comes around to see his son and she starts thinking it's her he's coming around to see. She's never had a boyfriend. I'm sure it was very flattering to her. But imagine her with a strapping man like that! He'd eat her alive. He'd never be satisfied.

Now, Shoe—" She smiled. "Shoe was another story."

"And Shoe left him."

"Precisely." She raised her index finger triumphantly. "Shoe left him. No man would walk out on Shoe."

"Left him because she was afraid of him."

Mrs. Tumarkin scoffed extravagantly. She seemed to be enjoying herself, and it was no wonder. Shoe was still her favorite subject. "Shoe wasn't afraid of anybody."

It wasn't fair, Johnny thought. Growing up, Shoe had never been close to their mother. Shoe made her too nervous. It was only when Shoe moved away that Mrs. Tumarkin began to admire her. And she only looked down on Ida because she'd stayed.

"Shoe was so afraid of him she didn't want him to know she had his son."

"And I can't for the life of me see why."

"You can't."

"You couldn't ask for a better father figure: confident, charismatic, generous, warm."

"He's also a liar. A manipulator. An egomaniac, and a bully."

"Nonsense. And most importantly, he loves Moses. He adores him."

"He adored Ida too, in the beginning."

Her head wagged from side to side. "A son is not a girlfriend. Perhaps she needed to mete out her favors a bit more sparingly."

Even after Mrs. Tumarkin had finished talking, her head kept bobbing slightly. Yet her hair was still, straw-like and slightly matted against her head.

Johnny realized he was staring and looked away. But in the ensuing silence he rose to his feet and slowly backed away from the bed. By the time he reached the door his mother was sleeping again, her mouth gaping open. He hurried away down the hall, headed back to the warmth and sounds and life of the kitchen.

I should have seen this coming, he thought. But in a way he had. When Shoe died, he had forecast the demise of his family. It was just taking a little more time than he'd first thought.

Johnny reached the kitchen, where Ida was recounting dreams, scary dreams, about vampires and giant bugs, laughing and gesturing. Emily imitated some monster's deep, booming voice. Moses guffawed and fell off his chair. And Johnny, leaning against the doorframe, held up a hand to shield his eyes from the brightness, which for a moment left him blind.

He hardly slept that night. Just before dawn, he gave up trying. He rose, stepped over Moses and his sleeping bag, shaved, set out the new clothes he had bought, then headed downstairs to fix a pot of coffee. On his way to the kitchen he spied Ida in the semidark of the family room, lying on the floor in front of the lit-up Christmas tree.

He went over and sat down beside her. "I'm surprised you got the tree up," he said. "What with everything that's been going on."

"I thought it was important," she said. "To do everything right."

"For the hearing?"

"In case we lose," Ida said. "In case this is the last Christmas we have him with us."

Johnny noticed then she wasn't looking at the tree, but at the ceiling. He tipped back his head and saw the warm wash of lights reflected above them.

"Ida," he said.

"Hmm."

"How have you lived with Mom all this time?"

"It wasn't always like this," she said. "Everything was easier when Shoe was alive. Besides, it never used to matter what Mom said. I never doubted myself."

Johnny nodded. "Good," he said.

Ida turned her head and smiled up at him. "That's all changed, though," she said.

"Maybe you should leave."

"I might," Ida said. "Guess I'll have Max to thank for that."

"I think I hated him from the first moment I laid eyes on him."

"Maybe earlier," Ida said. "I'm sure Shoe's opinion of him must have carried some weight."

"Not with you," Johnny said.

"Well," Ida said dreamily, "I'm an independent thinker."

"But he's such a raging asshole, Ida."

"He's not, though. That's the thing. If he were that simple, he'd be less dangerous. He's complicated."

"He's not so complicated," Johnny said.

"Well, he isn't simple. A simple person doesn't set out to destroy someone they love."

Johnny looked at her in disbelief.

"I know he loves me," she said. "It was love, and love doesn't just stop. Maybe it never stops, completely."

"He wasn't faithful to you; he wasn't faithful to anyone."

"No, I know."

"All right," Johnny said. "Then the thing you've gotta ask yourself is, what is that kind of love good for?"

"I don't know," she said. "But that's a separate question."

CHAPTER TWENTY-SEVEN

The hearing took place in the Hamilton County Courthouse, a formidable building in the center of that town, twenty miles from their own. Ida had driven past it many times, but had never been inside.

What she still envisioned, in those months and weeks before the hearing, was that magical day when Max would enter the courtroom and all of this madness would come to an end. He would enter alone, pushing himself through tall swinging doors, doors that would silently fall shut behind him. His eyes would scan the room, meet hers, and a silent understanding would pass between them. Then she would rise from her chair and cross the room to take his face between her hands, the hands he loved, and she would hold that face until all the strain had left it. She would hold his face until, at long last, he grew calm.

When Ida and her family arrived at court, there were no swinging doors and no silence either. The real door, which was unremarkable, stuck slightly when opened and creaked when closed. Their eyes never met. He didn't seem to know she was there. And Max was never alone. Always his parents flanked his right side. On his left, always the two beautiful women, both tall and slender, but the one who was his sister a little wiry, like him. The other one looked fragile, like some exotic plant. That one was his fiancée.

Much of the morning was taken up with testimonials from Max's parents about his character, his love of children, his love of life. After them a child psychologist took the stand. Based on interviews with Moses, he said, it was his professional opinion that the Tumarkins showed symptoms of a dysfunctional family. The grandmother rarely left her bed. The aunt lived with her parents and didn't hold down a job. They didn't go to church, but went to the cemetery all the time. Then he talked about the bond that had grown up between father and son, and recommended Max be given custody.

Sometimes between the testimonies of one person and the next, Ida found herself staring at the different members of Max's family. They all looked sane enough, this small entourage that swirled around him now, all sane except for him. Every gesture, every turn of his head she could see now was imbued with his particular madness, but it was not a madness detectable to the untrained eye, not one the court would recognize. Max had already lied and he would lie more, but Ida didn't suppose lies quite equaled perjury, not from a man who might believe his lies somehow got at the truth.

And she understood that at this hearing, it was her own sanity his lawyer, the judge, these strangers were evaluating. Her siblings used to tell her not to care what people thought, but in the end it turned out that you had to care, care very much, or Ida had to care, at least, forced now to somehow defend her life.

"I can't defend my life," she wanted to tell the judge. "I never knew I would have to. If I had known, I would have lived it differently."

Max's fiancée was lovely on the stand, in a long blue dress that matched her eyes. His lawyer asked how long she and Max had been dating. Four years, she said. When Max's lawyer asked if there had ever been trouble with other women getting crushes on her intended, she smiled.

"Is that a yes?"

"Yes," she said.

"How often does it happen?"

"All the time," she said. "He has that effect on women."

"So it wouldn't surprise you if, say, Miss Tumarkin there, who's never had a boyfriend, suddenly gets shown some attention by your fiancé and conceives some idea about their relationship?"

"No," she said.

Ida looked on her less with jealousy than pity. If anything, Ida wanted to save her. To save her from him. Him from her. To save both of them from each other. Until his testimony, it seemed to Ida she was the only one who understood him well enough to do it. After his testimony, she would understand him well enough to know he could not be saved.

Max took the stand before the morning break, head

held high, and scanned the courtroom. His eyes seemed to touch every person there except Ida. He never looked at her.

"I want to begin in the beginning," said his lawyer, "back in the time you were with Susan Tumarkin. You had no intimation she might be pregnant when she left the town in Idaho where you met?"

"Absolutely none."

"Did you find her sudden flight from the state strange?"

"Well, it surprised me, of course. But from what I knew of her, I wouldn't call it uncharacteristic behavior. She wasn't stable. Besides, I think she was scared."

"Objection," said Frank Hurley. He can't testify to her state of mind."

"I'm going to overrule the objection at this point," the judge said. "I'd like to know why Mr. Frost thought she was scared."

Max nodded gravely. "We were in love, and that wasn't her style, and then she got pregnant and that definitely wasn't her style, and I think she knew when I found out about our baby, I'd want to marry her and that scared her even more."

The judge sat forward. "Explain," she said.

"She couldn't let herself have anything she wanted. She thought that made her weak."

"And you believe she kept the child secret from you the next six years for the same reason?"

"That I don't know," Max said. "Maybe she changed her mind and then didn't know how to find me. I used to move around a lot, for my work. It doesn't concern me anymore. I'd never let my son suffer for her mistakes."

Ida heard a strange noise and looked to her left. Johnny was grinding his teeth. She put a hand on his arm.

When the judge sat back, Max's lawyer resumed. "So, six years go by, the mother dies, and a few months later you come looking for your son. How did you find out about him?"

"I read about her murder in the paper," Max said. "The article also mentioned the people who survived her."

"Where were you living at the time?"

"Boston. The story got picked up by the wire. It mentioned the age of her son, and that he had no father, and then I started to wonder."

"So you located his mother's family. Why?"

"I had to know if he was mine."

"No paternity claim was being made on you? No demands for child support?"

"No," Max said. "Until her death last year, I didn't know I had a son."

"So you might have easily dodged all responsibility for this child, isn't that true? Weren't you tempted to just let it go?"

"Not for a minute."

The lawyer looked pleased. He nodded at Max. "Thank you. No more questions."

Frank Hurley approached the box where Max sat. The two men eyed one another, the lawyer rapped his fist against the wooden rail, then turned and paced away.

"Isn't it true, sir, that in addition to establishing a relationship with your son, you established one with Ida Tumarkin?"

"Only in connection with my son," Max said. "I saw a lot of my son from November on, so incidentally, I saw her too."

"You did not spend time alone with her?"

"On several occasions I did," he said. "I needed to tell her I was the father. And I wanted a sense of their family. Miss Tumarkin was always very obliging. I learned most of what I know about their family from her."

"Miss Tumarkin has listed off nearly forty occasions when she says she was alone with you."

Max shrugged. "She's confused."

"Is she? Or are you? What about Oscar's, a bar in her hometown?"

Max looked genuinely amused. "I've been there several times. Not forty!"

"How many times with Miss Tumarkin?"

"One," Max said. "As I said, I had to tell her I was the father."

"Mr. Frost. I have more than one witness who can testify you were courting Ida Tumarkin for a period of at least four months. Are they confused as well?"

"Misled, perhaps."

"By Miss Tumarkin?"

"Perhaps."

"Toward what end?"

Max laughed softly. "You'd have to ask her that."

The lawyer turned and gave Max a sidelong look.

"Have all the women in the Tumarkin family met with your disapproval?"

A look of shock erupted across Max's face. "Only insofar as they influence my son," he said. "They are not bad people—they are dysfunctional people."

"All women, though."

Max smiled. "I adore women," he said, "if you're trying to suggest I'm some kind of misogynist. My mother, my sister, my fiancée are all with me in the courtroom today. You can ask any of them. I have always loved women. I have always tried to protect women close to me from any kind of harm. They know this. I think that's a natural instinct for any self-respecting man."

The lawyer shot up the flat of his hand. "What about a self-respecting woman who doesn't want to be, as you say, protected. Is that natural?"

Max shrugged. "Then she can protect herself, I guess."

"Unless she's your woman, perhaps?"

Max narrowed his eyes at Frank Hurley. "I don't know what you mean."

"You say that Susan Tumarkin fled because the prospect of her own happiness scared her. Perhaps she, too, was somehow confused?"

"Yes," Max said.

"And your son, sir, is he 'confused' when he has said in three separate interviews that he wants to stay with his aunt?"

"He doesn't know what he's choosing," Max said.

"When will he know? When he changes his mind and

says he wants to live with you?"

"He wants to live with me now," Max said. "But he's still living in their house. What else can he say?"

Again, the lawyer rapped his fist on the rail. "I'm done," he said. "No more questions, your honor."

Perhaps it was spite that drove him, Ida thought. But once Max testified, his spite no longer left her any hope. His spite was not romantic. It was not forgivable. And ultimately, it was not important. As she endured the humiliation of his testimony, and then further humiliation as her very sufficiency as an adult was put on trial, Ida thought fondly back to a time when she might have thought it was the worst thing, to be stuck up in front of people like that, to speak her answers into a little black microphone while a blank-faced woman tap-tap-tapped away.

Now Ida knew that was not the worst thing. Her pride, her dreams, her secrets were not at stake, but her Moses.

CHAPTER TWENTY-EIGHT

During the morning break, Emily hurried up to Johnny in the hallway outside their courtroom. Her eyes glittered.

"I need to tell you something," she whispered.

"Okay. Hey, what are you doing for lunch?"

Emily grabbed his arm and dragged him away from his family, and over to a stone bench against the wall. They sat down together, but she didn't look at him. She was looking over his shoulder, back down the hall. "We don't have much time," she said. "I've been subpoenaed."

"What? When did this happen?"

"Weeks ago. I would've told you sooner, but I didn't want to freak you out."

"But what for?"

"According to Max, I'm the only one Shoe ever told why she left him. He seems to believe if the real reason for Shoe's flight were known, it'd help their case. Shoe might be dead but she's still the mother. I doubt her wishes will weigh in custody, but I guess he's covering all the bases.

Max probably figures if her reasons for rejecting him could be discredited, that could mean another strike against your family, another strike for him."

Emily glanced over his shoulder again. "Oh shit. Here he comes."

Johnny grasped the sleeve of her coat, and was momentarily distracted. The coat wasn't warm enough. She probably didn't have a winter coat anymore, he thought. She'd been in the desert too long.

He turned to see Max's lawer approaching, hands in his pockets, sporty and casual. Johnny noticed that when the lawyer looked at Emily, there was a gleam of something like appreciation in his eyes.

"Emily," he said.

"Good afternoon, Michael." She smiled, ladylike, and rearranged her skirt as he took a seat on her other side.

Johnny and the lawyer pretended not to notice one another. Instead, Johnny leaned his head against the wall and closed his eyes in disgust. He wondered what the lawyer thought of Max. Did he know him and somehow approve of him, like Max's fiancée? Then again, what if he secretly despised him too, and was just doing his job? Wasn't that worse?

"Are you ready to testify?" the lawyer asked Emily.

"No," she said. "But I'm all dressed up, despite that fact."

When the lawyer laughed, Johnny felt like throwing up. He opened his eyes again so he could have the bathroom door in his sights, but ended up eyeing the lawyer instead. He was not much older than Emily, a decent-looking bastard, and well-groomed, but Johnny couldn't fault him for that. The job probably required it.

Johnny faulted him for everything else, though, and when the lawyer grinned at her—a wry, boyish grin—he was dumbfounded. My God, he thought. He's going to ask her out! But a moment later, Johnny changed his mind.

"You're a journalist," the lawyer said. "Isn't it your job to present the facts?"

"It's also my job to make sense of them," said Emily, still smiling. "If I can't, I'm not convinced it's responsible to put them out there."

"Like with the story you wrote about your friend's death?"

Emily's smile evaporated.

"What do you mean?" she said.

"I mean are you sorry you wrote it?"

"You mean am I sorry your client saw it?"

"Yes. Okay."

"Yes, I am."

"Trying to expiate now for your sins?"

"Oh, I don't know about that."

"But you're angry. You're angry that you were the instrument for bringing Max to his son. You're angry at fate."

"I don't believe in fate."

"Fine," said the lawyer. "At circumstance, then."

"Of course I am," Emily said. "But I wouldn't testify in any case."

"Your reluctance to testify makes me wonder if you

yourself don't have much faith in your friend's reasons for skipping town on my client."

"I've absolute faith," Emily said. "More all the time."

He sighed. "You know you're not accomplishing anything this way. Your testimony isn't crucial to our case."

"I wonder why I've been subpoenaed, then."

The lawyer rose. He brushed at his suit, although as far as Johnny could tell, there wasn't a speck of alien matter on it. "It wasn't my idea," he said.

Emily and the lawyer nodded to one another. He turned and walked away. Once he was out of view, her head dropped into her hands. She patted her cheeks several times. "Some charmer, eh," she said, then clicked the heels of her shoes together and started to rise.

Johnny grabbed her hand.

"You don't think they'll be able to use your testimony against us?"

"Of course they would," Emily said. "I have no faith in the world understanding Shoe."

That's right, Johnny thought. Why should they understand her when her own brother had failed to?

"You're going to lie, then?"

"No." Emily smiled, first at him, then at the ceiling. "That would be perjury."

Inside the courtroom, Emily took the witness stand. Max's lawyer approached her again, but this time without the grin.

"Miss Barker, did Susan Tumarkin ever tell you why

she left Max Frost and kept the fact of their child a secret from him for the remainder of her life?"

"Yes."

"Did she tell anyone else?"

"Not to my knowledge."

"What did she say?"

"She said he wanted to control her. She believed he'd want to control their child as well."

"Did she say how he sought to control her?"

"Step by step." Emily's eyes shifted to Ida, then to Max's fiancée. "That way you might not notice until it was too late. Or at least you felt it was."

"I'm afraid you're still speaking in generalities."

"I'm sorry," Emily said. "In this case, I think they're more helpful than the specifics."

"That's for the judge to decide."

"It doesn't matter what he did to Shoe—I'm sorry, Susan. It's what it signified. If you want specifics, just ask Ida Tumarkin what he did to her."

"Right now I'm trying to ascertain what inspired the wishes of the mother."

"Susan's mind worked in an unusual way," Emily said. "I don't think I could do it justice."

"No one is asking you to," said the lawyer. "I'm asking you to provide some specifics to the court."

Emily shook her head.

The lawyer paced away from her, then turned back, as if she were a puzzling work of art that needed the right perspective.

"Is there any reason you're reluctant to testify today?"

"I just want what's best for Moses."

The lawyer threw his hands up in the air. "In other words, you don't want Mr. Frost to get custody of his son."

"That's true," Emily said.

"To what lengths would you go to try to obtain that result?"

"What lengths are available to me?" Emily asked.

The lawyer cast a glance at the judge, but it wasn't necessary. The judge was already leaning toward her microphone, though Emily herself was only six feet away.

"Miss Barker," the judge said grimly. "Are you threatening to obstruct justice?"

"I have no wish to obstruct justice, your honor. Justice is dear to my heart."

"Justice, in your mind, is seeing the boy go to his aunt."

"Remain with her, yes."

The judge sat back.

"How long have you known Ida Tumarkin?" asked the lawyer.

Emily hesitated.

"Isn't it true that you and Ida Tumarkin have never resided in the same state? That you never even met until her sister's funeral?"

"That's true," said Emily, "but—"

"Just answer the question, Miss Barker."

"I'm trying."

"Aren't you trying to play God in a case involving two parties you know virtually nothing about?"

"I'm trying to honor the mother's wishes."

"Do you believe the dead take priority over the

living?"

Emily shook her head. She looked out into the courtroom, saw Johnny, looked away.

"No," she said. "But sometimes a person's good judgment outlives them. Lawyers rely on precedents set by dead men every day. And in this, I rely on a dead woman's judgment."

"Were her instincts so infallible?"

"Shoe didn't live according to her instincts. Most of her opinions about the world came from observation and extended reflection."

"When lawyers review a precedent, Miss Barker, it isn't enough to know a court's final decision. They have to know the facts of the case, the circumstances behind the earlier decision."

Emily's face spread into a familiar smile. It was also a dangerous smile, though Johnny had always thought it beautiful despite that. Its danger, he saw now, was its beauty.

"I understand you," she said. "And yet in this case, I think it would be better to avoid the facts, as you call them. I don't think they will illuminate the truth."

The lawyer rolled his eyes, then brought them to rest on the judge, her mouth a flat line. The judge leaned toward Emily.

"That is not your determination to make," she said.

Emily nodded, apologetic. "With all due respect, your honor, it's going to have to be."

The judge called for a recess. Then she, the two lawyers,

and Emily disappeared through a door. When they returned a half-hour later, Emily was not with them. The judge announced that Miss Barker had refused to cooperate and been found in contempt of court. She would remain incarcerated until morning.

Johnny rose to his feet. But it was then that Max's lawyer called his final witness. When Johnny heard the name, he felt a wave of sickness like he'd felt when they found Shoe's body. He sat back down as his mother, seated beside him, rose to her feet. She set a hand against his shoulder to steady herself, then Mrs. Tumarkin made her halting way to the front of the courtroom, where she was guided to her seat and sank down in it.

Johnny watched her collapse in on herself. He took in her black hair, her bloodless skin, and knew that here, they would kill two birds with one stone, for putting his mother on the stand would discredit both the aunt and the grandmother. He wondered how long this attack had been in the making. Maybe Max had laid the groundwork with that first prescription, back when he and Ida were still together, just in case.

Johnny looked at their own lawyer, sweating one minute, trying for Perry Mason the next, flustered by Max, and now, it seemed, dumbstruck. He had been a family friend for as long as Johnny could remember, had eaten dinner at their house. Johnny had gone to school with one of his daughters. He was a good man, a kind man, but he was outgunned.

Respect was an odd thing, Johnny reflected. He respected the man's decency. Yet in this context, decency wasn't called for. In this context, it was Max's lawyer who commanded respect, because force was on his side, and force was what seemed to matter here. Johnny supposed this meant that in some way he respected Max as well. After all, Johnny bothered to hate him.

Max's lawyer began, and Johnny watched another layer of his family's destiny laid bare.

"Hello, ma'am, how are you feeling today?"

Mrs. Tumarkin turned her eyes, dark and heavy, on the lawyer. "Tired," she said.

"You've been depressed since your daughter was killed."

She gave him a baleful look.

"My condolences," he said.

Mrs. Tumarkin swallowed painfully, either from sadness or because her throat was dry. "Thank you," she said.

"We want to talk to you today about your other daughter, Ida."

"I know that." Mrs. Tumarkin nodded her drooping head.

"In fact, ma'am, your daughter Ida has never lived away from home. Is that correct?"

Mrs. Tumarkin didn't answer. Her head dropped back. She was asleep.

"Mrs. Tumarkin." The lawyer leaned toward her. His voice was loud, but striving to be gentle. "Mrs. Tumarkin."

Her eyes snapped open. For a moment she looked alarmed, then her lids began to lower again.

"Please try to stay awake," he said. "I won't take up much more of your time, but I need to ask you one question."

Mrs. Tumarkin nodded.

"Do you yourself believe your daughter Ida would make the best guardian for your grandson?"

Mrs. Tumarkin smiled. The question seemed to please her. "The trouble," she said, temporarily animated, "is that she hasn't seen the world. And that's the key."

The Tumarkins' lawyer did not cross-examine the witness.

Lunch that day was awful. The family didn't know where to eat, so Ida led them to a diner around the corner and down the street. She walked briskly, ten steps ahead of everyone, babbling over her shoulder about wigs and pie. They slid into a bright blue booth and Johnny and Professor Tumarkin grabbed for menus. Neither man could look Mrs. Tumarkin in the eye—not that it mattered, since she couldn't keep her eyes open. Ida, on the other hand, stared at her through most of the meal, so oddly calm that Johnny could hardly look at her either.

His father could. His father tried engaging Ida in cheerful conversation. He asked about anything and everything he'd never asked about before: her paintings, the Christmas presents she'd bought for Moses, about Henry, who was keeping an eye on Moses that day after school, until they got home.

At first Ida smiled politely, too distracted to respond. She couldn't seem to tear her eyes away from her mother until finally, through some force of will Johnny saw pulling at the muscles of her face, she did. She turned her gaze full on her father, reached across the table, and took his hand.

"It's okay, Dad," she said. "I know you love me."

Johnny jumped up to find the restroom, but not before he saw his father's face bloom with surprised pleasure, think better of it, then fade and focus on his plate.

When the court readjourned that afteroon it was Professor Tumarkin's turn at the stand. Shoe had always called him the innocent, and Johnny saw it in his face, something earnest, still lacking in suspicion, even when Max's lawyer approached.

"How old is your daughter, professor?"

"Well, now, she just had a birthday." Johnny's father frowned. "Thirty-four."

"Thirty-four." The lawyer seemed to mull this over, as if it were a curious fact, indeed. "Never had any desire to strike out on her own?"

He shrugged.

"I'm sorry, the reporter can't record a shrug."

"I'm sorry." Professor Tumarkin turned his head toward the reporter, alarmed, then back to the attorney. He hunched his shoulders and leaned forward in his seat so that his mouth was up against the microphone. "Apparently not," he said.

"What sort of parenting values did you instill in your daughter?"

"Not many," said the professor.

"No?"

"It wasn't necessary. She came by them naturally, as I think most young people do, until they have those values bred out of them by society. But perhaps my daughter had some values in greater abundance than the average girl—gentleness, honesty, sincerity. My daughter is the most unaffected woman I have ever known."

"Unaffected?"

"Yes."

"Is that more important to you than, say, her holding down a job?"

Professor Tumarkin screwed up his face. He peered up into one corner of the courtroom.

"Yes," he said finally.

"A higher value than self-reliance? Than independence? Than being self-supporting? Than knowing that when you die, your daughter can take care of herself?"

"These need not be conflicting values."

"But in the case of your daughter, sir, they have been."

"I disagree," said Professor Tumarkin. "You will never convince me it was not in her best interests to let her stay at home."

"And in the interests of your family?"

"I don't see how you can separate them. What's best for the child is best for the family."

"Isn't that a dangerous maxim?"

"It isn't dangerous. It's difficult, sometimes, of course, to determine what 'best' is."

"Perhaps you find it difficult to determine where your grandson would be better off, what with your own family so divided."

Mrs. Tumarkin dozed beside Johnny, her head to one side. He saw his father's eyes rest there before they moved on to him.

"Well," said Professor Tumarkin. "It's not my determination to make."

"Your daughter, professor. Does she often behave in a manner that appears to be inappropriate for the situation?"

"What situation? What do you mean?"

"On April 11 of this year—Easter Sunday—didn't she spend all of that day, from sunrise to sunset, at your town's cemetery, waiting for your deceased daughter to rise from the dead?"

"We all did. The whole family. But I can explain."

The lawyer smiled blandly. "Please."

"It was Easter. Moses had a notion that if Christ rose from the dead on Easter, maybe his mother would too."

"Who gave him such a notion?"

"Oh, I doubt anyone gave it to him. Religion puts strange ideas in people's heads."

"Such as?"

"Well, such as that one. But Moses is very young."

"What other strange ideas does Moses have?"

"Oh, I don't know. He's quite normal, I think. Quite well-adjusted."

"But you said religion put strange ideas in his head."

"Not Moses in particular—anybody's head. I mean, it's preposterous. People killing their neighbors because one god says to worship him on Saturday and another god wants to be prayed to on Sunday…"

"If it were up to you, would you raise your grandson to be free of religion?"

"Well, ultimately, it's up to him."

"But you yourself are not religious? You don't believe in God?"

"No."

The lawyer nodded. "Thank you, sir," he said.

Court adjourned early that day, because the judge had a previous obligation. The two families filtered from the courtroom, then outside to their separate vehicles, parked in the same lot, not thirty feet apart. Johnny watched Max drive his family out of sight, not in the car Johnny had seen at Easter but in a big, shiny SUV. Maybe it belonged to his fiancée, Johnny thought. Or maybe business was looking up.

Johnny turned to Ida, who raised one hand to him in farewell, exiting the lot. His mother was in the backseat, Professor Tumarkin in the front seat beside Ida, having abandoned conversation and instead leaning down to fiddle with the radio. Johnny threw on the hood of his parka and started walking.

He got directions from the Santa Claus on the corner, stopped off at the closest grocery store, then set out for the jailhouse. It was three in the afternoon, but the sun was already low in the sky. They were rapidly approaching the shortest day of the year.

At the jail, they led him to a holding cell. Emily was alone inside it, lying on a bench, watching TV without the sound. She didn't see him, and Johnny didn't say a word. He didn't know what to say.

Finally she sighed, sat up, looked around. She got off

the bench, wandered over and leaned up against the wall, near the bars.

"I came to see if you needed anything," he said.

Emily shook her head.

"Something to read?" He reached in his backpack and pulled out a Spiderman comic book.

"Sure," Emily said. "I used to love to read."

She took the comic book and began to leaf through it. Johnny wrapped his hands around the bars and watched in silence.

Emily licked an index finger and turned a page. She chuckled at something, then wandered away, back to the bench, and sat down. She leaned her head against the cinder blocks and sighed.

"How'd it go today?" she asked. "After I left, I mean."

"Mom testified after you."

"Really? I thought your dad was supposed to be the first one up."

"He was," Johnny said. "For our side."

Emily put down the comic book. "You mean to say they subpoenaed her too? What for?"

"I don't think they subpoenaed her," Johnny said.

"Well, what did they ask her?"

"They asked her who she thought should get custody."

Emily stared at him. "And she said Max."

Johnny nodded.

Emily let out a long breath. She shook her head. Then she walked back over to where he stood, his hands still gripping the bars, and wrapped her own hands around his.

"Thank you," Johnny said.

Emily didn't ask what for.

They stood like that a long time, until their foreheads came together, not quite touching through the bars. Johnny closed his eyes. When he felt her hands drop away, he opened his eyes again to see she'd retreated back to her bench.

"So it's down to Ida now," she said.

"It should have been down to Moses. He's alreadyseven. If they'd listen to what he wanted we could've skipped this whole circus."

"They may listen to him when he's older."

"He may change his mind by then."

"He may," she agreed.

"In which case, we'll have lost him."

"Maybe then he wasn't ours to keep."

"What I don't get about Max is that people seem to like him," said Johnny. "His own family likes him. How do you fool your own family?"

"Maybe he didn't fool them."

"What are you saying? You think he threatened them, blackmailed them somehow into testifying for him?"

"I doubt it," said Emily. "I'm just saying there's no accounting for taste."

That reminded him. He rummaged in his backpack a second time while Emily looked on, despondent. When he brought out the pear, she turned pale.

"I couldn't find a ripe one," he explained. The one he held out to her was green. "When summer comes, we'll find an orchard where they're yellow."

She wouldn't look at him, just stared at the pear as if she were in pain. Johnny didn't know what to do. He stooped down and pushed the pear gently between the bars of her cell, then straightened up again and slowly turned around, until he'd made a circle. He studied the television without the sound. When he looked back at her she was looking at him. He forced a smile, then let it go.

"We're wasting time," he announced. "What's the point?"

Emily held his gaze, but blankly. He tried to clarify.

"I was mad about a lot of stuff," he explained. "But I was never mad at you."

Emily didn't blink. He tried again.

"I want to be with you. And make you happy."

She dropped her head, looked shyly back down at the comic he had brought her, then picked it up and hid her face. "You already have," she said.

"Oh," Johnny said. "That was easy."

She lowered the comic just enough to peer at him over the top. "Was it really?" she asked.

"Oh, well," he said. "Maybe not."

CHAPTER TWENTY-NINE

The day Ida took the stand, every streetlamp in downtown Hamilton was hung with its own wreath, every pole wrapped with its own tinsel streamer, sparkling red and gold. That morning on their way to the courthouse, the Tumarkins passed a man on a street corner in a standard-issue Santa Claus suit, ringing his bell. Ida dug into her pockets and scrounged up a quarter, two dimes, four pennies, and the same lozenge she'd found in her peacoat the winter before. She stared at the lozenge. She thought about saving it. She unwrapped the lozenge and popped it in her mouth, before she could change her mind.

The wrapper she dropped in the nearest trash can, the coins in the man's black pot, though not for good luck. She had never really believed in luck; she had always believed in destiny. Her destiny was proving far darker than she had ever envisioned.

The night before, she'd phoned the county jail and talked to Emily.

"You want to look motherly, but also chic. A with-it mom, Ida. That's who you'll be tomorrow."

Today that's who she was. But Ida hadn't realized how much she had counted on Emily being in that courtroom until now, when she was not. Moses was not there either, of course, but in school where he belonged—another week of second grade before the Christmas holiday—and so she kept a photo of him, a wallet-sized portrait they had taken at school that fall, in her breast pocket, over her heart.

It was not a good picture. She had taken a dozen better ones herself. His hair was tamed, his face was lit unnaturally, and they'd made him smile in a way that, while not exactly insincere, was not Moses' smile. It was this smile she imagined her nephew wearing on his face if Max won custody. Moses would wear it as they drove away with him, as he turned to watch her receding through the window of the black SUV, and wear it each time he saw her forevermore, not because the smile—this wrong smile—was meant for her, but because it had become permanently affixed to his face.

It was the smile Max would want for him, practiced, consistent, and in control. Those few photos she had of Max were all like this one of Moses. Before the camera, she never once had gotten Max to smile a real smile, any more than he had spoken a real word in the courtroom.

She carried the wallet-sized photo because it was the only one small enough to fit in her pocket. She slipped into a bathroom stall just before her testimony and looked at it once more. From her purse she also pulled an older, larger snapshot of him and Shoe, which she contemplated while her lips moved silently, as if she held one of Henry's holy cards.

When she came out of the stall, Max's fiancée was standing at one of the sinks, washing her hands.

"Do you know what Emily Barker meant?" asked Ida, not knowing where to start. There was too much, and it was all too important. "About the step by step?"

She tried to make her voice gentle. She kept her distance, as if this delicate woman were some wild animal, easily scared away. And still his fiancée's blue eyes skidded around the room the moment she saw Ida framed there in the bathroom stall.

"Don't talk to me," she said.

"I think you do know," Ida said. "Or you're afraid I do."

The other woman said nothing.

"At first, he makes you feel like you're embarking on a great adventure, as if your whole life were just preparation for the day when he found you. That's what I thought."

The other woman turned and reached for a paper towel, but there were none. She shook her hands in front of her.

"But it's his adventure," Ida said. "It will always be his adventure. Wouldn't you rather have one of your own?"

The woman rubbed her wet hands into her long hair, a lighter shade than Ida's, but just as heavy. "No," she said. She tossed the hair back from her face—like a model, Ida thought. Maybe she was one. "What difference does it make?" she added, a kind of afterthought, then for the first time she met Ida's eyes in the mirror.

"Our lawyer's going to rip you up out there," the woman said.

And perhaps he did. Sitting in the witness box, feeling one leg go to sleep and letting it, Ida kept thinking the lawyer's insinuations must wind down soon. When they didn't, she recalled her last night with Max, that night at the farmhouse when he'd roared in her face until she thought she'd lose her mind. By comparison, the lawyer's questions seemed to her inoffensive, his tone almost kind. Thinking this, a strange smile broke across Ida's face and the lawyer smiled back, bewildered but almost charmed.

True, he pried into aspects of Ida's life that she never would have thought he could, pried without apology or shame. Max had told him where to dig, into parts of her Max once seemed to cherish. But cherish had been his word. Ida should have known you couldn't trust a man who used a word like that. Shoe would have known better.

Then she had to remind herself that Shoe had not known better, not soon enough. Neither sister had figured Max out until it was too late. Shoe had gotten pregnant. Ida had given him access to Moses, enough access that now, in court, Max could claim a relationship with him, which might help him get custody. She'd given him access to her mother, and he'd turned that to his favor too. She'd given him access to herself, so that now his lawyer asked her about things that seemed to bear no relevance to Moses whatsoever.

They had exploited her mother for freakishness, and

now they were mining her for more of the same. Ida understood this, but didn't see a way to stop it.

He asked her why she visited the cemetery. He asked her what exactly it was she did in the woods. He asked her why she'd never graduated from college, never worked, never left home, why she painted, who her friends were, what she thought of God, what happened in that cabin at summer camp when she was ten.

"But don't most children that age have a healthy curiosity about sex?"

"Maybe so," she said. "It didn't seem healthy at the time."

"You weren't curious?"

Ida shook her head, and the lawyer pointed to the court reporter.

"Oh," Ida said. Then, "No."

She knew the basic facts of life when she went to camp. She didn't approve of them, but they had nothing to do with her, so she ignored them. After lights out, when one of the girls in her cabin read to them from a book for adults, Ida put her pillow over her head to block out the words. The other girls noticed and took her pillow away.

It wasn't much of a story. She'd once told it to Max, but only because of what followed, her great adventure with Shoe. The lawyer wouldn't care about that, though, any more than Max had.

"Perhaps you were unduly modest?" he asked.

"Perhaps I was," she said.

The lawyer faltered for a moment, and while he did,

she watched Johnny rise to his feet again. He had objected once already, and the judge had warned him then it would have to stop. He was not in a position to do so. Yet here was Johnny, addressing the judge a second time.

"I object," he said.

The judge peered down at him. "Mr. Tumarkin. You're either disrespectful or just plain foolish. You can take your pick. Now resume your seat."

When Johnny stayed standing, the judge leaned back on her bench. "Or if you'd rather, you can go join Miss Barker at the jail. I won't ask you again."

Johnny resumed his seat. Max's lawyer resumed his questioning.

"And you've never had a boyfriend," he said.

Ida shook her head.

"Pardon me if I seem surprised, Miss Tumarkin, but an attractive woman of thirty-four who's never had a boyfriend is something of an anomaly."

Ida could see he was waiting. She sat perfectly still and waited too.

"No sweehearts at all?" he finally prompted.

"No sweethearts," she said.

"Yet I've gathered from other people's testimony that you considered Mr. Frost your beau for a while."

"Well, he never considered me his," Ida said. "As he's testified."

"That isn't the question at hand, Miss Tumarkin. In the interests of the child, it is important for the court to know how you perceive your relationship with the child's father."

"Mr. Frost and I were in love," she said. "He told me he wanted to marry me. Then he changed his mind. We don't have a relationship now."

"And how did you feel about Mr. Frost?"

"I loved him and wanted to marry him."

Without meaning to, Ida looked at Max. He finally looked at her. And in a way, it happened just as she'd imagined: They'd reached an understanding. But she did not rise from her chair or cross the room or take his face between her hands. Max shifted his gaze. The moment passed.

"Miss Tumarkin, are you aware that Mr. Frost perceives your relationship with him differently?"

"I am aware of his testimony," Ida said.

"He says his relationship with you was purely platonic."

"Well." Her voice grew quiet and she smiled. "We're in court."

The lawyer raised his arm, and with some peculiar flourish of his hand, turned to the judge, as if that answer had illustrated something they had both suspected all along.

"No more questions, your honor," he said.

Ida stepped down.

The final witness was the custody analyst, the woman who had interviewed them all and talked to Moses about what he wanted. Her recommendation, to Ida's surprise, was that he stay with the Tumarkins.

"This boy has lost his mother in one of the worst

ways possible. He is still deeply bound to her. For him, now, his mother's family, home, and way of life is the next best thing."

Ida thought about her sister, the one who'd always wanted to protect her, the one whose protection she'd lost. It was always about me, she thought with a kind of wonder, a kind of scandalized shame. She'd been the queen of her country. She'd never wanted that to change.

Her life—the one Max had forced her to examine— was one long effort to protect herself. But that effort wasn't flawed, she thought, for any of the reasons he had cited. It was only flawed because that life was not what life was meant to be.

She didn't care anymore about losing Shoe's protection. What she missed now was Shoe. She had a feeling she would miss her more and more.

Ida looked around the courtroom and the light felt different. It felt like the light of a brave new world.

Later that morning the judge announced her finding: Primary custody would go to Mr. Frost. Max's sister let out a cheer, then fell quiet. The judge turned and looked at Ida.

"This is no judgment on you," she said. "But Mr. Frost is his father. You are not his mother. As a result, the burden of proof lies with your family to show Mr. Frost is an unfit parent. That's a difficult burden to meet."

Since Max was moving to another state, weekly or monthly visits would not be practicable, she continued. Instead, Moses would visit his mother's family for four weeks in summer, one week following Christmas and one other holiday, to be decided upon, with weekly telephone visitation. The judge rose, they all rose, and she disappeared.

When she had gone, Ida saw Max crossing the room in great strides and headed right for her, a grave expression on his face. She turned and fled through the courtroom door.

He chased her down the marble stairs and through the main hall, which echoed loudly as their feet slapped the floor. Through the glass doors she could see the courthouse steps down to the street, and when she reached them, Ida leapt forward into thin air, where the morning's snow had turned to sleet. She felt something wet and icy on her cheek and then he caught her, not all of her, not even her, exactly, but her coat sleeve—the sleeve of her peacoat, the coat of a normal person—then her arm. When Ida tried to yank her arm away, he pushed her around a thick stone pillar, away from public view, and lowered his face into hers.

"You know what I wanted." His voice was half sob, half snarl, and his breath hung in the air, visible proof that he had spoken to her once more. "I wanted the three of us to live happily ever after, but you would not allow it."

Ida thrust an elbow into his stomach. But Max just moved his mouth over her ear.

"I offered you everything," he breathed.

Ida stomped on the bridge of his foot. Max laughed his glorious laugh, the one that she had loved so well, and let her go.

"God, I miss you," he said. Then he turned and jogged back up the stairs, into the courthouse, and was gone.

CHAPTER THIRTY

After Moses, Ida's dreams changed. There were no more dreams of Max, or of waltzing to the Blue Danube with some faceless, perfect stranger. She dreamed instead of her nephew, and all the things they wouldn't do. In one dream she taught him how to scramble eggs, in another, how to build a fire. She knew that she would see his face again, but not at that moment of discovery, when she lifted her hands from his bike seat and he sailed away on two thin tires, mouth open with surprise, then joy. Those moments would fall to Max.

It was not the black SUV that took Moses away, not Max's little car either, but a big plane bound for Atlanta. Max and his bride-to-be would fly with Moses out of Cincinnati, and then the three of them were boarding an even bigger plane to Orlando. Max was taking him to Disney World before the latter half of second grade got under way in his new school in Detroit. Later that day, Ida would ship boxes with Moses' things to the newest suburb of that city, where Max had just bought a house.

"I won't stay," Moses said on the drive down to the airport. "I'll come back to you."

"Oh, love," Ida said, and broke off to blow her nose. "You know we'll love you to death no matter what you do."

Moses did look back as he walked onto the plane, but he didn't smile that terrible smile. He didn't smile at all. He looked once, turned the corner, and was gone. Then it seemed to Ida that for the first time in her life, she was alone.

The next day Ida, too, left Ohio. She and Johnny packed up one of the family cars, the one she always drove. Her father told her he and Mrs. Tumarkin would make do with one car for a while. Ida and Johnny would head south first, to miss whatever snow might fly across their path, then west, through Texas, New Mexico, and into Arizona. Ida was going to live near Emily for a while. Johnny was too.

Before they left, Ida slipped out through the glass doors, between the towering sycamores with their smooth white limbs, and crossed the brown grass of the playing field. She reached her father's building in five minutes. Like all the other red brick buildings on campus it was built to look old, and some of them really were old, but not her father's. Ida climbed to the third floor and turned two wide corners until she reached the hallway that housed his office.

She knocked on his door, entered, and took the vacant chair—the same one she had taken as a child, with a view onto the playing field across the street—then looked around the room. Nothing had changed.

Her father's special period of history was post-Civil War America. He had posters and portraits and maps from that era hung on the walls. To Ida, the nineteenth century had always seemed a sweet, uncomplicated time, but then, she had never asked her father anything much about it until a few weeks ago.

"Oh, no," he said when she did. "It was a mess, like any other." Then he held forth for half an hour on the Industrial Revolution. She realized she was just getting to know her father—just getting to know there was a man in there to know—and now she had to leave. They might never live in the same place again.

Ida had often visited his office as a small child, then again in college, when she'd come to hide between classes, before she dropped out. None of the rest of the family ever really had. It was a separate world, and one he would leave soon for retirement. Then, if his wife was sufficiently recovered, he thought the two of them might see a bit of the world.

"Well." Ida spread her hands. "That day has come."

Her father nodded, smiling, but his shoulders sagged. "I don't understand what happened to this family."

Ida smiled too. "Do you want the long answer or the short one?"

"Short," he said.

"Bad luck," Ida said. "But I also did my part. I shouldn't have stayed on so long. Everybody sort of paid a price for my happiness, I guess."

Her father frowned. "Who put that thought in your

head?"

"Nobody," she began, then realized that wasn't true. "Max did," she said. When her father frowned again, she added, "The trouble with Max was, a few of the things he said were true."

"Well, if he ever said a true thing, I never heard it." Professor Tumarkin thought a moment. "What happened was your sister's murder. It broke your mother's heart."

But this explanation didn't seem to satisfy him either.

"Maybe it was me," he said. "Tying your mother down to this town all these years."

"My favorite town on earth," Ida said.

He nodded slowly, lost in thought. "Maybe she broke her own heart," he said quietly, then looked up at Ida, as if remembering she was there. "People can do that, you know."

Ida was about to reach across the desk and take her father's hand, resting there, but he removed the hand and dug in his pocket until he found his handkerchief. He blew his nose loudly. It was a sound, Ida realized, she would miss as much as any.

She smiled at him. "I'm sure it happens that way all the time," she said. "More often than not."

On her father's desk, amid piles of papers, sat a framed photo of his three children, taken some twenty-odd summers ago, in a canoe on a lake. Ida didn't recognize the lake—it was not the one near their house—though she remembered paddling. She noticed something blue on Shoe, picked up the photo, and took a closer look.

It was a ribbon, pinned to her sister's tank top. Perhaps they'd gone to fetch Shoe at the end of summer camp. Shoe always went to camp, though Ida had only gone once, and left eight days into it. She and Shoe had hopped a train to get her out of there.

In the photo, the other two were both looking at something off the front of the canoe, but Shoe sat in the back of the boat with her paddle raised, looking sidelong at the camera. A knowing glance. Almost a wink.

"Those were good years," her father said sadly.

"I know."

"Do you remember the time your sister brought the dummy home from school? And that dagger she'd made in shop? We didn't even know she was taking shop!"

"She wasn't," Ida said.

Her father decided to let it go. "Didn't you do a painting from that?"

Ida nodded.

"Do you still have it?"

"She gave that one away." Ida didn't tell him Shoe had given it to Max.

Professor Tumarkin looked disappointed. "Do you know," he mused, "your sister wasn't always like that. I mean, when she was Moses' age, she was different. Almost docile, in a way. Then something happened to her. She changed, almost overnight."

"Something did happen to her," Ida said.

They gazed at one another.

"I did a painting about that too," Ida said. "I'll show it to you before I go."

"You and your sister," he said. "There was always something between you."

Ida picked up the photo from the lake again. She studied it. Of course Shoe was just a young girl in the photo. That smirk could be deceptive. What could she possibly have known back then?

"There was," Ida said. "But I didn't know it."

She touched the tip of a finger to her sister's sly mouth, then set the photo back on the desk.

"Shoe knew," she said.

CHAPTER THIRTY-ONE

Moses started his new school in the second semester. Because his second grade teacher already knew everyone's name, she didn't take roll. She could tell who was absent just by looking out into the room. Moses was present, but on the third day, she called him up to her desk after school.

"I noticed on your work you sign your last name as Tumarkin."

Moses nodded.

"But on the roster, your name is Frost."

Moses shook his head.

"I met your father." She touched three fingers to her throat. "Max Frost."

Moses nodded. "But my mother's last name was Tumarkin."

The teacher lowered her eyelids, and Moses noticed that her lashes were strangely curled.

"In this culture," she explained, "children generally take their father's name."

"Why?" asked Moses.

"Because that's the practice. So your last name is Frost. Your father registered you as Moses Frost. That is your legal name."

Moses studied her eyelashes and wondered if they hurt. "I like Tumarkin better," he said.

"Fine," she said, and blushed.

But it was not fine. That Sunday evening after dinner, Max sat Moses down in his office. First he asked him about basketball, which they were playing then in gym. Moses told him he was doing pretty well.

"I know you are." Max pushed his chair back from his desk and propped up his feet. Moses turned and saw Max's Air Jordans reflected in the mirror that hung behind him on the office wall.

"I got a call from your teacher the other day. She said you don't want to use our last name. Don't you like it?"

"I like Frost," Moses said. "I just like Tumarkin better."

"What do you mean? Do you mean you like the way it sounds?"

Moses nodded.

"You're my only son," Max said. "My flesh and blood. I'm your father."

"I know," Moses said.

They studied one another with their light brown eyes. Neither blinked. After a while, Moses got the funny feeling they were having a staredown, though it hadn't started out that way. He stared until his eyes began to water, until Max broke his own gaze and set a hand on Moses' shoulder.

"Moses Frost," he said.

Moses smiled and shook his head.

"But what difference does it make?" cried Max.

Moses shrugged.

Each night before Moses went to sleep, Max came into his bedroom. Max had it all decorated for him when Moses arrived that winter. He'd let Moses take down one poster and put up a painting Moses had done in its place. But Max hadn't let him put up the one Aunt Ida gave him, and it had been the same with the nest.

Moses had found that later, fallen to the ground, some egg shards nearby. Moses had tried to put this on a shelf over his bed, but when his father had seen it there, Max made him take it outside. Disease, he said.

Max came each night and tucked him in. Sometimes they talked. Sometimes Max offered him advice, or told him a story. Except for Sunday nights. On Sunday nights Max called him into his office for The Discussion. Moses would usually be a little sleepy by then, and wearing his pajamas. They'd go back and forth. He noticed, these evenings, that Max always smiled the same peculiar smile. He did not know what it meant, but it didn't mean Max was happy, he knew that much.

As the weeks went by, Moses came to feel as if he'd stepped into one of the fairy tales he and Aunt Ida used to listen to on library headphones, that he was being tested, though he couldn't say why. He came to feel the mysterious responsibility he bore, and the burden of his choice, as Max slowly lost his patience.

It is important to resist, thought Moses. And he

thought he had, until one Sunday night in April, when Moses glimpsed himself in the mirror on Max's office wall, and felt more strongly than ever that he had stepped into a sinister fairy tale, where some spell beyond his understanding or control worked upon him. Moses saw his reflection, with that same peculiar smile of his father's on his own face.

He waited until his father had dismissed him to wipe the smile away. In the bathroom he climbed up on the sink so he could watch his mouth in the medicine cabinet mirror. He waited some time to see if the smile returned. It didn't, but Moses was not reassured. Brushing his teeth, he wondered if it was too late to run away.

Moses knew the story of his namesake. He understood that one day he would return to his people, that this exile wouldn't last forever. But he was tired of waiting. So Monday he made arrangements, looking in the Yellow Pages under "bus," calling the bus lines and counting his dollar bills. Tuesday he packed on the sly, using the gym bag his father had bought him for basketball. He smuggled in the nest from outside and laid it on top of the atlas his grandmother had given him that Christmas, the week before he moved away. It was not the old atlas with the duct tape, although he would've liked that, but a brand-new one, with actual photographs, and every country in the book still in existence.

"To Moses," she had written inside it, "my only grandchild. So he may see the world."

And so he would. He stayed up an hour past his

bedtime, studying those photographs by flashlight before he opened wide his bedroom window, dropped his bag the five or six feet onto the lawn and then himself. It was dark, but Moses didn't mind the dark. It seemed to him the good smells of springtime were stronger in the night.

He began by walking the four blocks to the bus stop, where the streetlamp didn't work. It looked to Moses like someone had smashed it with a rock, but that wouldn't keep the bus from coming. He would catch the last bus headed downtown tonight and when he got there, buy his ticket to Ohio, since that's all he could afford. The daffodils would be blooming on his mother's grave when he arrived. From there he would go on to Arizona with money from his grandparents or Henry.

He had thought about wearing his pajamas so that if he were caught, he could say that he was sleepwalking. But the bag belied this. He wore jeans and sneakers and a green plaid shirt instead. He wore a jacket with a Nike logo on the front, though he knew from watching the Weather Channel on his father's big-screen TV that where he was headed, he wouldn't need it.

He hadn't minded Detroit. He had friends at school, there was a ravine on the way home and once at night, he'd seen raccoons climb up out of the sewer system. His stepmom, who was pretty, smiled at him all the time, though they both knew he could no more be her child than she could be his mom.

Before she and Max were married, their last night in the hotel at Disney World, Max had told him not to miss his aunt. "We'll get you another mommy," he had said.

"The best mommy."

But Moses, so like his father in some ways, had no use for superlatives, or, really, for mommies either. He would only ever have one of those. That was all anybody ever got.

Once, camping high in the mountains beside a shallow lake, he had had to leave the tent in the middle of the night to go to the bathroom. It was cold outside his sleeping bag, and when he went to put his boots on, they were damp and clammy. Outside was even colder, but Moses could see the Big Dipper above him, and before him the outlines of everything. He heard the wind stir up the surface of the lake and move away from it, uphill into a stand of tall fir trees. He followed.

Underneath the firs he went about his business, still half asleep, when suddenly he heard the crunch of sticks behind him. It was an animal, a large animal headed his way. Moses pulled up his pants and turned to see what it could be. When the shape came out of the shadows, he realized it was his mom.

"Boo," he said.

She stopped in her tracks—one unmistakable hitch in her long stride, maybe three seconds—then started up again, snatching the hood of his sweatshirt as she passed by, snapping it gently against his head. Together they walked out from the stand of trees, back out under the Milky Way. She grabbed him up and settled him onto her shoulders.

"I thought you were an animal," he said, rocking above her, warm only where the backs of his legs pressed into her shoulders.

"I am an animal," she said. "Weren't you scared?"

"Scared of what?"

"Scared of me," said Shoe. "Scared I was gonna try to eat you. Scared I'd be some kind of animal you'd never seen before—a monster!"

"Nah."

Shoe slowed, and so did the rocking. "Don't you believe in monsters?"

"Nah."

When they reached the tent, she dropped slowly to her knees, bent her head, and Moses climbed off onto solid ground. In the tent they crept carefully around his uncle and back into their bags. Moses lay listening to the adults breathing, feeling the warmth slowly return to his fingers and toes. He thought his mother was asleep when she spoke again.

"That's my fault," she said.

Moses never asked her what she meant by that. But soon now, he would ask Aunt Ida. He waited in the darkness for the bus and he was not afraid.

ACKNOWLEDGMENTS

Big thanks to Lydia Millet and Kate Bernheimer, who never let me forget I write novels. An added thanks to Lydia for her open-handed hospitality. Your home became my home (twice) while working on this book, and the menagerie of desert animals right outside your door kept me enviable company through one long, hot summer.